Books by Tom Hoffman

The Eleventh Ring

The Thirteenth Monk

The Seventh Medallion

Orville Mouse and the Puzzle
of the Clockwork Glowbirds

Orville Mouse and the Puzzle
of the Shattered Abacus

Orville Mouse and the Puzzle
of the Capricious Shadows

Available on Amazon and Barnes & Noble

The Seventh Medallion

by Tom Hoffman

Cover design by Tom Hoffman Graphic Design
Anchorage, Alaska

Tom Hoffman
Visit my website at thoffmanak.wordpress.com
Printed in the United States of America

First Printing: January 2016

ISBN-13 978-0-9971952-2-4

With lots of love for
Molly, Alex, Sophie, and Oliver

A very special thanks to my wonderful editors
Beth, Debbie, Alex, Amanda, and Karen
for their invaluable assistance
and excellent advice.

Table of Contents

"We have not even to risk the adventure alone,
for the heroes of all time have gone before us.
The labyrinth is thoroughly known: we have only to
follow the thread of the hero path. And where we had
thought to find an abomination, we shall find a god.
And where we had thought to slay another,
we shall slay ourselves. And where we had
thought to travel outward we shall come to
the center of our own existence
And where we had thought to be alone,
we shall be with all the world."

– Joseph Campbell

Bartholomew the Adventurer
Trilogy • Book Three

The Seventh Medallion

Chapter 1

Thaumatar

"You're certain? You're absolutely certain this is the one?"

"Yes, I'm certain. You seem to forget I was deciphering ancient Mintarian star charts before you were a mouseling. Believe me, I know Thaumatar when I see it."

"Creekers, hard to believe we're orbiting the birthplace of inter-dimensional travel. The Thaumatarians dreamed up the World Doors back when we were still running around throwing spears at wild Nadwokks. We didn't even have fire back then. Heh, can you imagine eating raw Nadwokk for lunch?"

"Focus, Beinerr. Take us in closer, please. Reduce orbit to one fifty miles and scan for infrastructure. I'm not seeing any ships. There should be ships. Lots of ships. Unless they don't use them anymore – they could have some advanced form of travel we haven't even dreamed of yet."

"One fifty miles it is, esteemed Master Scientist Vahnar. Scanners on, as per your most excellent command."

Vahnar grinned. "Now *that's* the kind of response I like to hear from my senior nav-pilot. While you're at it, see if you can get my wife to come out here and take a look at Thaumatar. It's certainly more interesting than studying interstellar dust particles in that tiny lab of hers. Maybe she can use her gift to help us figure out what's going on here."

Beinerr gave Vahnar a sideways glance. He had his own opinions about Lybis' gift, but he knew well enough to keep them to himself. Beinerr had heard all the stories – Lybis saw events before they happened, she knew what people were thinking, she could talk to people in their dreams. He might only be a nav-pilot on a puny Science Guild survey ship, but he knew when something was creepy.

Beinerr swiped the holoscreen, then tapped it twice. "Attention Madam Lybis, Master Scientist Vahnar requests the pleasure of your company on the bridge as soon as you are able."

Vahnar laughed. "That should get her down here."

Beinerr's eyes were riveted on his scanner display. "This is odd. Broad spectrum scanners aren't showing any activity on the planet. Nothing in this quadrant anyway. No ships, no lights, no vehicles, no movement of any kind. I'm not liking this."

"Hmm, you're right, that is odd. Try scanning for life forms."

Beinerr tapped three circular discs on his console as he eyed the holoscreen. "Nothing. And I mean *nothing*. Not a mouse, not a bug, not a bird, not a plant, not even microorganisms. We're picking up plenty of infrastructure, but it looks ancient. Half the buildings have collapsed. I don't know how else to put it – the planet appears to be dead. Wherever the Thaumatarians are, they're not here."

"It has to be a glitch in our equipment. A species or a culture can fade away into history, but every single life form on an entire planet? If life force is anything, it's tenacious. We should be seeing something. Double check the scanners, then take us around the planet and we'll do a total field scan."

"Increasing velocity to seven point three, scanners on wide spectrum, total field. Life forms will appear as white blips on the bridge screen."

The main monitor on the forward bulkhead blinked on, displaying the planet's surface in sharp colorful detail as it passed below them.

Vahnar eyed the screen. "If I wasn't seeing it, I wouldn't believe it. Everything looks deserted and totally lifeless. Right there, that looks like it used to be a forest. The trees are dead and have fallen over, but they're not decaying, they look like they died last week. That can only mean there are no microorganisms and no insects to facilitate decomposition. I'm beginning to wonder if we should even do a planetfall. We have no idea what killed everything. I've never run into anything remotely like this before."

Beinerr and Vahnar watched mutely as the surface of the planet slipped silently past on the bridge monitor. They had not seen a single blip of white light to indicate an active life form.

Beinerr was startled by a rustling noise behind him and spun around. It was Lybis, wearing her white cloak and hood. When a mouse becomes a member of the International Quintarian Science Guild they are issued a traditional white cloak and hood, an age old symbol representing the purity of science. Most scientists never wear them again, but Lybis always wore hers.

Beinerr managed to give Lybis a pleasant smile, trying not to make it look too forced. He wondered to himself how Vahnar and Lybis had ever gotten together. "Greetings, Madam Lybis, you're just in time to—"

Lybis held up her paw, motioning for silence. Her eyes were fixed on the bridge screen, her face taut. "Wait. It won't be long now. Wait."

Beinerr's smile vanished. He glanced at Vahnar, who shrugged and turned to look at the bridge display. For several minutes the three of them watched the Thaumatarian landscape passing by.

Lybis let out a long slow breath. "Now."

There was a blinding flash on the screen and the image was replaced by a swirling vortex of white light. Seconds later the planet's surface reappeared on the monitor.

Beinerr laughed nervously. "A glitch, that's all. Sometimes the scanner feedback loop is—"

Vahnar shook his head. "No. Take us back. Find out what that was."

"It can't be life force. It would have to be as big as a planet. It's not possible." A deep wave of anxiety rolled through Beinerr. He did not like the feeling at all, and he didn't care much for Lybis' gift.

"Take us back over the area that flashed, and turn off the life form scanner so we can see what's down there."

Beinerr's shoulders tightened. "As you wish." He flipped on the inertia dampeners and with a low hum the ship came to a gradual stop one hundred and fifty miles above Thaumatar. Beinerr swiped the holoscreen and the ship slowly turned, retracing their path over the planet.

"Maintaining orbit directly above flash coordinates. The flash was directly below us."

"I don't see anything. There's some kind of big rectangular structure five or ten miles to the west, but the flash seems to have come from the desert."

"Switch on life force scanners."

The screen turned a brilliant white.

"Creekers. Switch them off."

The planet's surface appeared again. They were looking at a vast, barren desert. Lybis looked at Vahnar. "We have to go down there. We have no choice. Everything depends on what we do now. Everything."

Vahnar nodded. If there was one mouse in the world he trusted, it was Lybis. "Beinerr, take us down. Check the atmosphere for contamination. We still don't know what killed everything. Well... killed everything except something."

Forty minutes later the Guild survey ship touched down on the surface of Thaumatar. Vahnar stared out the porthole, eyeing the rolling sand dunes. To the west was the massive structure they had seen on the ship's scanner. It was at least five miles away but looked enormous even from this distance. A dark sand color, with steeply sloping sides, the monolithic structure stood at least three or four hundred feet tall. It seemed like an odd place for the Thaumatarians to build such a mammoth structure. He wondered if the building had anything to do with the enormous life force flare on their scanners.

"Air is fine, no contamination. You're good to go.

You might want to suit up. You never know, especially under these circumstances."

Lybis nodded. "Thank you, Beinerr, we'll suit up. You stay here and mind the ship. If anything happens, take her back to Quintari. Tell the Science Guild what happened. Give them all the data." Almost as an afterthought Lybis added, "I am getting a powerful sense of urgency, but it's confusing. The feelings are coming from several different times and places."

Vahnar and Lybis donned their protective suits, pressed a tab on the port bulkhead and watched the outer hatch unfold down to the desert floor. They were greeted by a blast of broiling hot desert air as they exited through the hatch.

Lybis and Vahnar made their way down the ramp to the sands below. Vahnar scanned the area for any possible threats, but saw nothing. "I don't even know what I'm looking for. Maybe an invisible Nadwokk the size of a planet." He looked around for Lybis. She had headed off across the dunes, one paw extended in front of her. Vahnar knew what she was doing. She was letting the universe guide her toward whatever it was that flared up on the scanner. With a sigh of resignation he followed his wife into the desert.

Chapter 2

The Black Sphere

Step by deliberate step, Lybis made her way across the dunes, her eyes closed, one paw extended out in front of her. She made a wide turn to the east, ascending a large sloping dune. Vahnar halted at its base, well aware that small sounds or sudden motions could pull Lybis from her altered state. She paused at the top of the dune, rotating slowly like some curious organic antenna. When her arm was pointing to the west, pointing toward the massive sand colored structure in the distance, she called out, "From there. It came from there." Without further explanation she headed east, trekking down the far side of the great dune.

Vahnar trailed after Lybis. As he was making his way up the sandy slope he heard her cry out.

"Vahnar! Come quickly!"

Vahnar instinctively pulled a silver cylinder from the black sheath strapped to his leg. He flicked it twice and the device telescoped out, emitting a low hum. As he dashed up the dune he twisted the Sleeper's control knob to maximum power. He'd never used a Sleeper in the field before, but every Science Guild apprentice underwent rigorous Sleeper training in the contact simulators. At low power it would do just what its name implied – cause the enemy to instantly fall asleep. At high levels the sleep effect became far more pronounced and at maximum level, quite permanent. When set to level twenty the Sleeper sent out a powerful electronic pulse beam which caused a fatal overload in the enemy's brain.

Vahnar raced up the sandy slope, calling to Lybis. He crested the dune, spotting her at the base, hunched down next to a large ruptured silver sphere. Lybis saw Vahnar's Sleeper and waved her paw. "I'm fine – put that thing away! Come look at this."

Vahnar studied the sphere as he made his way down the dune. It reminded him of a comm satellite he'd seen that had dropped from orbit and smashed into a mountainside on Quintari's third moon. This sphere was larger of course, about twelve feet in diameter, and constructed of an unknown alloy, but it did have a similar look to it. "It looks like it dropped orbit. Is it a satellite?"

"No, not a satellite. It's hollow. It must have hit this outcropping at incredible velocity to do such damage. It's not metal. I'm not even certain it's made out of physical matter as we understand it. It's an extraordinary object, possibly infused with extra-dimensional forces, almost as if–"

Lybis stopped in mid sentence, her head tilting, her eyes losing focus. Vahnar waited patiently for her to continue. Half a minute later she turned to him, shaking her head. "No. This sphere is not the source of the flare, it was only the container. Look here, the sand has been melted, probably a plasma field escaping from the ruptured sphere. We need to find what that plasma was protecting."

Vahnar was completely bewildered by this. "I don't understand. I thought we were looking for a creature – some massive beast filled with immeasurable amounts of life force. Wouldn't the crash impact have killed anything inside the silver sphere?"

Lybis didn't reply, but motioned for him to follow her. She stepped cautiously across the rocky outcropping back onto the sand. Twenty feet away she stopped and kneeled down, gingerly moving her paw back and forth above the sand. Without a word she lay on her stomach, her eyes just inches from the ground. She licked the end of her paw, and with a barely perceptible motion tapped it to the sand. She stood up and held out her paw for Vahnar to see. "Look."

Vahnar looked but saw nothing. "What? Is something wrong with your paw?"

"Look again."

Vahnar moved closer, his eyes fixed on her paw. "Uhh... you have sand on your paw?"

"Closer."

Finally he saw it. Among the scattered grains of sand on Lybis's paw lay one grain which was not the same as the others. It was the same size, but it was far from being sharp and jagged. It was a perfectly round Black Sphere. "I don't understand. What is it?"

"It's the reason we were brought here. This Black Sphere is what caused the scanners to flare."

Vahnar laughed. "That's silly. Whatever set off the scanners has to be gigantic, as big as a battle cruiser.

That thing isn't even alive."

Lybis gave Vahnar a gentle smile which he recognized instantly. She was about to tell him why he was wrong.

"The moment you told me we were searching for Thaumatar I began to feel uneasy – as though there was something I had forgotten. Something important. As the ship drew closer to the target quadrant I began having visions, both waking and dream state. During these visions I was witness to the last days of Thaumatar.

"The end of Thaumatar began with a stupendous explosion at the brown complex to the west of us. Something went catastrophically wrong there. The force of the blast shot the silver sphere many miles up into the atmosphere. When it came down it was traveling at an unnatural speed, far faster than it should have been, and smashed into the rocky outcropping. The outer silver sphere ruptured, spraying out ferociously hot plasma and sending the Black Sphere flying across the sand.

"When the collision occurred the Black Sphere was infinitesimally small. In fact it was not a sphere, it was a single point. A singularity. Several hours after the crash the singularity began to change, began pulling life force from the surrounding flora and fauna. First the plants and small insects, then the birds flying overhead. They all fell dead, dropping to the desert floor. From that moment on, the planet was in its death throes. Within three days there was not a single living entity on Thaumatar. The life force of every plant and every animal had been drawn into the singularity. When there was no more life to be absorbed, it stopped. It was larger now and the protective black shell had formed around it. Whatever the Thaumatarians were building destroyed them and their planet.

"The universe sent us to this place for one purpose – to retrieve the Black Sphere. It is imperative we take it back to Quintari for study. We must find out precisely what it is and what the Thaumatarians were trying to create. I don't wish to sound excessively dramatic, but if we leave it here it will destroy our entire universe."

Chapter 3

The Flickering Mouse

"It's paws down the best idea we've ever had. Everyone on the island will love it."

"Uhh... really? The *best* idea we've ever had? What about deciding to become treasure hunters and calling ourselves Thunder and Lightning? How about going with Bartholomew and Oliver and Edmund to the lost Mintarian underground city and finding the Seventh Key and all that treasure? What about the fishing boat we bought for our parents?"

Thunder rolled his eyes. "Urghh. You sound like old Madam Bletchley when she would correct me in class. Maybe it's not our *best* idea, but building a grand fishing pier right here for all the islanders is *one* of our best ideas. Just look at that sparkling blue water filled with fat tasty fish. We can afford to build a show stopper of a pier with all the gold and Nirriimian white crystals we found in the Wyrme of Deth. Not to mention we'll be more than famous. They'll probably make statues of us. Do you think I should wear my adventurer hat when I pose for mine?"

Lightning snorted. "They'll probably want you to pose with a sack over your head so your statue doesn't scare the mouselings."

"Excuse me, I seem to remember a certain young lady mouse who said I was–" Thunder stopped, his eyes fixed on the lake.

"What is it? What are you looking at?"

"What? Nothing, I wasn't looking at anything. I was just thinking."

"You saw her again didn't you? Are you going to tell the Thirteenth Monk about her? You should tell him. I would, if I was seeing... *a ghost.*"

"It's not a ghost! It's a lady mouse all dressed in white floating above the water. And flickering. She flickers like a candle."

"Oh, and would you care to explain how that is *not* a ghost? Does she wave her paws at you and moan? Does she have ghost fangs?"

"I told you before, she doesn't have fangs. I don't think it's a ghost. She seems friendly and I think she wants to talk to me. Anyway, I'm not scared of her."

"Maybe you should ask Clara about it. She would know."

"I guess I'll tell the Thirteenth Monk. He told me to let him know if I see anything strange. Besides, we haven't seen Bartholomew or Clara since we got back from the lost city. We got that letter from Oliver though, the one that said the flying carriage company is doing well and so are the two Edmunds. It sounds like Edmund the Explorer is getting used to living in our world. It's a big change from the world he lived in fifteen hundred years ago."

"I hope he finds Emma."

"He will. Clara said he will, and she's always right."

"Let's go get breakfast. We're having snapberry flapcakes today. So yummy."

"Would you eat a snapberry flapcake if it had a big furry green caterpillar crawling across it?"

"Would I have to eat the caterpillar or could I flick it off the flapcake?"

"You could flick it off, but you'd still have muddy caterpillar footprints all over the snapberries. Plus, there *might* be more caterpillars stuffed inside the flapcake."

"Eeew. Would they be cooked or alive?"

"That makes a difference?? Gakk!"

"I'll race you home. Loser has to wear a frilly purple dress when we pose for statues!"

As they darted across the Island of Blue Monks toward their home, Thunder's thoughts turned to the Flickering Mouse he had just seen. He had only recently told Lightning about her, but in truth it had been many weeks since her first appearance. For some reason she always appeared at the lake, floating six or eight feet above the surface, her body flickering like a candle next to a drafty window. Sometimes he could see her mouth move but couldn't hear any words, and sometimes she would gesture for him to come to her. But where should he go? What was she? Was she from this world?

Since their return to the island, Thunder had visited the Thirteenth Monk numerous times and had learned a great deal more about seers. He had a series of exercises he did every night now to hone his skills, to make his visions sharper, the voices clear.

The Thirteenth Monk had showed him how it was possible to see an event which hadn't occurred yet using Clear Vision, a term Thunder had not yet shared with Lightning. He was still a little embarrassed by the idea of being a seer. He didn't want to be different, didn't want the other mice on the island to think he was spooky or creepy, especially that lovely young mouse who worked at the bait shop. Everyone on the island knew about the strange things the Blue Monks could do, but that was different. They were the Blue Monks, and for the most part they kept to themselves.

Thunder had continued his tutoring under the Thirteenth Monk once he realized it was quite easy to conceal his gift from mice who were uncomfortable with that sort of thing. He learned from the Thirteenth Monk that seers often had other abilities besides viewing future events. Some could enter the minds of sleeping mice and communicate with them during their dreams. There were seers like Bartholomew and Clara who could see the thought clouds of other mice, draw them close and read them. This was a skill Thunder was currently trying to learn. He had seen his first thought cloud only two weeks ago at the monastery. The Thirteenth Monk had clapped him on the back and said, "It won't be long now, my friend. No indeed, it won't be long now." Thunder wasn't quite sure what he had meant by that, but he was proud he had seen the thought cloud. His thoughts of the Thirteenth Monk were disrupted by the sound of Lightning's taunting screechy laugh.

"Ha ha, I can see it now, clear as day – a towering statue of Thunder the Great Treasure Hunter wearing a purple frilly dress!" Lightning had reached the front porch mere seconds before Thunder.

"No problem, can I borrow one of your purple frilly

dresses?"

Lightning was preparing to pound Thunder on the arm when their mom called out, "Breakfast!" Seconds later they were seated at the kitchen table.

Lightning's mom patted them both on the shoulder and laughed, "My two favorite treasure hunters – I hope you're not too famous to eat my snapberry flapcakes."

Thunder closed his eyes, breathing in the delectable aromas wafting over from the wood stove. There was nothing in the world like fresh warm snapberry flapcakes. His thoughts turned to the new fishing pier they were planning. How long should it be? A hundred feet? Two hundred feet? He began to imagine what the pier would look like. It should be massive, with great stout pilings strong enough to withstand any storm. There should be plenty of benches where mice could sit and relax on a sunny day, even if they weren't fishing. Maybe they would have slides and swings for the mouselings to play on, and fenced areas for the very little ones. As he visualized the pier, its image became clearer and clearer in his mind. He could see at least a hundred mice on it now, mice who were sitting and chatting, mice who were fishing, mouselings playing on the swings. The image grew sharper still, and he could see the sky was gray and stormy. That was not good, it should be a sunny day. He visualized a clear bright day, just as the Thirteenth Monk had taught him, and soon the gray clouds vanished, replaced by a brilliant cerulean blue sky. The image of the pier was now radiantly clear in his mind. He could almost feel the smooth wood planks beneath his feet, hear the screeching of the birds flying overhead as they dove down to pluck the fish from the sparkling water.

Then it happened. Thunder was standing on the pier. The breakfast table was gone, Lightning was gone, the aroma of snapberry flapcakes was gone – all replaced by the pungent smell of salt air and the sounds of laughing mice. He could hear and see everything as though it was real. This was without a doubt his strangest experience ever. Was the pier real? Was he visiting the future, visiting the pier after they had built it, or was he just imagining this?

He decided to look for clues. He would start by wandering around the pier to see if he recognized any of the mice. Could he talk to them? He noticed an older madam mouse walking in his direction. Creekers, it was Madam Bletchley, the teacher who had given him so much trouble in school. He loved to complain about Madam Bletchley and how strict she was, but he had learned more from her than any of his other teachers. As she approached him he tried to smile as pleasantly as he was able. "Good afternoon, Madam Bletchley, I do hope you're enjoying this lovely sunny day. It's quite a marvelous pier, is it not?"

Madam Bletchley walked right past him as though he wasn't there. This was unexpected. No one could see him here. Was he a ghost? Thunder walked over to an old mouse fishing off the side of the pier. "Excuse me, I couldn't help but notice there's a giant Nadwokk about to bite your ear." The old mouse never even looked up. He was softly humming to himself as he fished.

Thunder was now thoroughly confused. What was this place where no one could see him? Maybe it was the future but he didn't exist here since he was a visitor from the past. Maybe his physical body was still sitting at the breakfast table waiting for the snapberry flapcakes. That made a kind of sense to him. When he thought about it, he liked the idea of being invisible. He strolled down the pier looking closely at all the mice. He recognized almost all of them as island mice. Not a single one reacted to his presence, even when he called out and waved to them. Except for one.

She was standing in a group of mice with her back to him, but he would recognize her white cloak and hood anywhere. It was the Flickering Mouse, but she was not flickering now. She was real, solid, and nothing at all like a ghost. Thunder knew what was going to happen next. He was both thrilled and terrified. She spun around and looked directly at him. He could see her mouth moving, but this time he could hear her words.

"Vahtees! My dearest Vahtees, you can finally hear me, see me. I have waited such a long time for this moment."

Thunder stared blankly at her. Who was Vahtees? Was she looking at someone behind him? He turned around, but there was no one there. He turned back to find the Flickering Mouse standing directly in front of him. There were tears in her eyes.

"Vahtees, I am Lybis. I am your mother."

Chapter 4

A Tale of Sacrifice

Lybis gingerly touched her paw to Thunder's shoulder. "There's no need to say anything now. I understand how confusing this must be for you, and I know you don't recognize me. Sit with me on one of your lovely benches and I will tell you a story."

Thunder could not tear his gaze from Lybis. His thoughts and feelings were racing. He didn't remember her face, but there were other things, small things, like the way she took his paw and led him to the bench. The starchy smell of her white cloak. He never forgot smells. A sudden vision appeared to him – he was at the beach on a hot summer day. He was embarrassed that Lybis was wearing her white cloak. Another mouse was there – was it his father? Vahnar. Vahnar. The name had come from nowhere. Just popped into his head. Lybis and Vahnar. His parents. Lybis and Vahnar.

Lybis sat on the bench holding Thunder's paw. "I knew I could find you in the future. I am a seer. Not the most powerful seer in the world, but still a seer. You have inherited this from me, and one day your abilities will far surpass mine. You and your friend Lightning will bring a great change to Nirriim." She paused for a moment, looking into his eyes.

"I will tell you how you came to be in Nirriim. Your dear father Vahnar is gone. That is part of the story I am going to tell you. It is a long story, but we have all the time we need. We can stay here as long as we wish. When you go back you will return to the moment you left. The snapberry flapcakes will still be cooking and you will remember everything we talked about.

"The Black Sphere. That is where it all began. Your father and I were on the planet Thaumatar, the birthplace of the World Doors. We found a tiny Black Sphere no larger than a grain of sand containing an inconceivable amount of life force. It was created by the Thaumatarians, but it was a creation which brought a cataclysmic end to their civilization. All the life force in their world was drawn into the Black Sphere. When Vahnar and I found the sphere I knew we had to bring it back to Quintari for study. That is where you were born. On the planet Quintari. It's beautiful there. When you were small you would point up to the five moons and–" Lybis turned away, putting her paws to her face as though she was going to cry, then turned back to him. Thunder shifted in his seat as he waited for her to continue.

"I'm sorry. It is difficult to speak of those times. They were the happiest days of my life – Vahnar and I were so proud of our little Vahtees." She gently caressed his arm and continued. "Our journey from Thaumatar to Quintari took over two weeks, even at the fantastic speeds our ship was traveling.

"During the voyage a hidden truth about the Black

Sphere was revealed to me. I sat quietly with the sphere resting in my paw and brought my thoughts to a standstill, allowing only the presence of the Great Universe to enter my awareness. I let my consciousness travel into the Black Sphere, and what I saw there astounded me. Within it I found a universe filled with trillions upon trillions of stars and planets and galaxies, a universe where time was passing at a far greater rate than ours. I realized the life force from Thaumatar had not simply been absorbed, but had taken up residence within this new universe. Life force can never be destroyed, but it can be transferred from one body to the next. Billions of years had passed inside the Black Sphere since its creation. Physical life forms had evolved on countless planets. Civilizations had come and gone. The Great Universe showed this to me in the blink of an eye. It also showed me why I had been brought to Thaumatar.

The Black Sphere was expanding. Slowly at first, but soon it would reach critical mass and the sphere would expand at speeds beyond our comprehension. Our universe would be destroyed in the process, our life force absorbed by the Black Sphere. I had no idea why the Thaumatarians would create such a monstrosity, but I did know we had to stop the sphere from expanding. I told Vahnar everything I had discovered.

"When we returned to Quintari we immediately informed Manghar the Science Guild Master of the Black Sphere and the terrible danger it posed. Like us, he found it to be both frightening and fascinating. For many months we studied the sphere. Eventually we determined that the black outer layer of the sphere was a failsafe put in place by the Thaumatarians to prevent it from expanding in the event of a catastrophic failure such as the one they experienced. It had worked well enough so far, but it would not last much longer. The Thaumatarians may have had a backup plan to further contain the sphere, but we had no idea what it might be.

"What Vahnar and I had not counted on was Manghar telling Counselor Pravus about the Black Sphere. If I had to name one mouse in this world who I consider to be truly evil, the name would be Counselor Pravus, Chief of the Imperial Military Command. He cares only for power and the ceaseless expansion of the Quintarian Empire. Mice mean nothing to him. Lives mean nothing to him.

"When he learned about the Black Sphere, Pravus saw the potential for an unimaginably powerful new weapon. If they could control the Black Sphere they could drop it on an enemy planet and cause it to absorb all the life force on that planet. Their enemy would be gone, but the planet's infrastructure would remain untouched. The lifeless planet could then be colonized and reseeded with our native plants and animals. Within a relatively short time the empire would have a new planet, a new source of raw materials, and further expansion of Quintarian enterprise and industry. With such a weapon nothing could stand in the way of the empire. To our great dismay, Manghar approved of Counselor Pravus's plan and directed us to weaponize the Black Sphere.

"Vahnar thought it morally untenable to destroy worlds simply for economic benefit of the empire, but he wisely kept these thoughts to himself. He was not the only scientist to harbor these feelings, and after some time a group of seven like minded scientists joined forces to form a secret alliance. All seven, your father included, knew something must be done to prevent Pravus from gaining control of the Black Sphere, and together they formulated a plan.

"Vahnar would take the sphere to another world and hide it where Manghar and the military would not be able to find it, even when using their full spectrum scanners. Once the scientists understood the inner dynamics of the sphere, they would retrieve it and eliminate the threat of expansion and the threat of life force absorption. Only Vahnar knew where the sphere was hidden, and he created a cleverly disguised map detailing its precise location, a map meant to be used only in the event of his death. Each scientist received a silver medallion with a small eye embossed on it, the original mark of the Thaumatarians and a mark still used today by many mystical guilds. Individually the medallions were of little value. It was only when all seven medallions were united in a particular fashion that the map would be revealed.

"Several weeks after the medallions were distributed to the scientists, Vahnar requisitioned a scout ship, telling Manghar he was taking his son to visit relatives on the fourth moon of Quintari. He had often taken you there in the past, so Manghar's suspicions were not aroused. Once you and your father were on the ship, he headed to the fourth moon, circling around behind it. Hidden from the main Quintarian comm scanners, he created a spectral doorway to Nirriim large enough for the ship to pass through. Unfortunately, the creation of this spectral doorway did not go unnoticed by the Imperial Military Command."

Lybis stopped for a moment. "Vahtees, what I am

going to tell you now will be difficult for you to hear. Your father lost his life on Nirriim, sacrificing himself to prevent your death at the hands of a biohunter."

"He saved my life? I still have nightmares about something chasing me through the jungle. What are biohunters?"

Lybis's expression grew dark. "They are an abomination created by Counselor Pravus – a genetic aberration whose sole purpose is tracking down and killing fugitives."

"Oh."

"Vahtees, I know your father hid the Black Sphere on Nirriim, but I have no idea where. He was adamant about being the only one to know its location. He knew if Pravus uncovered their plan the other scientists would surely be interrogated, but this way they could not reveal the sphere's location. Once the sphere was safely hidden he had planned on returning to Quintari with you, but fate intervened, as it has a way of doing.

"It turned out a military attack vessel had followed Vahnar through the spectral doorway into Nirriim, and after several days of searching they spotted him on their scanners. Vahnar tried to escape but the scout ship was no match for the attack ship and they quickly caught up to him and opened fire. He went down in the jungle near the Island of Blue Monks. The records show he was badly injured in the crash but managed to get you out of the ship, telling you to run as fast and as far as you could.

"The attack ship landed and took your father aboard for questioning. They were well aware you had been on the scout ship with him and it was Pravus who ordered the biohunter to be sent after you. They told Vahnar if he gave them the location of the sphere they would call off the biohunter, but Vahnar didn't believe them. Vahtees, I don't know how your father did it, but he managed to set off a massive explosion on board the attack ship. It ended his life, but it saved yours. All biohunters are equipped with an internal failsafe system. When the direct connection is broken between the biohunter and its controller, the creature dies. When your father blew up the ship, the direct connection to the biohunter was broken."

Thunder was silent. He could not look at Lybis.

"It's all right, Vahtees. I wanted you to know what your father did and how much he loved you. How much we both loved you. How much I still love you."

"Bartholomew told me the day would come when I would learn how I came to be lost in the jungle and understand the significance of the silver medallion. I wear it every day. I never take it off. Maybe if I hadn't run off when–"

"Don't. If you had stayed, both you and your father would have been killed by Counselor Pravus. Always remember your father knew how much you loved him, and he also knew you would one day become a great seer. The signs were clear from the time you were a mouseling."

"Oh. I'm glad he knew. Both of those things."

"There is something else. Something more pressing. I truly hate to ask this of you, but I am also fully aware it is your destiny. You must bring the seventh medallion back to Quintari and join it with the other six medallions to reveal the location of the Black Sphere. You must do this before it is too late, before the sphere expands."

"Will you be there, on Quintari? Where are you? How do I find the other six medallions?"

"I am on Quintari, but I will not be able to greet you when you arrive. I am being held in Tenebra Military Prison along with the other six scientists. We have been here since Vahnar's death. The other six medallions were all taken by–" Her voice became strangely garbled.

Thunder's heart sank. She was flickering again.

Seconds later Lybis vanished and Thunder found himself sitting at the breakfast table, the air filled with the delightful aroma of warm snapberry flapcakes.

Chapter 5

Dear Oliver

Dear Oliver,

I imagine you were very curious about the contents of this letter. I hope you weren't afraid to open it. Ha ha! I know how much you dislike surprises. You needn't have been anxious, Oliver. I've become a rather good judge of rabbits over the years, and I have found you to be one of the kindest and most thoughtful rabbits I've ever met. Not to mention what a brilliant scientist you are. I will confess it is your purity of heart which draws me to you most of all. And of course how much you love my éclairs. Ha ha! Maybe one day I'll even share the secret ingredients with you! Maybe!

I would dearly love to see you here in Grymmsteir more often, Oliver. I could also visit you at the Fortress of Elders if you like. I would enjoy seeing how you make all those flying carriage Pterosaurs – but please don't ask me to ride in one of those fantastic contraptions! I'm afraid I like my feet firmly planted on the ground. What I'm trying to say is that we share the same feelings for each other. I have known for a long time that you were someone very special in my life.

There is something else I would like to ask you, as you are the only adventurer I know besides my father. I know I haven't told you much about him, but I think it's time I did. Oliver, my mother died when I was very young. I was raised by my father, Arledge Rabbit. He was an adventurer, a free spirit, a duplonium prospector and a treasure hunter, a rabbit who was always searching for the great prize which would change his life, bring him happiness. I accompanied him on many trips into the wilderness in search of duplonium and ancient bits of lost technology from before the Age of Darkness. I suppose many of the objects he found were from these Elders you have told me about. Truthfully I was not much of a treasure hunter, but I liked being with my father and seeing him happy. One day I will show you the duplonium bracelet he made for me. I cherish it to this day but I do have to be quite careful when I wear it! (KA-BOOM! Ha ha!)

I have not seen my father in over three years. The last time he went out treasure hunting he left me behind. He said the trip he was planning would be far too dangerous for me. He had heard stories of a lost city deep in Opar, far to the west of Grymmsteir – a city which had been decimated during the Anarkkian wars. He was certain he could find valuable ancient tech there which would make us wealthy. I didn't want to be wealthy, I just wanted him to stay home, but I knew I couldn't keep him from going. I could not change the kind of rabbit he was. I know now you must accept and love rabbits as they are, even if their view of the world is far different from your own. My father took his journal and his pack and gave me a very long hug. I never saw him again.

After the money ran out I tried selling headache medicine, a concoction discovered by my father on one of his trips. He swore by it, and it worked quite well, but as it turned out the key ingredients were nearly impossible to find, so I moved on to something simpler. I began baking éclairs and selling them at the market. To my great surprise they were wildly successful, and it wasn't long until I opened my own shop. The rest is history. Or at least it was until three weeks ago, when a ragged old prospector came knocking on my door. He presented me with my father's journal. He found it in a cave almost seven hundred miles west of the Grymmorian border, deep in central Opar. There was a note tucked in it containing my name and address, along with the promise of a substantial reward if the journal was returned to me. The prospector refused the reward, saying that returning the journal was simply the right thing to do. He refused to take my credits, but I made certain he left with enough baked goods to feed a small army. It was the least I could do to repay such kindness and integrity.

My father's journal. Where do I even begin? Most of the entries describe his journey across Opar. He was right, it was a very dangerous land. Time and time again he was forced to hide from unscrupulous, even murderous treasure hunters and a wide assortment of terrifying beasts. He mentioned something about large silver colored spiders which gave me a dreadful case of the shivers. After many months he finally reached his destination. He wrote in the journal he had found the lost city of Cathne, destroyed long ago by a fleet of Anarkkian flying ships. The journal also ended with a cryptic note. "Dearest Beffy, I have lost the map but I hope one day you will recover it." This made no sense to me. What map did he mean and how would I ever recover it? I wondered if he was... delirious, or worse, at the time he wrote it. I went to bed that night feeling quite forlorn. I had hoped to find out what had become of him, but all I knew for certain was he had found his lost city of Cathne.

In the middle of the night I woke with a start. A voice in my dream was saying over and over 'Recover it'. It took me a few minutes to realize what it meant. Recover it. Recover it. Re-cover it. The cover of the journal! The map had to be hidden inside the cover. I jumped out of bed and raced to the journal. Oliver, when I unstitched the cover and removed it, I found the map and a letter from my father hidden inside. I could not stop crying. It's all very strange, but I know where he went now. Well, not precisely where he went, but how he went there. He said in the letter that by chance alone he had entered a large collapsed building in Cathne while fleeing from some of those dreadful silver spiders. Ducking down behind a huge mound of rubble he found a doorway which opened up into the lower section of the building. He did say the top half of the building was a bright blue color. He lit a torch and headed deeper into the building. The level he was on had scarcely been touched by the Anarkkian attacks. He made his way through a maze of corridors and hallways, searching dozens of rooms, finding nothing of great value. When he passed through a set of blue doors at the end of the last corridor he found himself facing an extraordinary sight – a wavering blue translucent wall. He poked it with a stick, which moved easily in an out of the blue wall. He even touched the wall with his paw and it caused him no harm. He realized he could walk through the wall if he wished. That was when he saw the figure on the other side. He couldn't tell what it was, other than it walked on two legs, was very short and thin and... bright. He called out but there was no reply. There is not a rabbit in the world who is more curious than my father, and he was compelled beyond reason to discover what lay beyond the wavering wall and who, or what, the mysterious bright figure was. That was when he drew the map and wrote his final letter to me.

He combed the area and found a small cave where the journal would be safely sheltered from the elements, leaving with it the note containing my name and address. That was where the old prospector found it. My father returned to the blue striped building and walked though the rippling wall. What happened after that I cannot even imagine.

Here is my question, Oliver. Do you think it's possible my father might still be alive? Could he still be somewhere behind that wall? I know I'm asking for the impossible, but I wanted to know what you think. You are an adventurer and a scientist and I trust you to give me a truthful answer, no matter how painful it may be.

With all my love,
Madam Beffy

"That's an astonishing letter, Oliver. The blue wall she describes reminds me of the granite wall we use to enter our home here in Pterosaur Valley, although I believe it may have quite a different purpose. I am getting a peculiar feeling about it. I feel quite drawn to it. What do you think, Clara?"

Clara closed her eyes for several long moments. When they blinked open again she said, "It was no accident that the journal was returned to Madam Beffy or that she took the time and effort to write such a lengthy letter to Oliver about her father, Arledge Rabbit. Bartholomew, I believe you should travel to Cathne with Oliver and Edmund the Rabbiton and begin the search for Madam Beffy's father. He is most certainly an integral part of this chain of events. I will not be going to Cathne with you. I must stay here and wait. When the time comes it will be clear what I need to do."

Oliver stood up, pacing nervously back and forth. "Great heavens, do you think this means Madam Beffy's father might still be alive after all this time? If this is true we must leave as soon as possible. Hold on, I have an idea – our new prototype Mark X Pterosaur needs to be flight tested. It's far quieter and faster than our current line of Pterosaurs, and I'm certain she'll maintain a cruising speed of almost one hundred miles per hour. If we take the Mark X, it shouldn't take us any time at all to reach Cathne, not to mention we'll be warm and safe inside the cabin and far from those dreadful silver spider creatures Madam Beffy mentioned. Just the thought of them gives me a case of the willies. We can land next to the building with the blue stripe, make our way through the maze of corridors, step through the blue wall and look for Madam Beffy's father. Then, quick as a flash hop right back into the Pterosaur and be home again. It couldn't be simpler. This could be the least adventurous adventure we've had yet."

Bartholomew looked dubious. "I do envy your optimism. I suppose it all depends on what we find on the other side of the blue wall. That is the missing part of the equation – we will be entering uncharted territory with no idea of what awaits us. I do like your idea of taking the new Mark X Pterosaur for a test run. It should get us there quickly and safely. We can pack whatever gear we need here, then take your Pterosaur back to the Fortress of Elders and pick up Edmund the Rabbiton and the new Mark X Pterosaur." Bartholomew grinned. "I can't wait to tell Edmund where we're taking the Mark X for it's maiden flight. He'll pop that purple feathered adventurer's hat on his head before I can finish saying 'Opar'."

Chapter 6

Up, Up and Away!

"Edmund, did you pack an extra hat in case you lose yours?"

"I think you know quite well a true intrepid adventurer never, ever, loses his hat, so there really is no reason for me to pack a spare one. Besides, if that unlikely event should occur you could shape a new one for me in the blink of an eye."

Edmund the Rabbiton grinned as he climbed the narrow ladder into the Mark X Pterosaur. His eyes scanned the ship's surprisingly plush interior. "Oliver, this is quite a luxurious craft compared to the one which carried us to Nirriim."

"You mean the ship we crashed in that dreadful sandy desert after you sent us through your frightening spectral doorway? The ship which was devoured by the terrifying Wyrme of Deth in Nirriim after you sent us through your frightening spectral doorway?? That one?" Oliver threw back his head and roared with laughter.

Edmund ran his fingers across his chin. "Let me

think... who *was* the captain of that ill fated craft? Please correct me if I am in error, but isn't the captain of the ship always held responsible for any–"

"Well, it most certainly wasn't *my* fault the duplonium engines all failed the moment we entered Nirriim. I could not possibly have–"

Edmund the Rabbiton let loose his unique staccato laugh, a laugh that brought to mind the raucous cry of the colorful Kukululu bird found deep in the rain forests of Nirriim.

"Ha ha ha ha! Ha ha ha ha! As you can see I am getting quite adept at humorous repartee. Edmund the Explorer has been instructing me in the finer points of humorous interaction between rabbits. Did you see how I cleverly turned the tables and made you feel responsible for the demise of our ship, even though the actual cause was obviously the divergent physical laws of Nirriim? I have also learned quite a number of jokes from Edmund the Explorer which he assures me are extremely humorous. Would you like to hear the one about three drunken lady rabbits who walk into a pub filled with mice?"

"Oh, dear, I think not. We have far too many things to do before we leave. No time for jokes, I'm afraid. We mustn't be late. Madam Beffy's father could be there waiting for someone to rescue him."

"Perhaps you're right. I will scan Madam Beffy's map into my Interworld Positioning System and calculate the most efficient and safest route to the lost city of Cathne."

"Excellent, while you're doing that I will check the diagnostics on the Mark X to make certain everything is functioning smoothly. We have integrated a few systems into the Mark X from the ancient blinker ships we found on the fourth sub-level of the Fortress. There is now an anti-grav assist module which makes her much quieter, faster, and more efficient than the previous Pterosaurs. Augustus C. Rabbit is doing a marvelous job of running the company, so I have no qualms about leaving him at the helm during my absence."

Oliver slid open a large panel from the port side of the ship. "Hmm... everything seems to be functioning properly. The new self-diagnostic systems the engineering Rabbitons installed certainly simplify maintenance. I believe we are ready to go whenever you are, Bartholomew, so it's up, up, and away!" He chuckled to himself as he watched Bartholomew load the rest of their gear into the starboard storage compartments.

Bartholomew maneuvered the last adventuring pack into place. "You're as efficient as ever, Captain Oliver. This new ship is marvelous, by the way. How different it is from the old duplonium wagon we had on our first adventure."

"Quite so. I believe *we* have changed over the years as much as our mode of transportation has. Quite astonishing how little I really knew about the universe back then. I will never again fool myself into thinking I know everything there is to know."

"Well said, Oliver. I could not agree more. Edmund, are we ready?"

"Quite ready. This small green dot on the holoscreen is our Mark X Pterosaur. I have linked the ship's navigation system to my Interworld Positioning System and set a course which will take us directly to Cathne.

No navigation on our part will be necessary."

"Amazing, you are a wonder."

Edmund beamed, obviously pleased at Bartholomew's compliment.

Oliver took his place at the main console of the ship. "Take your seats, my adventuring friends. We're off to the lost city of Cathne to rescue Madam Beffy's father!"

With a muffled humming sound the sleek silver Mark X Pterosaur took to the skies. As the ship's velocity increased a clear canopy slid smoothly forward from a hidden compartment at the stern of the craft.

"Wonderful! The new canopy works perfectly – no loud roaring wind for us! We'll hardly have to raise our voices, even at speeds approaching one hundred miles per hour. How high will we be flying, Edmund? Not too high, I hope. I believe the altitude providing the most advantageous view of the landscape below is approximately five hundred feet."

Edmund nodded. "Precisely. I have set our speed fifteen percent below maximum cruising velocity, and she'll mimic the topography of the terrain below us at a constant altitude of five hundred feet for the entire voyage to Cathne. It should be a smooth ride all the way there."

Conversation dwindled as the trio of adventurers grew entranced by the lush forests and sparkling rivers passing below them. The hours flew by unnoticed until Edmund called out, "We've crossed over from Grymmore into Opar. We'll see a few small towns and villages along the Grymmorian border, but I don't believe we will encounter any as we move deeper into Opar. Edmund the Explorer described to me in great detail how the land was decimated by the Anarkkians during the war. Cities were obliterated and the great civilization of Opar was left in ruins. Horrific poisons were spread across the landscape by the dreaded Anarkkian cloud bombs. Centuries later there were still vast swatches of lifeless terrain to be found within Opar. Even today few dare to enter this forgotten territory other than bold treasure hunters such as Madam Beffy's father."

Oliver gave a sigh. "It's incomprehensible how any living creature could do such things to another. Wait, what is that?" He pointed to a large dark splotchy area of ground below them.

Bartholomew studied the peculiar landscape as they passed over it. "It could be the result of one of those Anarkkian cloud bombs you spoke of. There's no vegetation at all that I could see. It could be a trick of the light, but I think I saw some movement down there. I suppose it could be treasure hunters."

Oliver looked dubious. "Why would treasure hunters be interested in contaminated areas such as that? Wouldn't they be searching through the ruins of ancient cities?"

Bartholomew shrugged. "It's hard to know. Maybe they're just passing through. Anyway, I'm not really sure what I saw."

Edmund was unusually silent. He had noticed the movement also and zoomed in with his enhanced optics to identify the source. His eyes widened when he saw it, but he said nothing. There was no reason to unduly alarm the others. He would tell them later, perhaps after they had safely returned home with Madam Beffy's father.

Their first Oparian sunset was a magnificent display of nature's boundless beauty, and following a glass of tasty white wine they unfolded their beds and retired for the night. Edmund had no need for sleep, but lay on his back gazing up at the brilliant stars above, wondering if any of those far off worlds could be inhabited by other living Rabbitons like him. There were times when being the only living Rabbiton on Earth made him ache with a dreadful feeling of profound loneliness.

* * *

Bartholomew was strolling through the Timere Forest. He liked the forest. There were lovely birds twittering about and glowing beams of sunlight streaming down through the trees. He hummed to himself as he meandered along the forest path. "Hm hmmm hmmm... I do love a nice walk beneath the towering pines..."

"Ah, greetings Bartholomew. Having a pleasant little sojourn here in the forest?"

Bartholomew turned toward the sound of the voice, his eyes coming to rest on Bruno Rabbit.

"Hello, Bruno, lovely to see you. Such a nice forest."

"Indeed. You don't seem surprised to see me here."

"Surprised? Why would I be surprised?"

"Well, it's your dream, not mine."

"Mm hmmm."

"You don't know you're dreaming do you?"

"I'm sorry, what did you just say?"

"I would like you to do something for me. I would like you to stare at your paws. Focus on them, force

them to become sharp and real, see every hair."

"Okay."

Bartholomew looked at his paws. At first they appeared soft and fuzzy and it was difficult to focus on them, difficult to make them stop drifting about like two furry clouds. When they finally did become sharp and crisp and clear something quite extraordinary happened. A brilliant rush of awareness flooded through Bartholomew. He was really there in the forest, fully present in the moment. The entire forest had become as sharp and as clear as his paws. The path he was strolling on had become real. He could see clearly the smallest details, smell the pine trees, feel the soft blanket of pine needles beneath his feet, the warmth of the sun on his fur. "What is this? Where am I? Bruno? Bruno Rabbit? Did you bring me here?"

"Ah, there you are. Awake at last. You have finally woken up inside one of your dreams. Excellent. Now, I would like you to answer one very simple question for me. Why do—"

Bartholomew's eyes darted anxiously about the forest. "This is a dream? I have woken up inside a dream? How is that possible? What does that even mean?"

"There's nothing to it. When you focused on your paws, you brought to bear your full awareness and consciousness, making the dream seem real."

"This is amazing! It's like I'm really here in the Timere Forest. I can't wait to tell Clara about this."

"Clara has been doing this since she was a bunny."

"Oh."

"Now, are you ready to answer my question?"

"Of course. I think. Are you really Bruno or are you

a dream Bruno?

"Is there a difference?"

"Umm..."

"Here is my question. Why do you walk in your dreams?"

"Well... what? What else would... umm... to get somewhere?"

"Think, please. There are no laws of physics in your dreams. No gravity. No equal and opposite reactions, no bodies tending to stay in motion. There is no physical matter here, only thought. Why do you tromp along the forest floor instead of soaring and swooping through the trees like some great long eared bird? What is it that keeps your big furry feet planted firmly on the ground?"

Bartholomew looked puzzled. "Hmm... you know, you might be on to something here. If this is a dream, and I'm quite certain it is, the laws of physics and motion really do not apply here."

"And so..."

"Um..." Bartholomew clapped his paws together. "I've got it! The laws of physics here are my own creation. I am bringing them with me from the waking world and allowing myself to be controlled by them. This is incredible! Why have I not thought of this before?"

"And what can you do about these self-imposed restrictions?"

"Well, for one thing, since there is no gravity and this is my dream, couldn't I jump as high as I want?"

"Why just jump? Couldn't you fly?"

"I don't see why not." Bartholomew raised his arms and grinned. Bruno watched Bartholomew's features

blur as he shot up into the air at precisely four thousand two hundred twenty-nine miles per hour, shrieking like a terrified little bunny.

Bartholomew woke up to find himself back in his bunk on the Mark X Pterosaur as it hummed along beneath the glittering night sky.

Chapter 7

Clonk it!

As the Mark X Pterosaur skimmed along through the clear blue Oparian skies, Bartholomew sat hunched over in his comfortable lounge chair, deep in thought. "That dream I had. It seemed so real. And Bruno Rabbit. If it really was him and he is able to enter my dreams, that in itself is incredible. There has to be more to this. I know Bruno Rabbit, and every action he takes has deep purpose. He would not make such an effort simply to teach me how to fly in my dreams. I'm missing something, I know I am. I wish Clara was here. She's so much better at understanding these things than I am."

"Bartholomew, look at this! The auto-nav is taking us through a fantastic gorge. It's quite marvelous. See how the stratified layers of rock are so clearly delineated? Fascinating!"

Bartholomew sat up, his attention now on the chasm they were passing through. Oliver was right – the layers of multicolored rock running across the deep vertical walls were strikingly beautiful. The ship was cruising at the preset altitude of five hundred feet and the canyon walls extended upward at least another three or four hundred feet. "Magnificent, Oliver. The gorge is at least eight or nine hundred feet deep and at least half a mile wide. Look down there at that river running through the canyon. It reminds me of those dreadful rapids along the Halsey River."

As Bartholomew and Oliver were gazing down at the roaring river, Edmund was looking out across the bow of the Mark X. Something in the distance had caught his eye. It was well over a mile downriver but he could see some sort of gauzy material stretched across the entire gorge from top to bottom and side to side. "That's very odd indeed. Look up ahead. There's something blocking the gorge. It looks like a sheer fabric of some kind. I'll magnify and display the image on the holoscreen." Seconds later the trio stood staring at the display.

"Great heavens! It's some kind of gigantic net. Who would do such a thing? Who would put a great net across a canyon? Edmund! Take control of the ship and get us out of this blasted gorge before we hit that dastardly creation!"

Edmund sprang to the main console, his fingers a blur as he tapped on the grid of colored discs. He grabbed the number one control stick and pulled back. "Nothing is happening! I can't control the ship! I can't override the autonomous nav system!"

"We'll be there in less than a minute! There's nothing you can do?"

"I've tried everything. The engineering Rabbitons must have installed a faulty failsafe override module. We're going to hit the net at almost ninety miles an hour!"

Bartholomew grabbed Oliver's paw. "Okay, we're going to blink down to the bottom of the gorge. Edmund, you stay with the ship. You're indestructible so you'll be fine. Once the ship hits, hold on to the net then climb down. We'll find a way out." With a brilliant flash of light Bartholomew and Oliver vanished, reappearing a split second later next to the raging river five hundred feet below the Mark X. They watched anxiously as the sleek silver craft shot toward the enormous net. Time seemed to slow down as the ship hit the glistening white ropes. The net easily withstood the impact of the craft, absorbing the force of the collision by stretching backwards several hundred feet, then snapping back to its original position.

"Look, the ship didn't fall! It must have gotten wedged between the ropes on the net. There's Edmund – he's okay."

Oliver and Bartholomew could see Edmund climbing to the top of the dangling craft. He stood on the bow of the ship and waved to them, then flipped on his voice projection system and called out, "I'm going to jump to the net and climb down! I'll be there in a moment!"

Edmund sprang from the bow to the net, grasping the heavy rope with both hands, positioning his feet on the ropes below him.

"He made it!"

"Why isn't he climbing down? What's he doing?"

"I can't tell. He's fiddling with something, he's moving around in a rather odd fashion. What is that Rabbiton up to?

Edmund's magnified voice boomed out across the

enormous ravine. "I can't pull my hands or feet off the net. I don't wish to cause any undue alarm, but I'm quite certain this is not so much a net as it is a gigantic spider web. I saw a spider as we passed over that contaminated area yesterday. They're extremely hard to see, but quite large, at least fifty or sixty feet across. You might want to keep your eyes open for the one who made this web."

"Great heavens, did he say spider web? A fifty foot spider? That's quite absurd. It's simply physiologically and anatomically impossible for an arachnid to grow to–" Oliver stopped. His eyes were on the far wall of the great canyon on the other side of the roaring river. He shook his head, frowning. A large section of the stratified rock wall seemed to be wavering like a sail in the wind. "I think I my vision may have been affected when you blinked us down. That rock wall seems to be..."

Oliver let out a terrified shriek. "SPIDER! GIGANTIC SPIDER!!"

Bartholomew had just started to turn when a red beam of light shot across the river, hitting him square on the back. The force of the beam blasted Bartholomew across the rocky canyon floor and sent him crashing into the gorge wall. He tumbled motionless to the rocky floor. Oliver's eyes were wide and desperate. "Bartholomew! Bartholomew! EDMUND! Bartholomew has been injured!"

Unfortunately for Oliver, Edmund was still five hundred feet in the air, stuck to the monstrous web, watching helplessly as Oliver ran toward Bartholomew. The nightmarish eight legged monstrosity was now clearly visible and was heading toward Oliver. The roaring river presented no obstacle to the great behemoth. Its enormous silver legs allowed it to amble across the wild river like a rabbit fording a shallow stream. Oliver reached Bartholomew, dragging him behind a huge boulder at the base of the canyon wall.

"Oh great heavens, Bartholomew, please wake up! The spider is coming this way! You have to shape one of those defensive spheres around us. Please wake up!"

That was the moment Oliver heard a voice cry out. "Clonk it! Clonk it!" Oliver was close to hysteria, his head swiveling madly about looking for the source of the voice.

"Clonk it! Just clonk it!"

Oliver cried out, "Who are you? I don't know what that means! I don't understand what you're saying!!"

The massive spider was now only thirty feet from Oliver. Its body was coated with a gleaming silver material, sunlight sparkling and flashing off its eight massive jointed legs. Oliver gaped in horror at the six glowing red eyes sitting above the spider's enormous scissored poisonous fangs.

"Oh dear. Oh dear. This can't be real."

"Like this! Clonk it like this!"

A tall rabbit wearing tattered clothing leaped out from behind a nearby boulder and raced toward the spider. The spider was quick, but the mysterious rabbit was quicker. Right before she reached the spider the rabbit leapfrogged over a massive boulder onto one of the spider's gleaming silver legs. Scampering up the side of the great creature she stood on its back in less than a second, a jagged rock held high in one paw. With a loud cry she smashed it down on the spider's head, or as Oliver would later write in his journal, the spider's *prosoma*. The gigantic arachnid stopped, slowly sinking to the ground with a peculiar whirring noise, its six red glowing eyes fading to a dark shade of blue.

Oliver's eyes darted back and forth between the tall mystery rabbit wearing the tattered clothing and the monstrous silver spider. Finally they settled on the lovely rabbit who had saved his life. "You stopped the spider! You killed it using only a rock!"

"The Silver Legs is not dead. It will heal itself in one day and rise again."

"Bartholomew!" Oliver cried out when he noticed Bartholomew moving painfully to an upright sitting position. "Are you all right?"

"Uhhgh. I will be in a moment." He held both paws together until a golden light emanated from his body, then quickly faded away.

"Good as new." Bartholomew rose to his feet. Who is our lovely new friend, and what is that silver monstrosity?"

Oliver shook his head. "I have no idea. She popped out from behind a boulder and saved me from being devoured by the spider. She says she 'clonked it'. Apparently that means leaping on top of it and bashing it on the prosoma with a sharp rock."

The newcomer turned to Bartholomew and said, "I am called Renata. There is a yellow protrusion on top of the Silver Legs. If you hit it with a rock the creature will fall for one day, then it will walk again."

Oliver strode over to the immobile beast, running his paw over the gleaming outer skin. "Very peculiar exoskeleton. It would appear that it is–"

"Hello, down there! If you hadn't noticed, I'm still stuck to this web!"

Bartholomew grinned and waved to Edmund. "Oliver, any ideas how we can get him down?"

Renata provided a ready answer to Bartholomew's question. "Fire. The web's weakness is fire."

Bartholomew nodded, calling out, "Edmund, I'm afraid you're going to be taking a bit of a tumble!"

"Just get me down, please!"

Bartholomew flicked his paw and a brilliant beam of orange light sizzled across the canyon into the web. A ragged line of brilliant fire raced up the web, turning the whole structure to ashes in a matter of seconds. They watched as Edmund and the Mark X tumbled five hundred feet to the ground below, clouds of billowing dust and flying stones marking their landing spots. When the dust had settled Bartholomew could see the ship sitting on the river bank pinned between two immense boulders. Edmund emerged from behind one of the boulders, brushing the dust off himself. "Ah, lovely to be back on solid ground again."

Renata's eyes had widened when she saw the orange beam shoot out from Bartholomew's paw, but they widened even more when she saw Edmund. "Is that a Silver Legs? Shall I clonk it?"

Oliver chuckled. "There have been a few times when I desperately wanted to clonk him, but no need for that now. He is our dear friend Edmund the Rabbiton. You'll find him to be quite marvelous company, though at times he can be rather exasperating."

"He is made of the same substance as the Silver Legs. He is ancient tech, from before the Time of Darkness?"

"Indeed so, but he is also the only truly living Rabbiton in this world. If I'm not mistaken, our large eight-legged friend over there is also ancient tech. The moment I touched it I knew it was a machine. It has a rather marvelous camouflage system built into its outer defensive layer. Bartholomew, do you recall creating that invisibility sphere around our wagon at the Ferillium Inn? I believe this system functions in a similar fashion. Light enters one side of the spider and exits out the other side. The viewer does not see the spider, seeing instead what is behind the spider. Quite ingenious, I must say."

"The elders of our village told us many stories of the Silver Legs. They arrived during the Time of Darkness, sent here to destroy us. They live on, though the dark times have long passed."

Bartholomew nodded. "The Anarkkians must have brought them here during the war. Maybe Edmund the Explorer will be able to tell us more about them when we return. A more pressing matter is us figuring out how to get out of this gorge. Obviously we can't fly out, so—"

Renata interrupted Bartholomew. "I will examine your ship. I have a gift with ancient tech. I will repair it and travel with you. My family is gone. My village is gone. I have no reason to stay here." She turned quickly, bounding across the jagged rocks to the Mark X.

"Bartholomew, do you think we should let her touch the ship? Only the Engineering Rabbitons are capable of repairing an auto-nav malfunction. Suppose she..."

"What harm can it do to let her try? The ship is already out of commission. I also think it would be wise to let her join our party. She knows the land and can guide us to the lost city of Cathne. There may be areas it would be best for us to avoid."

The trio of adventurers followed Renata to the fallen ship. Both her paws were resting on the side of the craft. "Here." She slid open a wide silver panel revealing thick bundles of multicolored wires running to dozens of pale green cubes and three rows of striped blue cylinders covered with indecipherable symbols. Renata stood back and gazed at the impossibly complex electronic system, then pointed. "This one. This is the source of your problem." She reached in and yanked out one of the green cubes.

"Good heavens, are you sure we should–"

"Let her finish."

Renata tossed the cube over her shoulder into the river, her eyes still on the bundles of wires. She reached in, twisted a dozen sets of wires together and turned several of the striped cylinders. "Your ship will fly now. I will travel with you."

Oliver looked over to Edmund with a shake of his head. "Well, give it a try, my tall silver friend." His face wore a mask of doubt right up to the moment Edmund pulled back on the number one control stick and the Mark X Pterosaur gently lifted off the ground.

Bartholomew grinned. "What do you think? Do we have a new engineer?"

"Great heavens, Renata, how on earth did you do that? You must have read the Elders' original engineering texts. Your practical knowledge of engineering and mechanics is astonishing."

"I don't know how I am able to do these things. I simply look at the tech and then I remember. I remember how to fix it. I could do this even when I was a bunny."

Bartholomew looked at Renata through new eyes. "Fascinating." He couldn't wait to tell Clara about this. She would probably have an explanation for Renata's unusual ability. "Well, however you did it, you have saved the day, Renata. You are more than welcome to join our party. We were on our way to the lost city of Cathne when our ship malfunctioned and we ran into the spider web."

Renata hesitated, turning to look upriver. "I have lived here my whole life, but the time has come for me to put my home behind me. My village and everyone in it was destroyed by bandits almost six months ago. There was a rumor being passed around that we had discovered a hoard of gold from before the Time of Darkness. I was out searching for tech when the bandits came. When I returned, I found everyone dead, the village burned. The rumor was false – there was never any gold. I suppose the bandits were furious when they found nothing. They killed everyone."

Oliver's face softened. "Such a loss is unfathomable. I heartily agree with Bartholomew – you are quite welcome to travel in our company for as long as you wish."

Renata nodded. "It is my destiny. I will go to the lost city of Cathne with you." She stepped over to the ship's ladder and climbed into the Mark X.

Several minutes later the craft took to the air. Edmund called out to Oliver, "Steady at five hundred feet, traveling west toward Cathne at ninety miles per hour. I will keep our altitude constant at five hundred feet. Not to mention keep both eyes open for giant spider webs. Ha ha ha ha!"

Oliver did not hear Edmund's attempt at dark

humor. He was gazing down at the massive slumbering Silver Legs, its gleaming outer skin sparkling and glimmering brightly in the warm afternoon sun. It was hard to believe something so beautiful had nearly brought his life to an end.

Chapter 8

Clara's Visitors

Clara's eyes were on Pterosaur Valley, but her thoughts were of Bartholomew. He was sailing through the skies of Opar on his way to the lost city of Cathne and she had just received a thought cloud detailing the events of his journey so far. He told her about a strange rabbit named Renata with the ability to intuitively diagnose and repair complex Elder technology. This had piqued Clara's curiosity and for the last hour she'd been contemplating what circumstances could have led to such a unique skill. So the brilliant blast of blinding light that exploded behind her, followed by a cacophony of wild bloodcurdling shrieks was the very last thing she was expecting at that particular moment.

Clara, however, had been tutored since she was a bunny in the mystical art of shaping by none less than Bruno Rabbit, arguably the greatest shaper of all time. Before the last piercing shriek had ended, Clara was surrounded by an impenetrable sphere of defense. She turned to see a blur of two dark figures tumbling across the floor toward her and watched with some curiosity as they careened into the intensely powerful energy field surrounding her.

"OW! I think I broke my ear! AHH, it hurts!"

"Umm... you can't break your ear. Ears don't have bones in them."

"Owww... what?? Of course ears have bones in them, how do you think they stand up straight?"

"They don't have bones. If you'd paid even a little attention in school you'd know they have cartilage in them, not bones. And you can't break cartilage."

"Oh, thank you very much, Mister Oliver T. Mouse. I don't care what you say, I broke my ear and it's your fault. I told you we shouldn't run through that crazy spectral whatever it's called the Thirteenth Monk made."

Clara flicked her wrist and the defensive sphere around her vanished. "Well, if it isn't my treasure hunting friends, Thunder and Lightning. To what do I owe this extremely unexpected and rather rambunctious visit? Did I hear you mention something about the Thirteenth Monk sending you here?"

"Clara, could you look at my ear? I think I broke it."

Clara couldn't hide her smile as she stepped over to Thunder and gently examined his ear. "You'll be fine. You may have just twisted it when you hit the defensive sphere. Now, tell me why the Thirteenth Monk sent you here."

Lightning couldn't answer fast enough. "Thunder's real mom said he has to take his silver medallion back to Quintari and join it with the other six medallions that are hidden somewhere so we can find the map and do something to the Black Sphere before it explodes and destroys the universe. Destroys it. Totally. Destroys it."

Lightning dramatically raised one eyebrow.

Thunder pushed Lightning aside and took over. "So we went to see the Thirteenth Monk and he said we should come and see you because you would take us to Quintari and help us rescue my mom and keep the Black Sphere from expanding and sucking up all the life force in our universe, and that includes us."

"Okay. Thunder, Lightning, I want you both to sit down on this couch. Thunder, you need to start from the beginning and very slowly tell me the whole story. Leave nothing out."

Almost an hour later, after hearing about Thunder's meeting with Lybis on the pier of the future and how Vahnar had hidden the Black Sphere on Nirriim and sacrificed his own life to save Thunder, Clara was satisfied she knew everything Thunder and Lightning knew.

"Your visit is the event I have been waiting for. Somehow your Black Sphere is connected to the disappearance of Madam Beffy's father, although how two such disparate events could possibly be connected currently eludes me. But, we shall press on nevertheless and when the time is right all shall become clear. I will go to Quintari with you, which won't be as difficult as it sounds. Bartholomew and I have read the journals and documents Bruno Rabbit left behind when he moved to the City of Mandora. In one of the journals he noted that World Door Three opens directly into Quintari. It is clear our first objective should be the prison where your mother is being held captive. The location of the other six medallions remains a mystery, but I imagine your mother will be able to help us with that. Lightning, you have told your parents where we're going?"

"Yes, I told them we were both going to Quintari with you."

"Excellent. We need to move forward with all possible haste. I am getting powerful feelings of great unease surrounding this Black Sphere. I don't believe we have much time. We should get a good night's sleep and in the morning blink to the World Doors in the Swamp of Lost Things. The third door will take us to Quintari, although precisely *where* it will take us on Quintari I have no idea. But, as dear Bartholomew always says, "If we knew what was going to happen, it wouldn't be an adventure.""

Thunder was the first to rise the next morning. He'd had a difficult time falling asleep, plagued by an unending stream of questions running wildly through his head. How would they ever rescue Lybis from a high security military prison? What about all the guards? How would they even find the prison? And where were all the other medallions? And if they did eventually find the Black Sphere, what would they even do with it? Then he remembered something the Thirteenth Monk had said to him.

"Thunder, a thought is an action you take, no different from picking up a stone or drinking a glass of water. You are the one who decides what you are going to think. Don't let your thoughts jump around like a wild monkey leaping from branch to branch. You have the power to control your thoughts. This is something you must learn." The Thirteenth Monk also said, "A mouse can only think about one thing at a time. If you're thinking about *this*, then you're not thinking about *that*." Thunder decided he would make a conscious effort to think about something else other than their impending trip to Quintari. When he finally drifted into the world of dreams his mind was filled with pleasant thoughts of the new fishing pier he and Lightning were planning to build.

After everyone had risen Clara shaped a hearty breakfast and one hour later they blinked to the Swamp of Lost Things.

"Aghh!" We have to walk through this smelly goopy muck? Gaak!"

"I bet some creepy snake thing with big poison fangs will slither into your boot and then.... SNAPPY SNAPPERS!" Lightning let out a shriek of laughter. Thunder was not amused.

Clara shushed them. "Quiet, you two. There's a time for humor, but that time is not now. We need to find the World Doors." She pulled out Bartholomew's old pair of World Glasses, the ones he had found in the Skeezle Brother's shop. She donned the glasses and looked around. She had tried to blink them close to the door and she wasn't far off – the ancient wooden door was floating above the swamp less than fifty feet away. "This way." Clara pointed toward the door.

When they arrived Clara pulled the golden key out of a flapped side pocket. She held it up and grinned. "We don't want to lose this. You remember what happened the last time one got lost."

Thunder snorted. "I remember we each got a bag of gold nuggets and Nirriimian White Crystals!"

Lightning tapped Clara on the arm. "I can't see the World Door. How do you know it's here?"

Clara handed Lightning the World Glasses. "Both of you take a turn looking through these."

"Whoa! I can see it, plain as day!"

Clara slipped the glasses back into her coat pocket and swung open the World Door.

For a number of reasons Clara was a rabbit who was not often surprised, and on the rare occasions when she was surprised, she was quite good at concealing it. This was not one of those times. This time she let out a piercing yelp and stumbled backwards, bumping into Thunder, who then tripped over Lightning's foot and plunged into the foul muck. Lightning managed to dodge the falling Thunder while keeping his eyes on the hallway, trying to get a glimpse of what had startled Clara. One of the doors was wide open and a long green scaly tail covered with thousands of thorn-like yellow protrusions was poking out. The creature was slithering through the doorway, but froze when it heard Clara's yelp of surprise. Then, with a peculiar rustling noise, a mottled green and brown scaly face with two bulbous yellow eyes peeked out from behind doorway. When it spotted the trio of adventurers the beast made a shrill whistling sound, jerking its head back behind the door. Seconds later the tail wiggled out of sight and the door slammed shut.

Lightning could barely speak. "Oh, creekers. Oh, creekers. Please don't tell me that was door three."

Clara was herself once again. "No, we're in luck, that was door two. How odd – all this time I've never thought about all the other creatures who might be using the World Doors. I'm surprised we've never run into one before." She grinned at Thunder and Lightning. "Surprised *and* delighted!" Lightning cackled with nervous laughter and stepped up into the corridor, his eyes flitting from door to door. "We should hurry, Clara. We need to find that Black Sphere."

Clara smiled, inserting the gold key into door three. It opened with a soft click, accompanied by a captivating melody reminiscent of the ocean's wordless song of incomparable beauty. Lightning bolted through the doorway.

Chapter 9

Paradise Lost

The truth of the matter was Lightning had darted through door three because he was afraid the frightening green lizard they had just seen would make another appearance. That did not happen, however, and Lightning's fear evaporated like morning fog in the warm afternoon sun the moment he stepped into Quintari. Before him lay the most beautiful beach he had ever seen. Glorious white sands sloped gently down to an equally glorious emerald green ocean. Small waves rhythmically lapped up against the shore, leaving ripples of bubbling foam as they slipped back into the sea. Radiant sunlight glinted off exquisitely formed seashells scattered along the glistening sandy beach while soft tropical breezes swirled across the rolling dunes.

Lightning let out a great long sigh. "Creekers... double creekers! Now *this* is more like it. I might just have to move here."

He heard Clara and Thunder step through the World Door but couldn't tear his eyes from the impossibly beautiful vista that lay before him. He heard Thunder cry out, "Whoa! Now *this* is a beach. Let's go swimming!" He dashed past Lightning. "Last one in is a big hairy Nadwokk!"

Thunder dove straight into the sparkling sea, popping up seconds later, wiping the cool invigorating sea water from his face, the putrid swamp muck on his clothes washed away in moments. "Come on in, Nadwokk, the water is–" Thunder's face froze, his eyes riveted on what lay behind Lightning and Clara.

What lay behind Lightning and Clara was the other side of the very, very small island they were standing on. A very small island in a very, very, very large sea. "What... where's all the... how do..." Seeing the surprise on Thunder's face, Lightning spun around, quickly coming to the same startling realization as Thunder. They were standing on a minuscule island in the center of a vast ocean with no other land in sight.

"Creekers! What is this? They tricked us! Why would they put a World Door here? Arggh! I do not like Quintari at all!"

Clara was equally surprised but far less concerned about their fate than Thunder and Lightning. They could always go back through the World Door to the Swamp of Lost Things and more than likely find another way to reach Quintari. Clara also had a deeper understanding of how the universe worked. She knew there were invisible strings connecting events which on the surface did not appear to be connected. The universe had brought them to this island. Why? A tiny island in the middle of an enormous sea on a strange faraway planet in another dimension. What could possibly be here? She scanned the horizon for movement but saw none. She called out to Thunder and Lighting. "All is not lost, my treasure hunting friends. Let's explore what there is of the island and see what we find."

Lightning looked up at the brilliant sun, squinting his eyes and putting both paws to his throat. His voice was dry and raspy. "Uhhh... thirsty... sooo thirsty. Need water..."

Thunder rolled his eyes. "We haven't even been here ten minutes and you're dying of thirst?"

"Excuse me, in case you hadn't noticed we're on a sun-baked desert island and the last time I checked there weren't any water fountains here."

Clara flicked her wrist and a small table appeared in front of her. Sitting on the table was a large pitcher of cold lemonade and three glasses. "Would anyone care for some lemonade?"

Thunder gave the most pleasant smile he was capable of. "Thank you so much, Clara, but I'm not really thirsty right now since we just had breakfast an hour ago, but it's entirely possible one of the other inhabitants on this sun-baked desert isle is quite thirsty and might like a glass. I'm going to go exploring now." He gave Lightning a severe look then burst out laughing. "Maybe I'll find a water fountain!" Thunder dashed up the hill toward the highest point of the island, which was only about twenty feet above sea level. The peak of the island was crowned with several dozen palm trees, most of them bearing bunches of hanging green fruit.

Thunder could see the entire island from this new vantage point. It was roughly an oval, at its widest point less than a quarter of a mile across. There were no other palm trees other than the ones growing at the top of the island. Thunder made a cursory exploration of the whole island, finding nothing except some rather exotic seashells. He thought about taking a few back to the lovely mouse who worked at the bait shop, but couldn't quite figure out how to carry them, especially since their adventure in Quintari had just begun. Finally he made his way back to the top of the island. The ground was littered with huge fallen palm leaves and Thunder picked up two of them, for a moment imagining himself using them as wings, soaring and gliding around the island, shouting down to Clara and Lightning as he flew past. He tossed them aside with a sigh. His search had proved to be less than successful, and it was with some frustration that he kicked a large palm leaf laying on the ground. Unfortunately, instead of kicking a soft and flexible palm leaf, his foot hit something beneath the leaf which was very hard and not in the least bit flexible.

"OOWWWWW!!" He really did think he might have broken something this time and was just about to holler for Clara when his curiosity took over. He pulled the palm leaves away to see what he had kicked. When he saw the source of his foot's painful encounter he stared at it blankly. Someone had left a square wooden door lying in the sand. Who could have left it? Was there someone else on the island? He decided to drag the door down the hill to show Clara and Lightning what he had found. When he tried to lift it, however, he made another startling discovery. It was not simply a door, it was a trapdoor – and beneath it was a three foot wide square shaft descending straight down into the island. On one side of the square shaft was a rickety wooden ladder that disappeared into the inky darkness below.

"CLARAAAAAA!! Come quickly!!"

There was a brilliant flash of light and Clara appeared directly in front of him.

"Whoa! Not *that* quickly!" Thunder stumbled backwards in surprise, almost falling into the open shaft behind him. "Look! Look what I found!"

Clara eyed the trapdoor and the vertical shaft with its crudely made wooden ladder. "Ahh. You've found the reason we're here. Run get Lightning. It's time to leave paradise."

Chapter 10

The Ballast Pump

"I was wondering. Could Lightning and I borrow the key to World Door Three once in a while? That way we could spend a day at the beach if we wanted to – maybe we could even bring some friends."

Lightning snorted, "Oh, like that precious mouse who works at the bait shop?"

Clara sighed. "We'll see. Right now I'm concentrating on not falling off this very wobbly ladder. We've already descended about a hundred feet and I can't see the bottom, and we can't blink down if I don't know where I'm going. Hold up for a minute." She flicked her wrist and a glowing ball of light appeared, gradually descending, illuminating the shaft as it went. After a hundred feet Lightning cried out, "Look, I can see the bottom!"

Ten minutes later they stood at the bottom of the shaft. Lighting leaned over, his paws on his knees. "Whew, that was tough. I hope we don't have to climb back up that thing."

Clara pointed to a tunnel entrance standing almost

eight feet tall and six feet across. Her glowing light drifted into the tunnel, illuminating a series of heavy wooden support beams crisscrossing the walls and ceiling.

"It looks safe enough. Someone went to a great deal of trouble to build this, but I can't imagine where all the wooden beams came from." Clara stepped into the tunnel. "Let's go, treasure hunters. There's only one way to find out what's at the other end."

The trio continued on for a half hour before they noticed a light coming from around a sharp curve in the tunnel. Clara put her paw to her mouth, signaling for Thunder and Lightning to move silently. The three adventurers inched forward, step by cautious step, until they reached the bend in the tunnel. Clara peered around the corner, then pulled her head back, an unreadable expression on her face. Thunder and Lightning looked at her questioningly. She appeared to be thinking, then shrugged and walked around the bend, followed by Thunder and Lightning.

When they rounded the corner Thunder saw a rather plump older mouse sitting in a wooden chair reading a newspaper, his feet propped up on a makeshift table. He wore baggy dark blue pants which had seen better days, a faded blue and white striped shirt and a pair of old fashioned gold rimmed glasses.

Looking up when he heard them enter the room, the old mouse eyed the three strangers with a perplexed expression. Seconds later a light of realization blinked on in his eyes. "Ahh, may I assume you are here to fix the ballast pump?"

Four things happened in rapid succession. Thunder looked at Lightning, Lightning looked at Clara, Clara looked at Thunder, and Clara looked back at the mouse wearing the blue and white striped shirt.

"Umm... yes, precisely, we're here to repair the broken ballast pump."

"Excellent, follow me if you will. The crew will be quite pleased. Quite pleased, indeed." The bespectacled mouse rose from his chair and headed down the tunnel with Clara, Thunder, and Lightning trailing behind him. After walking for about ten minutes through twists and turns they reached a great cavernous room filled with a mishmash of crudely built wooden furniture. There were bunk beds, tables, chairs, wooden chests, trunks, and cabinets. There were also seven mice sitting at tables, all dressed in a similar fashion to the first mouse, most of them with a glass of ale clutched in their paw. Some were reading books, some were reading newspapers, some playing cards. They turned in unison when the group of adventurers entered the room.

One of them called out, "Visitors? Where they from?"

"Good news, mates, she's here to fix the ballast pump."

As one, the group of mice rose to their feet and began clapping and stomping their feet. "Hoorah! I knew it wouldn't take long!" One of the mice called out to Clara. "Where'd you find it? How far from the island?"

Clara saw a blue thought cloud float out from his ear and drew it to her. She put a paw over her mouth and gave a small cough.

"Of course you're talking about the bottle with the message in it. Umm... we found it floating in the sea about a week ago, almost five hundred miles away. As soon as we saw you needed someone to repair your pump we headed this way. Unfortunately our boat sprang a leak and sank as we were approaching the island and we had to swim ashore. Luckily, we were able to locate the trapdoor leading down to the tunnel and found our way here."

Thunder's eyes widened. Clara's story was, without a doubt, the most unbelievably concocted and profoundly spurious tale he had ever heard. He waited for the mice to either laugh or pull out swords and attack them. They did neither. They all cheered, then offered Clara a glass of ale.

"Ale sounds wonderful, but perhaps we should get to work on that ballast pump."

The mouse wearing the gold rimmed glasses nodded emphatically. "An excellent sentiment. Work first, ale later." A few of the other mice booed him, calling out, "Ale first, work never!" This was followed by raucous laughter and several of the mice pounding their fists on the table.

The bespectacled mouse rolled his eyes. "Feel quite free to ignore them. Please forgive me, I was so surprised by your arrival I forgot to introduce myself. I am Captain Mudgeon, formerly of the Quintarian Imperial Naval Armada, at your service." He bowed deeply before Clara.

"A pleasure to meet you Captain. I am Clara Rabbit and these are my two assistants, Thunder and Lightning."

"Excellent, please follow me through this tunnel to the submarine."

Thunder stopped in his tracks. "Did you say submarine??"

71

"Yes, of course, why else would we need a ballast pump?"

"Creekers, a submarine!" He looked at Lightning with an enormous grin. Lightning frowned.

"You do know submarines go *under* the water, right? Not on top of it?"

"Of course, everyone knows that. Don't get all nervous ninny about it, it's no different at all than operating the Mintarian Wyrme of Deth we found on Niriimm."

Captain Mudgeon's ears perked up but he said nothing.

Several minutes later they entered another large cavern. This one however, contained an enormous grotto with a seventy foot long charcoal gray cigar shaped craft moored to a long wooden dock. "Here she is, and a finer submarine you'll never see. Other than the broken ballast pump, of course." He laughed loudly, slapping his leg.

Clara had not been idle during their walk to the submarine. She had been pulling thoughts from Captain Mudgeon, attempting to learn as much as possible about the submarine and the broken ballast pump. She smiled to herself. It would take her about ten seconds to shape the new parts. She had also discovered something very special about Captain Mudgeon. She now knew why the universe had brought them here.

Clara stepped onto the wooden gangway leading up to the submarine. "We'll take it from here, Captain. It should take us about an hour or two to repair the pump. Thunder, Lightning, let's go. We have work to do."

"Excellent, I'll be waiting back with the crew. Just give us a shout when you're done. I hope you won't charge us too much for all your labors." He chuckled loudly and headed back down the tunnel.

Clara swung open the outer hatch and entered the submarine. Lights blinked on, illuminating the interior of the craft. Thunder eyed the maze of valves, pipes, and gauges. "Creekers, this is amazing! I'm going to find the control panel."

Clara did her best impression of a stern, severe look. "Thunder, do *not* touch anything. Do you understand me?"

Thunder grinned. "Sure, I won't touch anything."

Lightning and Clara headed through the narrow passageway leading to the engine room. Clara eyed the two duplonium powered steam generators. "Those look quite similar in function to the motors Oliver had in the old Pterosaurs. Steam power drives the generators which makes electricity to power the electric motors. Here, this is the ballast pump. It pumps seawater in and out of the ballast tanks so the submarine will ascend or descend." She gazed at the pump for a moment then flicked her paw. With a flash of light four new parts blinked into place. "Hmm... that's a little too obvious." She flicked her wrist again and the shiny new parts were now coated with a layer of grimy black oil and grease. "That should do it." She picked up a large pipe wrench and handed it to Lightning. "Take this and pound it against the bulkhead every so often for about an hour, loud enough so they'll think we're working on the pump. I'm going to go make sure Thunder isn't touching anything."

"Umm... the bulkhead?"

"The wall. Pound it against the wall."

Clara made her way back down the passageway to

the bow of the submarine. She found Thunder standing in front of a large semicircular control panel. He turned at the sound of her footsteps and grinned. "This is amazing, Clara. I think if I had to I could run this. Oliver taught us everything about the operating procedures and mechanics of the Wyrme of Deth, and this doesn't look much different."

"Thunder, the one very important difference is, this is Captain Mudgeon's boat. When we go back we'll talk to him. I have a very good feeling he will help us. Who knows, maybe he'll even let you have a turn running the ship."

An hour later Clara and Thunder headed back to the engine room.

Lightning was still pounding the wrench on the bulkhead and looking slightly dazed.

"You can stop now. I'm sorry we took so long."

Lightning kept pounding the wrench on the bulkhead.

"LIGHTNING, YOU MAY STOP NOW."

"WHAT? DID YOU SAY SOMETHING? I CAN'T HEAR ANYTHING."

"Oh, dear." Clara reached over and gently took the wrench from Lightning's grasp. Her paws glowed brightly and she placed one over each of Lightning's ears. The light flooded into his ears, then faded away.

"Whew, that's better. For a minute I thought I'd never be able to hear Thunder's dumb jokes again. Hold on, what was I thinking??" Lightning grabbed the wrench and started pounding the bulkhead again, then gave a loud screechy laugh.

Thunder rolled his eyes. "Some mice just never seem to grow up."

Clara gave the pump one last inspection and they walked back to the first cavern. Captain Mudgeon was leaning back in his chair reading the newspaper. "Ah, here they are. How did it go? Can you fix it? It's rather severely damaged, I'm afraid."

"It's all done, Captain. It should work perfectly now."

Captain Mudgeon beamed as the crew clapped and cheered. One of them cried out, "Ale for everyone!" This was followed by fists pounding on the tables. Captain Mudgeon rose from his chair and approached Clara. "I wouldn't be much of a captain if I didn't inspect the fruit of your labors. If all is as you say, we will gladly pay you a reasonable sum for your efforts."

Back at the submarine Captain Mudgeon carefully inspected the repaired ballast pump, running his paw across the new parts. "Excellent! Perfect. Well done, indeed. Now, perhaps you can tell me who you really are, how you got here, and how you managed to install brand new parts when you boarded this boat with nothing but the clothes on your back. Not to mention how you managed to complete a job in one hour that normally takes four engineers an entire day. I may not look like much, but you don't get to be a captain in the Quintarian Imperial Naval Armada by being a dimmer."

Thunder gulped.

Chapter 11

Captain Mudgeon's Story

Clara had known for some time that Captain Mudgeon was on to them. She had pulled enough of his thought clouds to know he was far cleverer than he let on, but she also knew he was a just and honorable mouse. She was not afraid to tell him the truth.

"Captain Mudgeon, I am a shaper. We have come here from other worlds seeking out one particular mouse. I cannot tell you the full story, but it is imperative that we find her as soon as possible."

Captain Mudgeon nodded. "I thought as much. Only a shaper could have done what you did. How did you get to the island?"

"Have you ever heard of the World Doors?"

"Of course, built by the Thaumatarians. There is a World Door on this island?"

"There is."

"Curious. I suspect this island has a far more colorful history than we will ever know. Who are you trying to find?"

Thunder spoke up. "I'm trying to find my mom. Her name is Lybis."

Captain Mudgeon turned quickly, looking at Thunder as though seeing him for the first time. "Lybis is a very odd name for a mouse, young sir. In fact, I have only met one mouse in my entire life named Lybis. She is currently a prisoner by order of Counselor Pravus in the Tenebra Military Prison on Betshannk Island in the middle of the Desparian Sea." Thunder could almost feel the piercing gaze of Captain Mudgeon stabbing through him. He looked down at the ground.

"Um... that's my mom. That's where she is." In a barely audible voice he added, "Could you take us there? I could pay you with the gold nuggets and Nirriimian white crystals I found on our trip to the lost Mintarian city."

Captain Mudgeon's faced softened, his eyes resting on Thunder. He was silent for a time, then spoke. "I will help you rescue Lybis. I am all too familiar with Tenebra Prison, and I also know and greatly respect Lybis as a mouse and as a scientist. I will confess to you here and now that I was a prisoner in that abysmal institution known as Tenebra Prison for five long years." Captain Mudgeon leaned back against the bulkhead. He looked ten years older and very tired. "Let's go to my quarters. I have some comfortable chairs there. We'll sit and I will tell you everything I know about Tenebra Prison."

Captain Mudgeon led the way to the captain's quarters near the bow of the submarine. He smiled. "I think you'll find the accommodations here somewhat more refined than those of the cavern. Please make yourself comfortable."

He waited until everyone was seated, then began.

"So... Tenebra Prison... where do I start? First, you should understand that Counselor Pravus and Chief of Science Manghar do not have as firm a grip on Quintari as they would have everyone believe. There is a great deal of dissatisfaction with the methods used by Pravus in running Quintari. Mice are tired of his ruthless behavior and the endless expansionism at the cost of so many thousands of lives. For many years his brutal activities were carefully concealed from the public, or twisted into honorable behavior by his propaganda machine. Over time, however, whispers and rumors surfaced regarding the true nature of his despicable actions. As you might expect he has been ruthless in retaliating against anyone who divulges the truth behind these villainous schemes. That's where I enter the story.

"There was a ship crossing the sea from Ovangt to Phenare. It was a pleasure ship carrying several thousand mice celebrating the lunar holidays. One of those mice was not concerned with the lunar transition, but was a soldier returning home to Phenare. A soldier who had stated openly he was going to reveal the true story behind a dreadful massacre which had occurred in Ovangt. Pravus told the public that rebel forces had slaughtered almost one hundred innocent mice, but the truth was far different. It was Pravus who had ordered the killings, his only purpose being to put the rebels in a bad light.

My submarine was cruising less than fifty miles from the ship when we received our orders. We were to send it to the bottom of the sea, with everyone aboard. There should be no survivors. We were to place blame on the rebel faction, stating categorically they had placed a massive duplonium bomb on board the ship, killing everyone and sinking the vessel.

"Since I was a mouseling the only thing I ever really wanted was to become a submariner. The very idea of cruising along beneath the vast Quintarian seas was profoundly appealing to me. My father had been a submariner in the Naval Armada and it was from him I learned honor, integrity, and above all, kindness to all living creatures. I carried these principles with me into the submarine service when I was of age, and I have never abandoned them.

"I could not believe I was being commanded to end the lives of two thousand innocent mice. I could not do it, and I did not do it. I announced to my crew that I was directly disobeying orders to destroy the ship and that I alone would suffer the consequences of my actions. I knew they would be severe.

"I turned the boat around and headed back to the base in Phenare. Pravus was furious. The true story of the massacre came out, but of course Pravus denied everything, saying the soldier had been paid by rebels to fabricate this preposterous tale. I was sentenced to twenty-five years in Tenebra prison for flagrantly disobeying orders. It was only my exemplary record and the great number of close friends I had in the Naval Command Center that saved my life. Pravus wanted to make an example of me, wanted me executed. Two days after the trial I disappeared into the dark hole known as Tenebra Prison.

"The prison sits in the middle of Betshannk Island in the Desparian Sea. The island is three miles across in both directions and nearly six hundred miles from the nearest land mass. It could not be more isolated. To make matters worse, the surrounding waters are filled with shreekers, thirty foot long predatorial beasts who roam much of the Desparian Sea, devouring whatever unfortunate creatures they happen to encounter. These extreme conditions virtually guarantee an escape free prison, and consequently the inmates are allowed to roam the perimeter of the island during their daily exercise period. Not a single prisoner had ever escaped from Tenebra Prison. Until I did.

"After several months I settled into a dreary and mind numbing routine. In the morning there was retraining, their attempt to teach me the error of my traitorous ways. I did my best to appear interested and not antagonize them. Punishment for misbehavior was brutal. There were many stories passed around of unruly prisoners being thrown into the sea and devoured by shreekers. I had no desire to end my days inside one of those hideous creatures.

"As time went by I acquired certain privileges, partly due to my good behavior and partly due to my former rank as captain. The most beneficial of these privileges was a job. Rather than be confined to my tiny cell for days on end I was given the task of distributing daily rations to the prisoners in my wing, over two hundred inmates altogether. Among that group were six scientists and a mouse named Lybis, a known high ranking member of the International Quintarian Science Guild.

"Great mystery surrounded these seven prisoners, as they were kept in strict isolation and no communication with them was allowed. The only other prisoner they ever saw was me. Every morning and every evening I would bring them their meals. I was not allowed to speak to them, but I always smiled at Lybis when I delivered the meals. After a time she smiled back. This went on for almost a year. Often times when I arrived I would find her seated on her bunk apparently sleeping, but the moment I looked at her she would open her eyes. It was quite unnerving at first, but I grew accustomed to this rather unusual behavior.

"Everything changed the day she passed me the note. One morning as I handed the breakfast tray to her she slipped a crumpled piece of paper into my paw. I said nothing, quickly stuffing it into my pocket. At the end of my duties I returned to my cell and read the note. All it said was 'pleasant dreams'. I had no idea what this meant and thought perhaps she had gone mad from the isolation. The truth was far from madness.

"That night a mouse wearing a white cloak and hood appeared to me in a dream. I recognized her immediately as Lybis. The dream became increasingly real until I no longer believed it to be a dream. Lybis waved her paw and two chairs appeared. She sat in one and motioned for me to sit in the other. She said this would be a safe place for us to talk. We had many long conversations in this unusual fashion, and over time grew to be close friends, even though I had never talked to her in the waking world. At first I thought I might simply be dreaming, but during one dream she looked directly into my eyes and pointedly said, 'wonderful conversation, don't you think?'. The next day when I delivered her meal she slipped me a second note. The note read, 'wonderful conversation, don't you think?'. I knew then that she truly was entering my dreams.

"As the months rolled on I learned a great deal more

about her. Almost every night she would appear and we would talk for several hours, often discussing her abilities as a seer and her career as a Guild scientist. It was all extremely fascinating and she taught me a great deal. I never asked why she was imprisoned, but one night she told me the whole story. I was appalled that Pravus would even consider using the Black Sphere as a weapon, but I can't say I was surprised. In hindsight I can see there were many future events Lybis was aware of, but events she did not share with me. She said all events are connected, but for the most part we must experience these events with no knowledge of the outcome. This is how we grow and expand our true inner self. I'm afraid that quite a number of the things she said were beyond my comprehension, but I thoroughly enjoyed our conversations. I believe she knew one day her son would come to me on that small island, but I have no substantive proof of that.

"As it turns out, I was not the only mouse whose dreams she was entering. There were others, including several of my old submarine crew members. It took them much longer to believe she was real, but once they did Lybis's plan began to take form. She had hatched an ingenious plot to enable my escape from Tenebra. As it turned out, my entire crew had been unanimous in their belief that I had made the right decision in not sinking the pleasure ship, and they were more than happy to help me escape. Almost six months later I was free, and I had made my escape beneath a bright midday sun, in front of over a dozen guards."

Captain Mudgeon grinned for the first time since he had been telling the story of his stay at Tenebra Prison. "Escape. Escape. Escape. The very thought of it was like some fantastical dream to me and I could think of nothing else. The great day finally arrived, beginning like a thousand other days before it. I woke up, delivered the morning meal, had my retraining session, then my exercise period walking the island's perimeter. A vital element of the plan was to be certain the guards were watching me. To that end, I stood on the edge of a small cliff and screamed at the top of my lungs. I could live no longer, prison was driving me mad and I would rather die than spend another minute in this torturous nightmare. Then I leaped into the sea, a sea swarming with the voracious predators known as shreekers. The guards watched curiously as I swam farther out, many of them grinning, waiting for the moment when a shreeker would drag me down. It didn't take long. I screamed horribly, wildly thrashing about, flailing my arms and legs, and finally disappearing in a red frothy foam beneath the waves. And that, my friends, was the utterly gruesome end of poor old Captain Mudgeon. At least it was to the guards who witnessed it.

"What they didn't see was one of my loyal crew members swimming beneath me wearing a very efficient Imperial Naval artificial gill breather, and carrying a spare one for me. He was the one who had pulled me down beneath the waves, not the shreekers, and he had also released a sack filled with blood red dye. As for the shreekers, every one of them within a half mile radius was lying on the sea bed sound asleep, courtesy of that wonderful silver stick known as a Sleeper – a device issued to all submariners.

"We descended to twenty feet and headed east, swimming for over three hours, watching as the fast approaching shreekers would abruptly lose interest in us, then drift gently to the sea floor below. We reached the submarine and entered the airlock through the upper escape hatch. So, there I was, the only prisoner in history to successfully escape from Tenebra Island and no one would ever know.

"What next? It was Lybis who told us about Paradise Island and its secret grotto. She had come across it during her years with the Science Guild and filed it away in her astonishing memory. That's where we went, and Paradise Island has been our home base until we were marooned here by a faulty ballast pump. My crew sent off a message in a bottle, which struck me at the time as overly optimistic, but I remembered Lybis telling me all events are connected. I did hear from Lybis in my dreams several times after we arrived here, but then she stopped appearing. I'm afraid I have no idea why. Perhaps her plans had all been set in motion."

Captain Mudgeon reached over and touched his paw to Thunder's shoulder. "You have a truly wonderful mother, Thunder. Or perhaps I should call you Vahtees. She spoke of you often, telling me how she tried night after night to reach you in your dreams. She knew it was only a matter of time before you would be able to see her and speak with her, and in that she was correct.

"So, that is my tale of Tenebra Prison, and the reason I would gladly sacrifice my own life to help rescue Lybis."

Chapter 12

The Ghost of Tenebra Past

"So Clara, how are we going to rescue Lybis and the scientists? I was thinking you could blink into the prison then blink them all to the submarine and we could escape that way."

"I'm afraid it's not going to be as easy as that. If we did that the Imperial Naval Armada would be after us the same day and I doubt we would be able to elude the entire Armada for long. Captain Mudgeon's escape was successful because the guards believed he had been devoured by the shreekers. If our plan is to be equally successful the guards must not suspect Lybis and the scientists have actually escaped."

"How can you do that? That sounds impossible."

"I'm working on a plan, but I'll need your help. Lybis and the scientists need to be in on it also, as they will play a crucial role in the escape." Clara grinned. "I think they're going to like this. Let's meet with Captain Mudgeon and Lightning this afternoon. I should have all the details of the plan finalized by then."

The following night Thunder went to bed early, but he did not go to sleep early. He lay in bed with his eyes closed, visualizing the pier he and Lightning were going to build. He had realized if he traveled into the future, to the very same day and minute and second as he had before, he would again find Lybis standing on the pier. He concentrated ever more deeply, bringing the dock into focus, using the techniques taught to him by Thirteenth Monk. It didn't take as long this time before he crossed over and found himself standing on the pier, basking in the warm afternoon sunshine. He spotted Madam Bletchley strolling toward him, just as he'd seen her before. He walked past the old mouse fishing off the edge of the pier and heard him humming his lovely tune. Thunder stopped for a moment. There was something about that song. This time the mouse looked up, smiled, and nodded to Thunder as he walked past. That hadn't happened the first time he was here. This time the old mouse could see him. He walked down the pier toward the group of mice congregating at the center of the walkway, spotting the white cloak and hood immediately. Lybis turned and waved to him.

"Vahtees! You found Captain Mudgeon! This is wonderful, I'm so glad. Please tell the Captain I'm sorry I've been out of touch. I was ill for a time and needed a great deal of rest. I'm fine now though. You were clever indeed to find me here. I will always be in this spot at this time if you ever need me."

"Captain Mudgeon told us about his escape from Tenebra Prison and Clara has hatched a plan for you and the six scientists to escape."

It took Thunder almost an hour to fully explain the

escape plan to Lybis. She was grinning, at times even laughing. "I love this plan. Your friend Clara is quite brilliant. I have another vital task for her, Thunder. We must retrieve the other six medallions from the storage area on Level 2 beneath the prison. The personal belongings of the arriving inmates are stored there, and that includes the six silver medallions. The guards were unaware of their real value and tossed them into a storage container with our other belongings. I don't know precisely where our storage compartment is, but hopefully Clara will be able to find it. Your presence has given me hope, something I have not had in years. I look forward to a time when I am free from this place and can put my arms around you in the waking world and hold you close to me."

"It won't be long now. The scientists can begin their part tomorrow night."

Lybis threw Thunder a kiss and faded away. Thunder was once again lying on his bed.

For such a massive complex, Tenebra Prison was extraordinarily quiet at night. Absolutely no talking was allowed and lights went out precisely at nine o'clock every evening. The only sound to be heard was the soft padding footsteps of the guards as they made their rounds up and down the long corridors. So it came as quite a surprise to the guards monitoring Lybis and the six Guild scientists when they heard a bloodcurdling scream coming from one of the cells. The guards raced down the corridor toward the source of the scream. One of the scientists was pressed up against the cell door, his eyes wide. "He coming! He's going to kill us! He blames us all. He's going to kill us!"

"Stop talking nonsense. Who's coming to kill you?"

"Captain Mudgeon. He's back. He's come back to kill us!"

The guard snorted. "That traitor is dead. I saw him die with my own eyes, torn to bits by the shreekers."

"Look, here. He was here, and he's coming back." The scientist pointed to the floor of his cell.

The guard gave an exasperated sigh but aimed his light into the cell. He froze. Three fish were flopping about on the floor in a tumble of wet seaweed. He looked at the other guard, then back at the scientist. "It's a trick. There's no such things as ghosts. Go back to sleep or you'll be joining Mudgeon in the belly of a shreeker."

Two nights passed in silence. On the third night the guards were again making their rounds, strolling along the corridor leading to Lybis's cell when they saw it. It was standing in the middle of the hallway about twenty feet away from them. A great hulking figure surrounded by a flickering blue light. The guards stopped dead in their tracks. One of them shined his light at the figure. The guard gave a startled wheezy gasp. It was Captain Mudgeon. It was Captain Mudgeon with long green strips of dripping wet seaweed trailing behind him. Two spiky fish were flopping crazily on the floor in front of him. One of the guards managed to squawk, "Creekers! It's him! It's Mudgeon!" The other guard tore a Sleeper out of his pocket and dialed it to maximum power, aiming it at the terrifying figure. When he pressed the tab there was a humming noise and the blue light around the figure flared brightly. Mudgeon's eyes glowed with a fearful red light and he began a strange ungainly walk toward the two guards, dragging one leg along the floor. His raspy moaning voice echoed throughout the corridor. "THERE IS NO SLEEP FOR THE DEAD. VENGEANCE WILL BE MINE. THE SHREEKERS HAVE SENT ME TO BRING YOU HOME TO THE SEA!"

The two guards turned and ran for their lives.

On the fifth night the guards peered around the corner down the hallway and saw Captain Mudgeon bathed in a blood red light, his paw pointed directly at them. More fish were flopping on the floor. This time the guards didn't even hesitate. They turned and ran.

On the seventh night Clara again blinked into the prison. This time, instead of formshifting into the ghostly Captain Mudgeon, she blinked down to Level Two of the prison. No guards were present, as the storage room was always securely locked. Clara blinked into the room. It was far larger than she had imagined, with thousands of small compartments, each containing the personal effects of a prisoner. She gave a sigh. "Why can't things ever be easy?" She examined a few of the compartments, which unfortunately were identified by number, not by name. "It seems I shall require some assistance from the universe."

Clara held out one arm and closed her eyes. She walked forward, gradually making her way down the long aisles filled with hundreds of small storage compartments. Finally she stopped in front of an oversized compartment. She flipped up its lid and peered inside. In the back corner, hidden under a mound of white lab coats she found six silver medallions, all identical to Thunder's. She whispered her thanks to the universe and carefully closed the container, sliding it back into place. With a brilliant flash of light she was gone.

The guards watching Lybis and the scientists were in a terrible quandary. They had told no one about Mudgeon's ghost or the flopping fish or the wet seaweed. They had returned only once to look for proof of the Captain's presence, but found none. The floors were dry, the seaweed was gone, the fish were gone. They were terrified and yet they could tell no one, for if they told such an outrageous story they would undoubtedly be thrown to the shreekers. Each night they cautiously approached the cell corridor, peering around the corner to see if Mudgeon was there. If he was, they made a hasty retreat. If he was not, they dashed past the cells just long enough to make certain the prisoners were still there. They did this every night until the night of the grisly murders.

On that fateful night the two guards crept towards the dreaded corridor, one of them silently motioning for the other to peek around the corner. Just as he was about to peer down the hallway there was a blast of brilliant blood red light, bathing the entire hallway in a ghastly and terrifying crimson glow. The guards were frozen with a paralyzing fear, physically unable to turn and run. Then the screams began, the most horrific shrieks of terror and anguish the guards had ever heard. Dreadful thumping and thrashing noises followed, then the moaning voice of Captain Mudgeon. "SPEAK OF THIS TO ANOTHER SOUL AND YOU SHALL SUFFER THE FATE OF THOSE WHO BETRAYED ME, DEATH IN THE JAWS OF A SHREEKER!!"

Mudgeon's words were still echoing through the empty corridor when the guards regained control of their bodies and dashed away.

When the morning watch arrived the guards

discovered the gruesome remains, although there wasn't really much left of Lybis and the six scientists. There was blood everywhere, splattered on the walls and floors, and mixed in with the blood were shreds of clothing and fur. All of the scientists must have met the same horrific fate.

The night guards were questioned, but claimed they had seen nothing out of the ordinary. Everything was calm when they had made their rounds. One of them had a theory, however. The one named Lybis, she had strange powers of mind control and dark evil magic. She must have gone mad and killed the scientists with her thoughts, then dragged their bodies down to the sea and fed them to the shreekers. Then, overcome with guilt or madness, she took her own life, leaping into the open jaws of a voracious deadly shreeker.

Sure enough, when the guards searched the prison grounds they found a trail of blood and fur leading to a small cliff overlooking the sea. Torn clothing belonging to Lybis had washed up on the bloody sand below. It was the only theory they had, and that's what went in the official death report sent to Counselor Pravis' office. The guards had feared deadly reprisal, but when Pravus read the report he simply shrugged. He was getting ready to execute Lybis and the scientists anyway. The Black Sphere was gone and he would move on. He had plenty of other deadly weapons in his arsenal.

* * *

Lybis held Thunder close to her for many long minutes. Their joyful reunion after they had blinked to the submarine was a sight Clara would never forget, and she was deeply grateful to the universe for reuniting the two mice.

Captain Mudgeon was tickled pink by Clara's story of his ghostly visitation, begging her to tell the story over and over. "Clara, tell me again what the guards did when they saw me!" Each time he heard it he roared with laughter.

Lightning still had a few questions. "Clara, where did all the blood and fur come from?"

Clara laughed. "I shaped it, of course. It served the dual purpose of terrifying the guards plus providing convincing proof that all the prisoners had been killed."

The six scientists gave Clara one hug after another, shaking her paw and thanking her profusely for helping them to escape.

After a great deal of discussion the six scientists decided to join up with the rebel forces in Ovangt, putting their efforts into ferreting out the truth behind the fabricated tales of propaganda spewed out by Pravus and his cohorts. One of the scientists had a brilliant plan to broadcast their findings across all of Quintari using an abandoned communications satellite still in orbit around the planet. Captain Mudgeon felt certain the vicious reign of Counselor Pravus was nearing an end.

Lybis would return to Pterosaur Valley with Clara, Thunder, and Lightning. Once they had used the medallions to discover the Black Sphere's hiding place they would still have to determine how to deal with it. Lybis spent long hours with the other scientists developing a plan to eliminate the threat of the Black Sphere's expansion without harming the universe within it. It was an extraordinarily complex problem and one which was not solved easily, but in the end they did come up with a viable solution.

Thunder and Lightning spent a great deal of time on the bridge of Captain Mudgeon's submarine as it churned along beneath the Desparian Sea. Once the Captain realized how knowledgeable Thunder and Lightning were on power trains and guidance systems he was happy to instruct them in the operation of the submarine. Within three days they were controlling the boat for hours at a time. The submarine was equipped with a large domed viewing port on the bridge and since they often cruised just below the surface, Thunder and Lightning had many spectacular encounters with Desparian sea life. This included sightings of the terrifying black shreekers who skittered through the water at astonishing speeds. One huge shreeker made a valiant attempt to devour the submarine and gave Thunder a terrifying front and center view of its gaping mouth and three rows of long curved razor sharp teeth.

After eight days at sea Captain Mudgeon's submarine finally chugged into the grotto beneath Paradise Island. For three glorious days everyone relaxed, basking in their newfound freedom, enjoying the island's sparkling emerald green waters and gleaming white sands. Thunder and Lightning spent long hours frolicking in the waves, often joined by Clara, Lybis, and at times even the rather staid scientists.

On the fourth day Clara and Lybis announced it was time for them to head back through the World Doors to the Swamp of Lost Things. There were many long hugs and heartfelt farewells. Captain Mudgeon promised to update Lybis on the status of Counselor Pravis after he had ferried the six scientists to Ovangt, where they would join up with the rebel forces.

That afternoon Clara, Lybis, Thunder and Lightning waved goodbye to Paradise Island and stepped through World Door Three into the foul smelling Swamp of Lost Things. Once they arrived in Pterosaur Valley they would tackle the thorny problem of precisely how to unite the seven medallions and what to do after they discovered the Black Sphere's secret hiding place.

Chapter 13

A Walk Through the Trees

Bartholomew Rabbit stood as still as a tree on a sultry summer's day, his arms outspread, his eyes closed, then floated silently up into the air, hovering twenty feet above the forest floor.

"Ah, excellent, Bartholomew. I see you've been busy since the last time we met here in your lovely Timere Forest."

At the sound of Bruno Rabbit's voice, Bartholomew quickly descended to the soft forest floor to find Bruno leaning against one of the forest's magnificent trees. Bruno was sporting his customary dark green cloak and hood.

"Thanks, Bruno. I've been practicing. I can wake up in most of my dreams now and I'm learning to overcome my self-imposed restrictions."

"Then it shouldn't be any trouble for you to push your arm into that tree trunk."

"Do what?"

"Push your arm into a tree trunk all the way up to your shoulder, then pull it out again. Or if that's too easy for you, try strolling right through a tree trunk." Bruno added, *"Because as you well know, the trees we're looking at here do not exist. All these magnificent apparent creations of nature are in fact nothing more than creations of your own mind."*

"Logically I know the trees don't exist, Bruno, but the idea of physical matter is so ingrained into my being I'm not certain I can abandon it."

"Give it a try. Of course, I wouldn't be much of a teacher if I couldn't do it myself." Bruno stepped away from the tree he was leaning against, then turned to face it. Without hesitation he strolled through the gigantic trunk and out the other side, then turned around and walked back through it again. *"Nothing to it. A bunny could do it."*

Something changed in Bartholomew when he saw what Bruno had done. He knew it was possible now. He had seen it. He floated over to a nearby tree. *"This forest exists only as a creation of my mind. None of it is real. I am pushing a nonexistent dream arm through a nonexistent dream tree. Nothing through nothing."* He held his paw against the tree, pushing it slightly, and felt the trunk give way. It was like pushing his arm through thick molasses, but it had worked. His arm had gone into the tree. He grinned and looked over at Bruno. *"It works!"*

"Of course it works. Now do it again, faster this time. Any resistance you feel is of your own making. You are the one resisting the idea that the tree and your arm are only thoughts."

After nearly an hour of practice Bartholomew could

put his arm into the tree and pull it out with negligible resistance. Bruno gave a great yawn.

"Now walk through the tree. Start by putting your arm through and let the rest of you follow. Your body is simply an extension of your arm."

Bartholomew gave Bruno a dubious look.

"DO NOT DOUBT YOURSELF!" The roar of Bruno's voice shook the forest. Pine needles fell like rain, the raucous cries of a thousand startled birds filled the air.

Bartholomew walked through the tree and out the other side.

"Excellent. Practice this until you can run in a straight line through the forest without feeling the trees. Then practice flying through the forest in a straight line until the trees you pass through are only a blur." Bruno vanished in a spectacular flash of green light.

Bartholomew awoke to the sound of the Model X Pterosaur humming along through the night skies of Opar.

Bartholomew was concerned that flying in the Model X would be too frightening an experience for Renata, but when the Pterosaur lifted off quite the opposite proved to be true. Renata was grinning like a bunny when they took to the air. She displayed no fear at all and was captivated by the landscape passing below. "This is wonderful! It feels almost familiar, this sensation of flying, as though I have experienced it before. I know there is a world beyond this one, a world we shall enter when it is our time – perhaps this feeling I have is an echo of our life in that Great Beyond."

Bartholomew could see there was greater depth to Renata than he had previously thought. She was more than just their guide through uncharted territory. "You may well be right, Renata. There is much about this universe which is unknown to us."

Edmund nudged the control stick to the left, making a slight course correction. "Bartholomew, if I am not mistaken we are approaching the outer boundaries of the lost city of Cathne."

"Slow us down to twenty miles per hour, Edmund. I want to get a good look at the city before we land. We're looking for a collapsed building with a bright blue band wrapping around the top section. Madam Beffy's father found the blue translucent wall beneath that building."

Edmund tapped the grid of colored discs, slowing the Mark X down to twenty miles per hour and decreasing their altitude to four hundred feet.

Bartholomew studied the approaching city. The scale of it was grand beyond anything he could have imagined, dwarfing by far the lost Mintarian city they had explored beneath the desert of Nirriim. Cathne spread out across the landscape almost to the horizon, but he could see only three major buildings left standing, buildings which Bartholomew estimated to be well over a thousand feet tall. He was eyeing the tallest of the three when a beam of red light sizzled past them, immediately followed by a second beam which blasted into the hull of the Mark X, rocking the ship wildly.

Edmund shouted a warning. "Silver Legs below!" He pulled back on the number one control stick and the craft shot up into the sky, knocking Oliver and Bartholomew to the floor. Only Renata remained standing. Within seconds the Mark X was out of range of the spiders' force beams. Bartholomew crawled to the edge of the ship and peered over the side. Far below he could see nearly a dozen of the mammoth Silver Legs congregating on a wide boulevard, several of the them firing their force beams harmlessly in the ship's direction.

"Edmund, see if you can put us down on the roof of that building. We can set up camp there. The Silver Legs can't get to us and we'll have a marvelous view of the city. We may even be able to spot the blue building from up there."

With Oliver's guidance Edmund set the Mark X gently down on the roof of the tallest building. After they landed Edmund noted the ship's altimeter read slightly over fourteen hundred feet. Oliver exited the Pterosaur the moment they touched down, eager to examine the construction materials and techniques used by the Oparians to create this towering structure. He flipped open his journal and pulled a pencil from his pocket. "This is quite astonishing! Think how different our world would be if it were filled with buildings such as this." Striding around the perimeter of the roof he jotted down note after note. With a few quick calculations he discovered the footprint of the building was a perfect square almost one quarter of a mile across. A squat rectangular structure at the far end of the roof caught his attention. "Edmund, look! There's a door over there leading into the building. Come with me and we'll see what we can find."

Bartholomew watched as Oliver and Edmund disappeared through the doorway, then turned his gaze to the sprawling city below. Renata took a spot next to him. "We are looking for a building with a blue stripe?"

"Yes, that's the building Madam Beffy's father

discovered. Beneath it he found a blue translucent wall. He walked through the wall but we have no idea what became of him after that."

Renata gave a nervous cough, then spoke in an oddly hushed, almost reverent voice. "You are one of the sacred elders from the Great Beyond?"

Bartholomew smiled. He didn't have to pull her thought clouds to know why she asked that. "No, I'm simply a shaper. Shaping is the process of converting energy from one form to another using the power of the mind. It's hard to explain, but it's just physics, not magic. When water turns to ice, it's not magic, it's the nature of things. Shaping is no different. Oliver can probably explain it far more clearly than I can."

"Perhaps I shall talk to Oliver then. When I saw you shooting the beam of fire at the Silver Legs' web, I hoped you had come from the Great Beyond. I would like to speak with such a being."

"I think most rabbits and mice would share your wish, Renata. There are a great many questions we would all like to have answered."

Bartholomew felt a deep sadness in her reply. "I do not have many questions I would like answered, only one."

Bartholomew turned at the sound of Oliver's voice. "Bartholomew! Look what we found in one of the rooms!" Oliver was waving a large sheet of folded paper, opening it as he and Edmund hurried across the roof to Bartholomew and Renata. "It's a map of Cathne! We discovered a room on the floor below us containing thousands of them."

"That's wonderful, Oliver. Here, I think this is the building we landed on. It's the tallest one."

"Yes, yes, of course it is, but you're missing the whole point."

"I am?"

"Good heavens, Bartholomew, it's right there in front of you! Look!" Oliver pointed to a tiny building on the map almost identical to a thousand others displayed in the highly detailed rendering of Cathne. The only difference was, the building Oliver was pointing to had a blue stripe around it.

"You found it! You are amazing, Oliver."

"Well, yes, but I will confess it was Edmund who first spotted it."

Edmund beamed proudly. "Now that we know its precise location, we should be able to see it from here." He strode to the east side of the building, carefully scanning the cityscape. "I found it. I have marked its location on my holomap. It should take us less than five minutes to reach it in the Mark X. We will need to keep our eyes open for Silver Legs of course."

Bartholomew shook his head. "Silver Legs shouldn't be a problem, Edmund. Now that we know they're here I can surround the ship with a sphere of defense. Their force beams shouldn't present any problems at all."

The adventurers decided their best move would be to have a good meal and a restful night's sleep before venturing into the building harboring the mysterious blue wall. Bartholomew shaped a table and chairs, plus all the ingredients Oliver needed to prepare one of his delicious gourmet dinners. The Mark X had a small galley on board which Oliver used to cook the meal.

There was a great deal of small talk over dinner, including much conjecture over what lay beyond the blue wall, and what the bright figure might be that

Madam Beffy's father had seen. Everyone did their best to make Renata feel welcome, asking questions about her life growing up in Opar. She seemed to enjoy telling her bunnyhood stories and many were quite humorous. There was no mention of the tragic events surrounding the loss of her family and village.

After dinner Bartholomew shaped several bottles of a lovely white wine, which went nicely with the spectacular Oparian sunset. As darkness was falling Edmund set up the tents and they retired for the night. The stars above sparkled brightly and the night air was calm and silent, so when the dreadful scream came it woke Bartholomew instantly. He blinked out of his tent in time to hear a second scream coming from Renata's tent. Dashing over to her tent he tore the flaps open and found Renata lying in her sleeping bag, eyes wide open, her face a mask of fear.

"Renata, what's the matter? Did you see something?"

Renata managed to shake her head. "No, no, I saw nothing. I'm sorry I woke you. It was a bad dream. I have them quite often I'm afraid. I'm fine now, thank you for checking on me."

Bartholomew did not question her about the nature of her frightening dream and he did not pull her thoughts to him. He assumed it had to do with the loss of her family. "Okay, but please let us know if you need anything."

Stepping out of her tent he found Oliver and Edmund anxiously waiting to learn why Renata had screamed. "She was having a bad dream. Everything is fine now." Returning to his tent he lay down and tried to sleep, but he couldn't get Renata's screams out of his thoughts. He was certain they had come from a far deeper place than where dreams are born.

Chapter 14

The Blue Wall

Bartholomew awoke to the sound of his tent flaps whipping about in a howling wind, rain drops spattering madly against the tent's canvas walls and roof. Thunder rumbled and growled in the distance. This was concerning to Bartholomew, as they had to fly the Mark X to the blue-striped building today. Even worse, when he stepped out of his tent he was nearly knocked over by the shrieking wind. With a flick of his wrist a defensive sphere blinked around him. He saw Edmund standing near the edge of the building eyeing the approaching storm. Bartholomew had never encountered a storm displaying this kind of raw fury. The entire western sky was pitch black, hundreds of ragged flashes of lighting crackling and shooting across the darkness, barely obscured by the dense undulating curtains of torrential rain. "Edmund, what is happening here?"

Edmund appeared to be unfazed by the monstrous fast moving storm front. "Ah, good morning, Bartholomew. I trust you slept well? I have been watching the storm approach for several hours. The lightning is quite spectacular, although it does bring to mind stories Edmund the Explorer told me of the deadly Anarkkian lightning attacks during the war."

"It looks dreadful! Do you think we can fly in it?"

"I don't see why not. I am quite indestructible, and you can simply create one of your defense spheres around the Mark X."

Oliver stepped out of his tent into the ferocious winds, holding one paw out in a futile attempt to block the oncoming torrent of rain. "Great heavens! This is quite fearsome! We should leave before it gets worse. We'll never be able to fly in such a maelstrom."

Bartholomew looked at the black roiling skies and brilliant flashes of lightning. "You're right. We need to pack up and leave immediately. We have no idea how strong the winds will become at this altitude or what will happen when the lightning reaches us."

Within fifteen minutes the adventurers were packed and loaded in the Mark X, the craft shaking and vibrating in the horrific blasts of wind and rain. Edmund shouted to Bartholomew, "Defense sphere! Put up a defense sphere!"

With a flash of light the sphere popped up around the Mark X, stopping the wind instantly. "I think that should do it. We'd better get going. Edmund, head for the building with the blue stripe."

Edmund pulled back on the control stick and the ship rose into the air. Even with the defense sphere the craft was being violently knocked about by the brutal winds. Oliver cried out to Edmund. "Take the ship down as quickly as possible! If the wind gusts gets any worse even the sphere of defense won't help us. The winds might not be as severe closer to the ground."

Edmund nodded, sending the Mark X out over the edge of the building and into a rapid nearly vertical descent. The wind seemed to be lessening as they sped downward.

"Excellent, I think that should–" Oliver's thought was cut short by an incomprehensibly brilliant flash of white light and a deafening thunderous explosion. The ship rocked wildly, almost colliding with the side of the building. "I can't see! Edmund, I think we were hit by lighting! Can you see where we're going?"

"I'm fine, My optical system was unaffected by the lightning. I am in complete control of the Mark X. Nothing to worry about."

Renata sat hunched over in her seat, paws covering her eyes. She had seen storms like this before and knew full well the extent of their terrible ferocity.

Edmund brought the ship down to an altitude of only a few hundred feet. Oliver's vision was returning. "This is better. Not so windy here." A flash of red light shot past the bow of the Mark X. Two more quickly followed. Bartholomew's defense sphere flared brightly for a split second when a third beam collided with the ship.

"Silver Legs! They're all over down there! They must have spotted our ship descending from the roof."

"We're fine, their force beams can't penetrate my sphere of defense. Edmund, take us to the building with the blue stripe."

"On our way."

Bartholomew watched as the nearly impenetrable curtains of pelting rain blasted against the ship's sphere of defense. "It's magnificent, in a terrifying sort of way!"

Oliver hollered back, "I most certainly agree with the terrifying part."

The Mark X shot across the cityscape for several more torturous minutes before Edmund called out, "I see it! Right over there! Keep your eyes open for a spot to land."

Oliver raised his arm and pointed. "There! Edmund, put her down in that open space near the big silver door. I believe that is the very door Madam Beffy's father used to enter the building." Oliver leaned forward in his chair, watching anxiously as Edmund maneuvered the ship through the fierce winds and sheets of pounding rain toward the building. "Oh my, I wish Madam Beffy was here to see this – to see what her father saw. I don't think she would care very much for this storm, however. I must remember everything we see so I can describe it to her."

Edmund's fingers were tapping madly across the grid of colored discs. Without looking up he said, "Perhaps we will find her father and Madam Beffy will be able to hear the story directly from him."

Even in the midst of this howling tempest, Oliver found himself deeply moved by Edmund's comment. "You have surprised me, my old friend. That is a very comforting thought and I thank you for it."

With a rattling thump the ship set down in a small clearing next to the building with the blue stripe. Bartholomew hollered above the roaring wind, "Here we are! Everyone out and into the building! We don't know how long it will take for the Silver Legs to reach us. Mind the wind! Cover your eyes!"

Bartholomew waited until the others had safely

entered the building. The buffeting wind and rain pounded against him as he scrambled down the ladder. He hit the ground just as a spider's red force beam shot past him and he instantly popped up a sphere of defense. Glancing back across the piles of rubble he could see at least six Silver Legs racing madly across the massive mounds of shattered concrete and steel, moving a great many times faster than the lone spider they had seen in the gorge. Dozens of force beams flashed past him, blasting the surrounding piles of building debris into clouds of dust whipped wildly about by the furious wind. Several of the beams bounced harmlessly off his sphere of defense. With one final look behind him he blinked into the building. Oliver, Edmund, and Renata were peering out the windows at the hoard of rapidly approaching Silver Legs.

Oliver let out a sudden anguished cry. "The ship! They're destroying my ship!" A cluster of the gleaming eight legged beasts had grabbed the craft with their scissored fangs and were tearing it to pieces. Oliver's prized Model X Pterosaur was no more.

Edmund voiced the question they were all thinking, "How are we going to get home now?"

Oliver could barely get the words out. "I don't know. I really don't know."

Bartholomew scanned the interior of the building. It must have been luxurious in its day, as it was clearly well appointed with wide marble staircases and plush carpeting, all covered now with a thick blanket of dust and debris. The level they were on appeared to be almost untouched structurally, unlike the floors above which had been severely damaged by the Anarkkian attacks. "Let's head through these doors. Madam Beffy said her father had gone through a maze of corridors before finding the blue wall." With a quick flick of his wrist several glowing orbs appeared, brightly illuminating the room.

Edmund pushed open a pair of glass doors and the party ventured deeper into the building. Renata felt as though she had entered another world. She had never seen a building as grand as this. "It is so large it's like being outside, and yet we are inside." She wrinkled her nose. "It smells old, like a hut after the long winter, a musty, ancient smell. I do not care for this smell."

They silently padded through hallway after hallway, stopping occasionally to look for clues as to the original purpose of the building. Edmund emerged from one of the rooms holding a pawful of folded papers. "I found a room containing thousands of maps. The writing is foreign to me, and the maps appear to be in a variety of different languages. They are not maps of Cathne, but they could be of other regions within Opar."

Bartholomew studied the maps. "You're right, there are numerous versions of the same map in different languages. I'll take a few with us. You never know. Perhaps one day we'll be able to translate them." Bartholomew slipped them into his adventuring pack and they moved ahead through the dusty corridors.

"Wait." Bartholomew held up his paw for them to stop. He was looking with some curiosity at a row of dust covered rectangular panels protruding from the corridor walls. "I think these are pictures." A wide orange beam shot out from his paw, moving across the wall. When it hit the panels the dust vanished. "Look! They are framed photographs."

"They're lovely!" Renata gazed at the images. "They're all landscapes, but I don't recognize the terrain. And those plants... I've never seen anything like that. These are not images of Opar."

Edmund pointed to one of the pictures. "The writing on them is quite indecipherable, just as the writing on the maps was. Perhaps it indicates the precise geographical location of each particular image."

Bartholomew clapped his paws together. "Travel posters! They are travel posters."

"Great heavens, Bartholomew, I believe you may be correct! Maps and travel posters. Do you suppose this was a train station? Perhaps it is similar to the gravitator transport system which lies beneath the Fortress of Elders."

"It's possible. We shall soon find out."

The party moved on, making their way down the musty hallways, walking for nearly a half hour before coming to a halt in front of a set of colossal blue metallic doors.

"The blue doors! Madam Beffy's letter said her father had opened a set of blue doors right before he found the translucent wall. A blue wall behind blue doors? Do you think that might indicate a color code of some kind?"

Bartholomew shrugged. "I don't know, Oliver. It certainly could be significant. I don't think we'll know anything for certain until we reach the rippling wall."

Edmund pushed one of the blue doors open. Bartholomew's two glowing orbs drifted across the threshold.

Oliver gave a loud whoop. "The blue wall! We're almost there. Madam Beffy's father could be on the other side of that wall."

The four adventurers stood facing the thirty foot long rippling blue translucent structure. It looked as though it was made of a viscous liquid eternally in motion, wave after endless wave smoothly rippling across its surface.

It was Renata who described it best. "It looks like someone turned a river on its side." Bartholomew's eyes swept the room, spotting a long curved counter running along the back wall. On the counter was a flat dish containing twenty or thirty short cylindrical objects. He blew the dust off them and picked one up. "They look like writing implements, some kind of pencil. This should work quite well." He picked up a handful of the colorful cylinders and stepped over to the rippling wall.

"Let's see what happens." Bartholomew tossed one of the cylinders at the wall. The path of the pencil was not affected in the least, passing through as if the wall wasn't there. He tossed in several more cylinders with identical results. Finally he looked at the others and shrugged. He reached out, gently moving his paw back and forth through the wavering blue liquid. "Nothing. I can't even feel it. My paw is completely unaffected by it. I have no idea what the purpose of it is, but it looks safe enough. It's certainly not a defensive barrier."

Edmund had been watching curiously as Bartholomew tested the wall. "I am indestructible, so I should go through first, then return and tell you what I have seen."

Oliver looked hesitant. "Do you think it's safe?"

"I am indestructible."

Bartholomew nodded. "It makes sense to me if

you're quite certain you want to do it."

Without another word Edmund stepped through the wall. Seconds later they could see something moving on the other side, but it was vague, more like a blurry wavering shadow. They waited for Edmund to return through the wall. Five minutes passed with no sign of him.

"What is he doing? Why hasn't he come back?" Oliver's voice contained a note of growing panic.

"I think that's him!" Renata pointed to a shadowy form that appeared to be waving at them.

"Is he telling us to enter, or to stay away?"

Bartholomew answered. "We have to go through the wall no matter what Edmund is trying to tell us. It's why we came here, it's where we have been sent by the universe. We are here to find Madam Beffy's father. Everyone hold paws and we will go through together."

Seconds later they stepped through the wavering blue wall into the unknown.

The unknown was decidedly less frightening than Oliver had anticipated. They were standing in a large room bathed in warm yellow sunlight, numerous brightly colored comfortable chairs strategically placed about the area. Edmund was seated in a red lounge chair gazing out a wide picture window.

"Ah, there you are. I was trying to tell you it's quite impossible to travel back through the wall."

Bartholomew turned, stepping back in surprise. The wall on this side was frozen, unmoving. He reached out and tapped it with his paw. It was solid, impenetrable. A beam of green light shot out from his paw, but the wall was completely unaffected by it.

Oliver's breathing quickened. "How do we get

back?" He looked at Bartholomew with wide eyes.

Bartholomew put his paw on Oliver's shoulder. "We've been through worse than this, my old friend. We'll find our way home. We always do."

"Perhaps you're right. I should not worry so much. If Madam Beffy were here she would not be worrying. She would be enjoying the lovely weather." Oliver walked over to the panoramic picture window and stood for a moment basking in the warm sunlight. "At least that dreadful storm has passed, and the sun... the sun..." Oliver stopped, pointing mutely up at the brilliant blue sky.

Bartholomew stepped over and glanced upward. He said nothing for a moment, then spoke. "Two suns. There are two suns in the sky. This is not Opar. We are most certainly a long, long, way from Opar."

Chapter 15

The White Triangle

Bartholomew leaned back in his chair, gazing absently at the ceiling. "Let's think about this. The bad news is we're very far from home, we have no idea where we are, and no idea at all how we're going to get back. On the positive side, the weather is delightfully sunny. That's something, I suppose."

Oliver's voice popped up from across the room. "A little too sunny, if you catch my meaning. At least the scenery is lovely for those of you who like barren gray rock and not a plant or a drop of water in sight. We don't even know if this planet has an atmosphere."

Bartholomew smiled at Oliver. "You make a good point about the lack of flora and fauna, but on the other paw we're safe inside this lovely building. The chairs are quite comfortable, don't you think?"

Renata nodded in agreement. "Yes, very comfortable. I wish we'd had chairs like this when I was growing up in Opar."

Oliver rolled his eyes. "I daresay comfortable chairs are the least of our concerns."

Bartholomew continued. "More to the point, then, I think we can assume the building with the blue wall was some sort of transportation center, along the lines of a railroad depot. When we walked through the rippling wall we were shuttled instantly to this planet. Which begs the question, why here? Why would anyone want to visit a barren wasteland such as this? The answer is, they wouldn't want to visit it. I believe this is a way station, a place to rest before changing trains and moving on to the real destination."

"And that destination would be..."

"I'm a little vague on that part, but I believe we should explore the rest of the building. There may be other shuttle walls we can pass though which will take us to more appealing locations. Since we haven't seen Madam Beffy's father here, we can logically assume he also must have moved on to another location."

Oliver perked up considerably at the mention of Madam Beffy's father. "That does make good sense. Let's try the doors at the rear of this room and see where they take us."

It wasn't long before the adventurers were marching down yet another corridor, peering into the multitude of darkened rooms they passed by. Bartholomew suspected they were offices, but were filled with unfamiliar electro-mechanical devices which they left untouched. Oliver had not forgotten the vaporizer rifle he accidentally fired on his first visit to the Fortress of Elders.

After passing through several large waiting rooms filled with plush reclining chairs, tables, and shelves piled high with an assortment of travel maps, they swung open a set of ornate silver doors and stepped into a vast circular room.

"Great heavens, you could hide ten marching bands in here. Look, way over there – more of your shuttle walls, at least a dozen. This is wonderful! Wait– how will we know which wall Madam Beffy's father passed through?"

Bartholomew shook his head. "Let's look at them. Maybe Arledge left us a clue."

As they walked across the enormous room Bartholomew counted the rippling walls. "I see fourteen transport walls in nine different colors, including four green walls and two blue walls."

"Oh, dear, our chances are one in fourteen of choosing the correct wall. Of course, if we were to split up, each of us going through a different wall, that would increase the probability of–"

"Oliver, we're not splitting up. Have a seat and relax for a few minutes while I try something. Lately I've been spending a great deal of time with Clara learning how to receive guidance from the universe. Perhaps some of the techniques she has taught me will provide us with some much needed insight."

Renata sank down into a large stuffed chair. "Ahhh, I do like these chairs. Much more comfortable than a burlap sack stuffed with dry leaves."

Oliver slumped down in a lounger across from Renata and chuckled, "I'm glad to see one of us is enjoying herself."

Bartholomew stepped to the center of the room, closed his eyes and let go of his thoughts. He seldom received messages from the Cavern of Silence anymore because his outer self and his inner self had almost completely merged, meaning that Cavern's thoughts were now his own thoughts. He voiced a silent plea.

"Universe, I need your help. I don't know which shuttle wall to go through. I don't know which doorway will lead us to Madam Beffy's father. I'm sure you know how much Oliver wants to find Arledge for Madam Beffy." Then he waited quietly. He became the observer, watching his thoughts flow past, waiting for whatever help the universe would send him.

A blurry image appeared in his mind, quickly sharpening into a scene Bartholomew recognized immediately, and one he could never forget. He saw himself on the ladder in his library pulling out a dusty red tome titled *The Collected Stories of Renegade Rabbit, Private Eye*. When he flipped the book open a small photograph of Clara fluttered end over end to the floor below. Tears filled his eyes. That small photograph had changed his life forever.

The message sent by the universe had been clear, but what did it mean? Was Clara involved somehow? How could she possibly know which door they should take? Why were the answers the universe sent always so cryptic? Bartholomew decided to inspect shuttle walls for possible clues. Perhaps his vision of Clara's photo would somehow lead him to an answer.

When he reached the first door he found an ornate metal stand holding a stack of folded maps. He examined one, noting the numerous photographs of snow capped mountain ranges. It would make sense that the maps next to each shuttle wall were maps of that wall's particular destination. This might help. He moved on to the next shuttle wall. The maps he found there contained images of a bleak desert environment with towering red spiky plants and long scaly black lizards. Not good. He'd had his fill of deserts on their trip to Nirriim.

One after another Bartholomew continued down the line of shuttle doors. The seventh door had a map filled with photographs of gorgeous lush gardens, teeming with brilliant multicolored blossoms and tall willowy green trees. It reminded him of the Isle of Mandora. "Lovely. Lovely indeed." He was turning to leave when he saw it. The instant he laid eyes on it he knew what it was, and he understood clearly the significance of the message the universe had sent him.

Bartholomew was looking at a tiny white triangle no more than a half inch wide sitting on the intricately carved stone tiles in front of the rippling green shuttle doorway. He stepped over to the undulating wall, kneeling down in front of it, and carefully touched his paw to the triangle, simultaneously pressing down and pulling it towards him. The white triangle he had seen was the corner of a larger piece of paper that had been tucked beneath the rippling doorway. Bartholomew picked it up and flipped it over. It was an old photograph of Madam Beffy. He had his answer. This was the door Madam Beffy's father had passed through.

Chapter 16

The Bee

Thunder tossed one of the silver medallions onto to the table in front of him. "Urghh! Stupid medallions!" He glanced toward Clara and Lybis who were sitting across the room, deeply engrossed in a conversation concerning the science of the Black Sphere. "Creekers, I've tried everything I can think of but I can't get the map to appear. Maybe these dumb medallions are broken."

Lightning looked up from his papers across the table. He set down his pen, glaring at Thunder. "Did you try stacking them like I told you?

"Of course I did. That's the first thing I tried."

"Did you stack them in any particular order?"

"There's seven of them. Do you know how many possible combinations of stacks that makes? I'd be an old gray mouse doddering around with a cane by the time I figured out the right order."

"Oh, why don't you tell me exactly how many combinations there are, Mister Oliver T. Mouse?"

"Stop calling me that! There's a lot of combinations,

that's how many there are. A lot. Besides, I don't think my dad would have made it *that* hard to find the map."

Lightning gave a long sigh. "Well, if you really must know, there are seven hundred and twenty possible combinations. You'd better get busy." Lightning cackled.

Thunder was about to give Lightning some very rude advice when he was distracted by a distant buzzing noise. His eyes darted around the room. "What IS that noise?"

Lightning gave an exasperated sigh, again looking up at Thunder. "What is *what* noise? In case you hadn't noticed I'm working on my journals. I'm going through all the notes I took about Edmund the Explorer's adventures and now I'm writing complete versions of his lost adventures in a second set of journals. I'd forgotten how many of them had—"

"You don't hear that buzzing noise?"

"No, I do not hear a buzzing noise. Maybe you have a bee stuck in your bonnet." Lightning gave another loud cackle, doing his best to irritate Thunder. The moment Thunder heard the word 'bee' was the moment Thunder saw it. It was not a normal Lapinoric bumblebee, it was a very, very large Lapinoric bumblebee, almost a foot long, and it was flying directly towards him. He leaped out of his chair with a high pitched yelp. "Look out! Giant bee!" He scrambled and skittered madly across the floor trying to avoid the mammoth buzzing insect.

Lightning let out another loud screechy laugh. "Good one! Nice try, Thunder, but I'm not falling for the old giant bee trick."

The huge bee turned, following closely behind

Thunder as he raced around the room. "Clara! Do something! Stop this bee!"

Clara and Lybis turned in tandem at the sound of Thunder's cries. They watched with concern as he darted and dashed about the room, hollering out something about a giant bee. "Thunder, what is it? What's wrong? What are you talking about?"

"Giant bee chasing me! I think it's trying to sting me! You have to stop it!"

Clara looked at Lybis. Lybis shook her head. "We can't see it. No one else can see the bee. Stand still for a moment and relax."

Lightning's grin rapidly faded when he realized Thunder was not play acting. "Creekers, are you all right? Are you going loopy?"

Thunder stopped, a wild look in his eyes. "It's almost here! Make it go away! It's huge! I don't like it!"

Lybis rose from the table and stepped quietly over to Thunder. "I think I know what is happening here. I want you to stand perfectly still, and relax. Let go of your fear while carefully observing the bee. Use all your senses, not just your eyes."

The enormous bee buzzed closer and closer to Thunder. The Thirteenth Monk had instructed Thunder well in the art of mind relaxation, an invaluable skill for any mouse, but an absolute necessity for a seer. Thunder let out a long slow breath, releasing his thoughts, watching as his dread of the bee faded away to nothing. He stood motionless as the mammoth insect drew closer. When it was only a few feet from him it slowed to a stop, its wings a blur as it hovered directly in front of him. He watched curiously, as if through someone else's eyes, as a large golden honeycomb formed beneath the bumblebee. Thunder could smell the sweet nectar. The bee's wings slowed down until finally they stopped, the bee hanging motionless in the air. Seconds later the bee and the honeycomb were gone.

Thunder did not move. Then, his eyes grew bright with realization and he spun around to face Lybis. "I've got it! I've got it!"

He dashed back to the table and spread out all the medallions. "Look! The medallions are hexagonal, just like the cells in the bee's honeycomb I saw. They all fit together perfectly!" He aligned the six medallions belonging to the scientists in a circle. In the center of the circle was an empty hexagonal shape. The seventh medallion fit perfectly into the empty space.

"Oww!" Thunder jerked his paw away from the medallions. Brilliant blue-white electric sparks were shooting out from the surface of his creation. The light from the sparks grew brighter and brighter until Thunder was forced to shield his eyes. When the glare finally dimmed he saw the seven medallions fused together, a three dimensional holomap slowly rotating above them.

"Creekers!" Lightning's chair fell over backwards as he jumped up from the table. "The map! You found the map to the Black Sphere!"

Lybis put her arms around Thunder. "I am so proud of you. The bee you saw was a vision sent by your inner self. For you to see with such clarity at your age is most remarkable."

Clara nodded, resting her paw on Thunder's shoulder. "It was no accident the day your path crossed with Bartholomew's at the Paw and Dagger Tavern."

Lightning dashed around the table, quickly examining the holomap. "You were right, Lybis, the Black Sphere is hidden in Nirriim, but it looks like it's almost two hundred miles west of the Island of Blue Monks. I've never been that far west." Lightning pointed to a red circle on the map indicating the location of the Black Sphere.

Thunder swept his paw through the map and it grew larger. "There. Now you can see the words. Next to the red circle it says *Bellumia 121577*, then some words I can't read, then my name, *Vahtees*. What do you think that means?"

Lybis shook her head. "I don't know, but I do recognize your father's atrocious writing – this was definitely written by Vahnar. Maybe he was writing a note to you, or perhaps it's the name of a town or village. Enlarge the map again."

Thunder's paw passed through the holomap. He frowned. "Nothing. It doesn't look like there are any towns out there, no villages or roads. There is a river with a name though. It's called the Surangi River. That sounds kind of familiar."

Lightning grimaced. "Did you even open your geography book in school? It sounds familiar because it flows within ten miles of the Island of the Blue Monks. If you take a small boat from the west side of the lake down the Brevis Tributary and you'll wind up in the Surangi. Make the map as big as you can and I'll show you."

Thunder's paw swept back and forth until the holomap almost reached the ceiling.

Lightning exclaimed, "Look! Right there, see? The

lake drains into the Brevis which flows into the Surangi."

Thunder nodded, but his mind was elsewhere. He had spotted something else on the holomap. "Look at this! A tiny silver dot inside the red circle, right near the edge of the river."

Clara examined the map carefully. "You're right, it's a small circle and it was drawn by hand. Vahnar must have put it there. Maybe the sphere is buried in a round container?"

Lybis put her paw on Clara's arm. "I'm so sorry to interrupt, but we really have to leave. Something has happened, I can sense it. The sphere has grown larger. We need to find it."

Clara nodded. "I'll get the key to Door Seven, we'll blink to the Swamp of Lost Things and enter Nirriim through the World Door. I can blink us as far as the Island of Blue Monks but after that we'll need to travel on foot. It's not safe to blink to an unfamiliar location."

Lightning pointed to the map. "We don't need to travel by foot, Clara. We can take my boat down the Brevis to the Surangi River. If you follow the course of the Surangi you can see it flows right past where the Black Sphere is hidden. It should only take us about four days to get there. We won't have to trek through any jungle at all."

Lybis clapped her paws together. "That's wonderful, Lightning. This cuts weeks off our travel time."

Clara returned moments later with the Seventh Key. "Are we ready? Everyone hold paws."

With a brilliant flash of light the four adventurers vanished, appearing less than a second later deep in the Swamp of Lost Things. Clara donned the World

Glasses, quickly spotting the doorway. "Right there!" She strode over to the door, opened it several inches and peered inside. She turned to Lightning and grinned. "Not a single spiky green tail in sight. Everyone in!"

Clara inserted the Seventh Key into the lock and the door opened with a soft click. Thunder smiled when he saw the familiar blazing sun and sand through the doorway. "Welcome to Nirriim! The good news is we don't have worry about the Wyrme of Deth anymore."

Clara stepped out onto the rolling dunes. "Bartholomew and I passed through here on our trip to the Timere Forest. He told me the story of his first visit with Oliver and Edmund, and as much as I would love to stroll through a burning desert and get attacked by a flock of deadly wild creekers, I believe we should blink to the Island of Blue Monks."

It took two hops to blink to the island and a ten minute walk to reach Lightning's home. Lightning's parents were thrilled to meet Lybis, although Thunder was uncertain how to introduce Lybis to Lightning's mom. "Um... this is my... this is Lybis, who..."

Lighting's mom laughed and put her paw on Thunder's shoulder. "It's okay, Lybis is your mom. Finding you was truly a gift, but I always hoped the day would come when you would discover your true heritage. I'm so sorry to hear about your father, but I am overjoyed that you found your mom. I know how hard it was for you all those years wondering who you were and how you came to be in the jungle."

Lighting's mom prepared a lovely meal for the adventurers and insisted they spend the night. The following morning they rose with the sun, packed, and headed down to the dock where Lightning's boat was moored. Thunder and Lightning stowed all their gear beneath the seats then bid their farewells. Lybis had tears in her eyes when she hugged Lighting's parents. "Thank you for everything you've done. I will keep them safe, I promise." She waved as Thunder and Lightning rowed the boat away from the dock.

An hour later their boat entered the Brevis Tributary and they were on their way to the Surangi River.

Chapter 17

The Surangi

The Surangi River was wide but flowed along at a good brisk pace. Lightning and Thunder took turns at the oars in case they had to circumvent any obstructions like fallen trees, which Lightning called sweepers, or protruding rocks, but most of the time they just let the river carry them along. Clara kept an eye out for any dangers which might require her shaping skills.

Lybis leaned back in her seat and watched the lush overgrown jungle passing by. "It's really quite lovely in its wild and untamed way. Sometimes I regret having spent so much time cooped up in laboratories and wish I had spent more time in the outdoors."

Clara smiled, "You followed the path you were drawn to. There is no fault in that."

"Hmm. You may be right – I can't imagine my life without science. Speaking of science, this is a good time to tell you what I discovered about the Black Sphere during my stay in Tenebra Prison. I will tell you I was not idle by any means during my confinement there. You know of my conversations with Captain

Mudgeon and the other scientists, but there is much more you are not aware of. Have you ever heard of a skill called the Traveling Eye?"

Before Clara could answer Thunder blurted out, "Bartholomew can do that! That's how he discovered the lost Mintarian city."

"Wonderful, then there is no need for me to explain what it is or how it works. When I entered Tenebra I had a basic understanding of the Traveling Eye, but lacked a certain proficiency in its practical application. The one thing I had plenty of in Tenebra was spare time, and I used it to improve my skills as a seer. It took the better part of a year before I could travel about at will, and almost another full year before I could cross over into other dimensions. I had a goal in mind from the outset, and that was to revisit Thaumatar. More specifically to thoroughly explore the facility where the Black Sphere was created. If I could examine the equipment and fully understand the processes used by the Thaumatarians to create the singularity, perhaps I could find a way to prevent its expansion.

"I spent several hundred hours visiting the facility, deconstructing the complex systems used to create the Black Sphere. The level of power necessary to create the singularity was simply staggering. In the core of the complex I discovered a mysterious black dome almost three hundred feet across. After a great deal of study I determined the dome itself was not made of matter as we understand it. Even as a field of consciousness I was unable to pass through its walls. I believe it was formed from an energy source the Thaumatarians had discovered in a parallel dimension. Such a dome was necessary to contain the staggering elementary forces needed to breed the singularity. I think the dome is constructed of the same material as the Black Sphere's outer protective shell, but of course the dome is far thicker and stronger.

"At night I would visit the Thaumatarian facility and during the day I discussed my findings with the other scientists. Our ultimate goal was to uncover the Thaumatarian's plan for the final disposition of the Black Sphere. We knew confining the universe inside the tiny black shell was only a temporary solution, and once the shell dissipated the singularity would expand. We were certain there was a second phase to their project which we were currently unaware of.

"I had almost given up hope when I discovered a set of plans in one of the upper level laboratories which clearly displayed the inner workings of the black dome. The dome held within it the energy of a hundred suns. That energy was used to contain a small multidimensional section of the Void, the space that is between all worlds, between all dimensions. Their eventual plan was to place the Black Sphere into the Void where it could harmlessly expand. There is a massive device sitting atop the black dome which until then had been a complete mystery to us. It turned out to have been designed for one purpose and one purpose alone – to inject the Black Sphere into the Void at close to the speed of light. It was the only way the Thaumatarians knew to place physical matter into the Void. Once there, the Black Sphere would expand and become simply one more universe connected to the Void.

"The Hallway of World Doors exists within the Void, each of its twelve World Doors opening to a connected universe. The Thaumatarians created doors to a dozen worlds, but theoretically there could be an infinite number of universes connected to the Void. I believe the creation of the singularity was simply an exercise for the Thaumatarians. They wanted to see if it was possible to create a new universe. Unfortunately, as you well know, it was an experiment which brought a sudden and tragic end to their world. The one thing which was never factored into their plans was the singularity's ability to absorb life force. I don't believe they ever recognized that possibility. Even the Thaumatarians made mistakes. With all the hours I spent examining the facility I was never able to determine the cause of the gigantic explosion, but the diagrams show there was a second dome used to contain the singularity before they projected it into the Void, and that was what exploded, blasting the Black Sphere into the desert."

By the time Lybis had finished her story Thunder and Lightning had lost interest and were having a contest to see who could spot the most fish in the river, which of course had led to wild exaggeration regarding both the size and quantity of fish sighted. Clara, however, was still listening intently to Lybis.

"Are you saying it would be possible for us to inject the Black Sphere into the void using the device built by the Thaumatarians?"

"Yes, that's exactly what I'm saying. Together, the other scientists and I reached the conclusion that using the injector is the only way to prevent the Black Sphere from expanding."

"And the only way to save our universe from destruction."

"Yes."

"If we even find the sphere, how would we get it to Thaumatar? We don't have access to inter-dimensional vehicles of any kind. That technology is far beyond anything we have in this world."

Lighting, who was leaning over the side of the boat trying to catch a fish with his paws, hollered out, "I know how to get there!"

Clara turned to Lightning, who had managed to grab a bright yellow fish but was having an extremely hard time holding the wildly flopping creature in his paws. "See?? I told you it was yellow with blue spots."

"You said blue polka dots. There is a big different between spots and polka dots. I still win for the most colorful fish. Stripes beat spots any day of the week."

Clara interrupted them. "Lighting, what did you mean when you said you know how to get there?"

Lightning tossed the yellow spotted fish back in the river and sat up. "In one of Edmund the Explorer's lost adventures he mentioned that some rabbits thought Door Number One opened up to the planet where the World Doors were created. He also said the few rabbits who entered World Door One never returned."

Clara touched her paw to her forehead. "They never returned?"

"That's what he said."

"Well, it's a start I guess. We'll have to cross that bridge when we come to it. Right now we need to concentrate on finding the Black Sphere. Once we have it we can take a peek into World Door One and see what it looks like."

As they drifted along the meandering river Clara found the passing jungle scenery to be quite relaxing.

They floated silently for mile after mile, weaving their way peacefully through the seemingly impenetrable jungle, listening to the raucous cries of the wild jungle birds and on occasion the dreadful growl or roar of some ferocious unknown jungle denizen. On the afternoon of their third day, the scenery had relaxed Clara so much that she curled up in the front of the boat for a short nap. It seemed to her as if she had just closed her eyes when she was awoken by Thunder tapping on her shoulder.

"Umm... what's that up ahead? I think it might be a bad rainstorm or something. I can hear the wind roaring."

"What? Rain ahead?" Clara sleepily focused on the enormous cloud up ahead. "That's odd. It looks like mist... like..." Clara's eyes popped open when she realized exactly what she was looking at.

"FALLS! FALLS AHEAD!"

Lybis sprang to her feet. "What? You mean a waterfall?"

Clara flicked her wrist and a long rope with a heavy metal hook at one end appeared in her paw. She calculated they had less than a minute until they reached the falls, and the boat was gaining speed with every second. She swung the hook around in a wide circle over her head and let it fly into the dense jungle, then yanked on the rope. It held tight. She murmured, "Thank you, Bartholomew." She was remembering his escape from the sinking duplonium wagon on the Halsey River. It was a rope just like this that had saved his life and Oliver's.

"Everyone hold on to the rope as tightly as you can and we'll all jump into the river! Do it now!"

Thunder and Lightning were beyond terrified. They could see clearly the magnitude of the falls ahead, and felt the boat rocking wildly back and forth in the rolling river. Nevertheless, Thunder and Lightning did not panic – they grabbed the rope along with Lybis and Clara, and the four of them leaped into the water. The current was swift and it was all they could do to hold on to the slippery wet rope. Lightning watched in horror as his boat went over the falls, disappearing into the mist.

Clara cried out, "Climb paw over paw until we get to the shore, then I'll help you out of the river!"

Clara's plan was working flawlessly right up until the rope snapped.

As the raging current sent them careening toward the mist, she managed to pop up a powerful sphere of defense around each of them, and as an afterthought filled the spheres with heavy padding. Four seconds later the four adventurers went barreling over the edge of the great falls.

* * *

When Thunder first woke up he thought he was having his old nightmare about the biohunter. He was lying face down in the foul smelling muck at the edge of the river. Was this the part of the dream where he jumps onto the floating log to escape the biohunter? Wait... no... his dad had killed the biohunter. Then he remembered the mist, plunging over the falls, the rocks.

"Unhh, ow, it hurts. I think I broke everything this time." He managed to lift his head up from the muck and look around. The towering falls were almost a half mile upriver. They looked at least several hundred feet tall, maybe more. It was hard to tell from this distance. It was a miracle he had survived, even cocooned inside Clara's sphere of defense. He spotted two long pieces of splintered white wood washed up on the shore. Lightning's boat. His beautiful boat. He felt dizzy, lightheaded. Maybe if he stood up... He managed to get to his feet and staggered forward a few steps through the mud.

The last thing he remembered was a strange chattering noise. He turned to see a six foot tall blue insect resembling a grasshopper come hopping out of the jungle. It was wearing silver armor. When it saw him, its chattering grew louder and it pulled a clear glowing cylinder from a black sheath strapped to its leg. That was precisely the moment Thunder collapsed into blissful unconsciousness.

The next time Thunder woke up he realized he was being dragged through the jungle by the huge blue insect. "Uhhh...bugs... I don't like bugs...all those legs...."

The blue insect stopped pulling him and began chattering loudly, just in time to see Thunder slump back down again, his eyes closed. The insect kneeled down next to Thunder and poked him with a foreleg. When Thunder did not wake up it shrugged and began dragging him through the jungle again.

The next time Thunder woke up he was lying in a bed, staring up at a shiny blue ceiling. "What? Where's Lybis and Clara and Lightning?" He tried to climb out of bed but realized he was far too weak. The room reminded him of Captain Mudgeon's submarine. Maybe someone had rescued him from the blue insect creature. If it had even existed. He gave a snort.

Probably he'd just dreamed the whole thing, some loopy nightmare, but he did have to find the others. If he'd survived the falls he was sure they had too. Anything else was impossible for him to even consider.

The door to his room swung open and a six foot tall blue insect wearing silver armor hopped in.

"You're real. Unhh." Thunder felt himself getting dizzy. He flopped back down on the bed.

The insect looked at Thunder for a moment then hopped across the room, chattering loudly. He leaned over, poking Thunder with his foreleg.

"Ow! What are you doing? Are you going to eat me?"

The insect put his head next to Thunder's face and made a peculiar sniffing noise, then chattered excitedly.

"Oh, no, no. Please don't eat me." Thunder's voice was a raspy whisper. It was all he could do to get the words out.

The blue creature stood up, chattering again and waving its arms. It turned away from Thunder and hopped out of the room, returning moments later holding a tall bottle filled with a thick red fluid. As it approached Thunder the creature shook the bottle and removed the cap. He leaned over and poured some of the viscous crimson fluid on Thunder's head.

"What is that stuff?? You're not putting sauce on me, are you? Are you putting sauce on me?? You're going to eat me with sauce?? Unnhhh.... I feel... I feel... I feel better! Hey, my head doesn't hurt anymore. What is that stuff? Here, put some on my knee, it hurts really bad. Plus my elbow. And I may have broken my ear. Right here, put some here."

The blue insect gently dabbed the red liquid on

Thunder's wounds until Thunder held up his paw. "That's good. I feel great. What is that stuff? You could sell that you know, and make a ton of credits. We could start our own business. What do you think?"

Thunder heard a door slam, then footsteps, then a very familiar voice.

"Hey, Hoppy, we couldn't find Thunder or Clara, but we did find footprints about a half mile from the falls that look like– hey, you found him!! You found Thunder! Thunder, are you okay? I was so... uh... well, you know... I'm glad you're okay."

Lybis ran to Thunder and put her arms around him. "You're safe. You're safe."

Lightning said, "Have you seen Clara anywhere?"

"No, I just woke up and found this... uh... insect fellow dragging me back to wherever we are."

"We think this is a ship of some kind. Hoppy found me on the beach and brought me back here. Lybis was still conscious and saw us. I was in really bad shape until he put that red stuff on me. I thought he was putting sauce on me. I named him Hoppy once I figured out he didn't want to have me for lunch."

The insect put the cap back on the bottle and then left the room.

"See you later, Hoppy! Hey, we should go looking for Clara. Maybe she blinked somewhere while she was going down the falls. Do you remember anything about the fall?"

"Not really. Just a little bit. It was scary."

"You got that part right. Let's go look for Clara."

The three adventurers made their way out of Hoppy's ship and headed down to the banks of the Surangi. They walked several miles downriver searching for signs of Clara, but found nothing, then turned around and walked back to the falls.

"Those falls are amazing. I can't believe we went over them in a sphere of defense and lived. They must be three hundred feet tall. The water is deep at the bottom though. That's probably what saved our lives. Wait, what is that?" Lightning darted down to the edge of the river and pulled out a soggy piece of cloth.

"It's Clara's hat." Lightning looked at Thunder with very wide eyes.

"Don't give me that look. Clara is fine. Her hat just fell off or something. Let's look around in the jungle right around here though."

Five minutes later Lybis cried out, "I found her! She's unconscious, but she's alive!" Together they carried Clara gingerly back through the jungle to Hoppy's ship.

"Hoppy! We found Clara! She needs help. Can you put that red stuff on her?"

Hoppy stepped out of his room and gave a start when he saw Clara. He motioned them to carry her quickly over to one of the beds where they set her down.

Thunder pointed to Clara, "That red stuff, we need to put that on her." He mimed opening a bottle and pouring it on her.

Hoppy held up one foreleg, then stepped out of the room. He returned a moment later carrying a device that looked like a vape pistol.

"What are you doing? Why do you have that? You need to put the red stuff on her head. It looks like she got hit badly. You don't need a vape pistol."

Hoppy chattered loudly and pushed his way past

Thunder and Lighting. He put the glass cylinder next to Clara's head and pressed the green tab. Rather than vaporizing Clara, as Thunder had feared, the cylinder glowed with a warm golden light. Hoppy moved the cylinder back and forth over Clara's head, then over the length of her body. He stepped back then picked up the bottle of red fluid and dabbed it on any obvious wounds. When he was done he placed a warm blanket on her and shut the lights off. He motioned for them to leave the room, presumably to let Clara rest.

Hoppy reached out with one of his forearms and gently patted Thunder's shoulder, then stepped into his room and closed the door.

Lighting looked at Thunder. "What should we do?"

"Maybe we should get Clara and leave. Hoppy might just be helping us so he can eat us later. With sauce." He gave his best taunting laugh.

"I knew I shouldn't have told you that. I think we should just wait here until Clara is feeling better, then build a raft and float down the river."

"Ever hear of something called shaping?"

"Oh, you're right, but Clara can't shape a whole boat. She said there are limits to how large an object she can make. She'll have to shape the parts and then we can assemble the boat."

An hour later they heard Clara call out from her room. "Hello? Is anyone there?"

They dashed into Clara's room and found her sitting up in bed. "You're all okay! I was so worried because we had no time to blink anywhere. The first thing that popped into my head was shaping the rope that Bartholomew had used in the Halsey River. I tried to blink as I was falling but hit something on the way

down and I must have been knocked ur
inside the protective sphere."

Clara rose from her bed, taking a f
at first, quickly realizing she was fine
dinner and after making plans for tł
for the evening. Thunder and Lightning speι.
hours sketching diagrams of a small but sturdy boat
Clara could shape for them.

The following morning Clara stepped out of her
room to the sight of Thunder standing next to a six foot
tall blue insect wearing silver armor. Clara put her paw
to her forehead. "Oh dear, I'm afraid I'm still not
feeling very–"

"He's real and he's not here to eat us." Hoppy
chattered loudly.

Clara studied the tall blue insect, noting his silver
armor. "He talks?"

"Just that chattering noise. I've never seen a ship
like this one before. I don't even know how it moves."

Clara sailed a blue thought cloud over to Hoppy.
When the thought touched him he turned in surprise.
Immediately a green thought cloud flew out of his head
and over to Clara.

"You can read thought clouds? This is marvelous.
Perhaps you can help me return home."

Clara sent out another thought. "Where are you
from? How did you get here?"

"Ahh. That is a rather convoluted tale, but I will do
my best to condense it for you. You might first want to
reassure your two young friends I have no plans of
dousing them in sauce and devouring them for lunch."

Clara laughed.

Thunder said, "What's he saying? Are you reading

thoughts?"

"Yes, I'll tell you later, but he needs our help getting home. He appears to be marooned here."

Hoppy took a seat and continued. "I come from a world quite different from this one, a world of warring nations. The fighting is endless, the wars rage on for years, and when one ends another begins. Every citizen is required to serve in the military, which explains my armor, and to some degree my presence here. I am a healer. You were most fortunate to find me, as our technology appears to be rather more advanced than yours. I know of no other way to say this – if I had not been here you would have died. You may make of that what you wish. Perhaps the universe was intervening in some way, perhaps it was simple coincidence.

"The warriors of my world believe it is a great honor to die in battle. They have nothing but scorn for healers, calling them cowards, and far worse. When they are wounded many decline my services, choosing death in battle over life. It seems a terrible waste to me and I have made no attempt to conceal my opinions regarding this.

"This building is my hospital, but it's also an interstellar craft capable of moving instantly from battlefield to battlefield. Our ships don't fly through the air from one place to another place. They are in one place, then they are in a different place. It's as simple as that. You are here, then you are somewhere else.

This hospital is compact and efficient, fully capable of healing thousands of soldiers, but many warriors don't believe hospitals should be allowed on the battlefield. I have used every means at my disposal to alter this archaic mindset, and recently I have been holding meetings with some of the warriors who are in favor of battlefield hospitals. This apparently angered a group of warriors who do not hold that opinion, and I believe it was one or more of them who reprogrammed my ship's holomap. When I tried to jump to a battlefield I found myself instead in the middle of this jungle. I suppose they had a good laugh about that. At least they didn't send me into dark space, or into the sun. They also removed the main power core so I could not return home. I used up my auxiliary power just getting here."

Clara was silent for a long time. "Why do you wish to return to such a world?"

"It is my home and I believe it is possible for our culture to change. Someone has to put an end to these barbaric beliefs. I have already persuaded hundreds of warriors to use the hospitals in the event they are wounded. The next step after making battlefield hospitals acceptable practice will be the greater task of awakening the individual consciousness of all beings, eventually bringing an end to wars altogether. I realize this will take many thousands of years and I will never see the results of my efforts."

Clara smiled. "In some ways our worlds are not so different. We have terrible wars also, though most rabbits consider them a necessary evil. You mentioned we might be able to help you. What can we do?"

"I need a power supply for my ship."

"Hmm. I am familiar with something the Elders created called a Cross Dimensional Energy Transfer Sphere, commonly known as a CDETS."

"That sounds promising. I'm assuming it simply siphons energy from the tenth dimension. I must say that seems an odd thing to carry around with you."

"I am a shaper. Do you know what that is?"

"There are tales told of shapers in our world, but most consider it a quaint and antiquated practice. Our science has advanced so far it is easier to use technology than something like shaping to perform most tasks. Unfortunately my ship is not equipped with a matter fabricator system. Are you saying you can shape me one of these CDETS?"

"I believe so. I have some understanding of them but I'll need to confer with Lybis on a few of the more technical aspects."

"This is wonderful. It appears our meeting was most fortuitous. There are times when it does seem as if the universe is conspiring to give us aid."

"I would agree. Now, let me find Lybis and I will discuss the best means to shape a CDETS. She can also help us to install the device."

The next afternoon Clara and Lybis presented Hoppy with a fully functioning CDETS. Together Hoppy and Lybis were able to configure the CDETS as a temporary working replacement for the ship's missing power core. Hoppy thanked Clara profusely for her help.

Hoppy's farewell ritual did not include hugs, but did involve touching his head to theirs and making a series of peculiar sniffing noises.

Thunder snorted, whispering to Lightning, "He's deciding which one of us to eat before he goes." None of them were quite certain how to say goodbye to Hoppy, so Clara sent him a thought cloud thanking him for everything he had done, especially for saving her life and healing the others.

With a wave of his forearms, Hoppy stepped into the boxy white ship. Moments later the edges of the craft glowed with a yellow orange hue and it simply vanished.

"Creekers, I bet Oliver would like a ship like that!"

Clara said, "I don't know, I think much of the pleasure for Oliver and for the rest of us is enjoying the scenery as we travel. We'd miss all that with a ship like Hoppy's."

Clara spent the rest of the day shaping the components for the stout little boat designed by Lighting. It would easily carry the four of them and was wider than their previous boat, making it more stable. Thunder and Lightning spent almost a full day assembling the craft with pegs and glue. After a coat of bright yellow paint they tarred the hull and the stalwart little craft was ready to become better acquainted with the Surangi River. Lightning checked for leaks, then loaded what little gear they had left into the boat. Clara would shape all the supplies they had lost when Lightning's boat went over the falls.

Lighting was about to push off when Clara held up one paw. "Wait! We've forgotten one of the most important things – naming our boat. Lightning, it's your design, what do you think the name should be?"

Lightning thought for a moment then leaned over to Clara and whispered in her ear. Clara grinned. "I like it."

With a flick of Clara's wrist two words appeared in large black letters on the stern of the craft.

THE VAHNAR

Lybis ran over and hugged Lightning. Thunder appeared to be sincerely moved by Lightning's gesture, blurting out, "Okay, I promise I won't pound you for at least a week. Thanks, Lightning."

Lightning pushed them off, quickly hopping into *The Vahnar*. Thunder was seated in the center of the boat, oars positioned in the oarlocks. Once Lightning was seated Thunder rowed them out to the middle of the river where the current was the strongest.

"Next port of call, the Black Sphere!"

Within a day the dense jungle foliage was replaced by thick forests of wide sweeping beetle nut trees, their broad yellow leaves standing in stark contrast against the brilliant blue sky. At times they could see through the trees to lovely hidden meadows filled with brilliant violet and yellow wildflowers. Thunder claimed he saw a ferocious wolf skulking among the trees, but Lightning didn't believe him, especially when Thunder said the wolf had glowing red eyes and was staring directly at Lightning and drooling.

The forests grew thinner and the trees more sparse until finally there were only broad grassy plains extending out as far as they could see. Lightning was quite adamant that he'd spotted several wild Nadwokks grazing while Thunder was busy rowing, but even Lybis seemed a little dubious about his claim. "I don't believe Nadwokks eat grass, Lightning."

"Well, I never actually said they were *eating* the grass. It's possible they were just poking around in the grass looking for the kind of food they do eat."

Traveling by boat was decidedly pleasant, and even with their unexpected delay at the falls it had reduced the length of their journey by many weeks. There were no rapids in this section of the river and the current was steady and smooth, but they still took shifts at the oars in case they needed to get to the riverbank in an emergency. Clara also had them practice blinking out of the boat as a group. No one wanted to repeat their experience of going over the falls.

On the third day of drifting through the open plains Thunder spotted something glinting in the distance, but couldn't make out what it was. The adventurers decided to pull up onto the sandy river bank and investigate. Lybis consented to this after Thunder and Lightning reminded her how much time they had saved traveling by boat. Also, she was quite certain the Black Sphere would remain dormant for two or three more weeks after its recent growth spurt.

It took almost four hours to trek across the open plains and reach the object Thunder had spotted. It was both larger and farther away than it had appeared from the river, being close to one hundred feet tall at its peak and three or four hundred feet in length. Thunder stared at it with a puzzled look, turning his head at an angle trying to gain a better perspective. "What is it? Some kind of building? It looks as though sections of it have been crushed and twisted."

Lybis knew right away what it was. "No, not a building. Vahnar would have loved to see this. I know it doesn't look like it, but it's well over a thousand years old. These were nearly immune to elemental damage. It's an Anarkkian Interstellar Battle Cruiser, and was more than likely shot down during the Anarkkian war. Who knows what it was doing out here, or why it was shot down."

"Can we go inside it?"

"I don't see why not. Don't touch anything though. These ships carried unimaginably powerful weapons. Anything of value was probably scavenged by the Anarkkians or the locals after the crash, but you never know. It's possible the ship crashed and there were no survivors. Hundreds of interstellar cruisers disappeared during the war and were never found. It was a time of chaos, a time of dreadful loss. Entire cultures blinked out of existence and even today, fifteen hundred years later, many worlds are still recovering from the war. Just look at Nirriim and Earth. Vahtees, your father was an avid historian and knew a great deal about the conflict. I could never get quite as excited about it as he did, but I did pick up a lot of knowledge from him about Anarkkian technology."

Thunder pointed to a gaping tear in the bottom of the ship. "We can climb in here." Thunder and Lightning scrambled up into the cruiser. Lybis called out after them, "Do NOT touch anything, Vahtees!"

Clara said, "I'll stay out here and watch for anything unusual. Call out if you need help."

Lybis followed Thunder and Lightning into the derelict vessel. As they made their way through the first deck level, Lybis said, "If I remember correctly, there were usually three levels on an interstellar cruiser. The lower level was for storage and troop transport, the midlevel for the main battle weapons, and the upper level for command and control, which included the ship's bridge."

The entire forward section of the ship had been nearly obliterated, leaving the decks twisted at odd angles and making passage through the wreck extremely difficult.

It was Thunder who spotted the first skeleton, immediately identifying it as Anarkkian from its two curved tusks. It was the first of many they found on the wreck, most of them on the lower level. Thunder and Lightning had seen a good number of Anarkkian warrior skeletons in the lost Mintarian city, but most of the skeletons here were in fragments due to the impact of the crash. A number of the rooms they passed through appeared to be troop quarters and these were the hardest to look at, most with several hundred shattered skeletons piled up against one wall. It was quite evident the crash had been completely unexpected, most of the troops still sleeping when the event occurred.

Lybis said, "I don't think there could have been survivors. I don't see how anyone could live through an event of this magnitude."

Thunder and Lightning climbed narrow twisted ladders up to the second level where the main battle weapons were located. Lybis pointed out the various weapon systems. "These are pulse beams which can vaporize a ten foot hole in the enemy's hull. They can also obliterate half a city while the ship is orbiting a planet. It takes a bank of over one hundred C-DETS to power a single pulse cannon. It has always saddened me to see such hard gained technology used for such senseless and destructive purposes."

Thunder scrambled over to a lengthy rack filled with four foot long clear glass cylinders. "Look, vape guns, just like the one we found in that blinker ship."

Lybis shook her head. "Leave them, even if they still have power it would be extremely dangerous to fire one after it was in a crash such as this."

"It looks like they stored the small arms here. There's three long racks of vape pistols too. And those four big blue cases. What do you think is in them? A big vape gun maybe?"

Lybis stepped over to one of the gleaming blue cases. She flipped the latches open and raised the lid. "Oh my, if this is not damaged... it is most certainly a gift from the universe and why we are here."

Lybis crouched down, running her paw across the object nestled within the box. "This should work. It should work. We'll need external power, but we can easily scavenge a half dozen pulse beam C-DETS for that. Hmm... coordinates here... that's good... universal sector modulation. Perfect! It really should work." She waved Thunder and Lightning away. "Stand back, I'm going to run a test. In fact, you should move into the next room."

She carefully studied the device until she found what she was looking for, a small red tab sitting near a long row of lights. Lybis tapped the tab twice, then pulled her paw away. There was a whining noise and a row of yellow lights blinked on. She tapped the red tab again and all the lights turned violet. One more tap and they blinked off. Lybis stood up and clapped her paws with excitement. "Vahtees, Lightning, you can come back in here. I need you to put this in our boat. We're going to need it later on. It's a miracle it wasn't damaged. While you're carrying it back to the boat I'm going to look for half a dozen C-DETS to power it."

"What is it? What does it do?"

"I'll explain later, but trust me, this is why the universe sent us here. It's what we need. Hurry, now. We have to move quickly."

Chapter 18

Bellumia 121577

"Are we there yet? Are we there yet?"

"Argh! It's not funny anymore! Stop saying that or I will pummel you to pieces!" Lightning wrestled Thunder to the floor of the boat and was about to pound him on the arm when Clara interrupted their wrangling.

"Perfect timing, Thunder. We are there yet. Although precisely where that is, I have no idea."

Thunder stood up as the boat scraped up onto the sandy shores of the Surangi River. "Why would Vahnar pick someplace like this to hide the Black Sphere? There's nothing here but hundreds of miles of grassy plains. Couldn't Counselor Pravus just use one of those scanner things to find the sphere like you and dad did?"

Lybis shook her head. "I have no idea. I do know your father was a brilliant mouse and if he hid it here he had a good reason to. We'll find out soon enough, I expect."

Clara hopped from the boat to the sandy shore. "Vahnar specifically wrote *Bellumia 121577* at this location on the holomap, plus he drew the red circle with the silver dot in it. Whatever we're looking for has to be around here somewhere. Let's spread out and see what we find."

Thunder and Lighting jumped out of the boat and dashed up into the shoulder high prairie grass. Thunder stretched his arms over his head. "Finally I get to run around instead of being jammed in that boat staring at your scary face."

Lighting smiled pleasantly, "Oh, and to which boat were you referring? Would that be the one I so thoughtfully named *The Vahnar*?"

Thunder grimaced. "I promised you one week without a pounding. I'm afraid your week is up." Thunder smacked his fists together. "And now you shall face the wrath of my deadly fists!" Lightning took off with a shrieking laugh through the tall waving grass.

"Come back and take your pounding like a mouse, you coward!" Thunder darted through the rippling grass chasing after Lightning, though the only part of Lightning he could see were his waggling ears.

As exhilarating as their race was, it was also very short lived, ending abruptly when Lightning gave a loud cry and his ears disappeared beneath the grass. Thunder stopped in his tracks. "Lightning? Are you all right? What happened?"

"Owww! I think I broke my feet!"

Thunder rolled his eyes. "Are you making fun of me? Wait there, little mouseling. I'll come and rescue you. Or maybe pound you into the ground like a big stake."

Thunder found Lightning sitting on a gleaming silver platform massaging his foot. The platform was circular, almost a foot tall and eight feet in diameter.

Lightning eyed the odd looking structure. "What is that thing?"

"I don't know, but I do know I almost broke my foot when I ran into it."

Thunder studied the circular platform. "Clara! Lybis! You need to come see this!" Lightning got to his feet to see what Thunder was pointing at. A single word was carved deeply into its brilliant metallic surface. The word was *BELLUMIA*.

"Creekers! We found it! This is the silver dot that Vahnar drew."

"We found Bellumia, but what *is* it?"

Clara and Lybis broke through the tall grass and hurried over to the platform. Lybis quickly kneeled down, studying the engraving.

"This is what Vahnar wanted us to find. I know what this is. Look here, right below *BELLUMIA*. These ten circular indentations. I've seen this in Vahnar's history books. I want you all to listen very carefully to what I am about to say. I can't overemphasize how careful we must be here. Under any other circumstances I would not dare to enter this place, but we have no choice. Not going in would mean the end of our universe. Walk quietly and do NOT touch anything." She looked Thunder and Lightning. Her face was humorless, almost cold. Thunder had never seen this side of Lybis. "Are we clear on this? Our lives are at stake."

"Yes, we're clear. But what is it? What is Bellumia?"

Lybis did not reply. She tapped the first circular indentation, then the second, then the first, continuing on until she had entered the six digit code Vahnar had left for them on the holomap –121577.

With a dull rumble the circular silver platform telescoped upwards until the eight foot wide cylinder had reached a height of almost ten feet. Two curved black doors silently slid open, revealing a circular compartment within, illuminated by an overhead ring of yellow lights.

"It's an elevator?"

Lybis nodded. "Yes, that's exactly what it is, and it leads down to a bunker. A bunker that hasn't seen daylight since its creation during the Anarkkian wars. I read about these in Vahnar's books. The Elders built them all across Nirriim and many other planets when an Anarkkian invasion was becoming a very real threat. These bunkers were not built to house troops, they held something far more dangerous. What resides below was meant to be the Elders' final ring of defense against the Anarkkians. This is where they housed the Autonomous A6 Warrior Rabbitons.

Lightning made a strange gulping noise. "Even Edmund the Explorer was scared of the A6 Rabbitons. Suppose they're still there? Suppose—"

"You don't understand, these are not ordinary A6 Warrior Rabbitons, they are Autonomous A6 Warrior Rabbitons. They make their own decisions, they choose what to destroy, who to kill, all on their own."

"Suppose they think we're the enemy?"

"Now you're beginning to understand. We will be facing two possible scenarios. The Autonomous A6 Rabbitons will either be activated or deactivated, which essentially means they will either be awake or asleep. Either way we have to go down there."

Thunder said, "Well, Vahnar went down there and survived, so maybe it will be okay."

"I hope you're right." Lybis stepped into the elevator, followed by Clara, Thunder, and Lightning. On the wall were two illuminated discs, the upper disc was yellow, the lower one violet. She tapped the violet disc and with a low whirring noise the car shot downward.

Thunder gave a sharp yelp. The car was descending so rapidly it felt as if he was falling. The feeling lasted for almost twenty seconds until the elevator finally came to rest at the bottom of the shaft and the two curved black doors slid open.

Clara peeped out into the darkness but could see nothing. A soft, mellifluous voice came out of nowhere.

"Welcome to Bellumia Bunker. Please mind the gap between the car and the platform."

Lightning jumped back, crashing into Thunder. Clara laughed nervously, then stepped out into the inky blackness. Hundreds of small lights blinked on high above them, revealing a vast rectangular concrete room at least one hundred feet wide and two hundred feet long with ceilings reaching up twenty or thirty feet. The room was empty save for two Blinker ships barely visible in the darkened far left corner. Each wall of the room held a mammoth pair of armored doors, all but one with a single yellow blinking light above the two doors. The doors at the far end of the room were topped with a solid violet light.

Lightning pointed to the two Blinker ships on the other side of the room. "Look! Blinker ships, like the one we found in the Timere Forest. Maybe they still work."

They padded quietly over to the two spherical ships. Lybis examined them, then shook her head. "These won't fly, they're too badly damaged. Perhaps they brought them into the bunker to be repaired, although I have no idea how they managed to get them down here. They must have another elevator somewhere."

Clara pointed to the door with the violet light. "I think we're supposed to go through that door."

Lybis nodded grimly. "That's where we'll go then." She strode across the stone floor to the set of armored doors with the violet light, studied the door for a moment, then tapped a disc on the wall. The massively reinforced doors torturously groaned open, revealing an intense darkness broken only by row after row of small yellow lights.

"What's in there?" Thunder squinted, peering into the darkness.

Clara flicked her wrist and a small glowing sphere appeared in front of her, floating through the open doorway and into the darkness beyond. Moments later the room was dimly illuminated by Clara's sphere.

Lightning could hardly speak. "Uh... uh... are those... are they..."

The hundreds of small yellow lights they had seen were the glowing eyes of row after row after row of Autonomous A6 Warrior Rabbitons.

Lybis whispered sharply, "Nobody move." Almost a full minute passed before she spoke again, her voice now barely audible. "I'm going in alone. I know what the sphere looks like. Stay here. If anything happens, do *not* come in. Clara, I know you are one of the most powerful shapers in your world, but your skills cannot compare to the power of an A6 Warrior. One blast of their vape beam would obliterate your sphere of defense and you along with it. There is no way to stop an A6 short of a fusion pulsar bomb."

"Even so, perhaps I should—"

"Clara, stay here. I'll be back as soon as I can."

Thunder and Lightning watched anxiously as Lybis slipped silently into the room filled with A6 Warriors. Thunder could feel his heart pounding. As Lybis approached the first row of Rabbitons it became clear just how large the A6 Warriors were. Next to an Autonomous A6 she looked like a tiny mouseling. The Autonomous Warrior Rabbitons were larger than Edmund the Rabbiton, standing nearly sixteen feet tall and eight feet wide at the shoulders. Each row held twenty A6 Rabbitons and Thunder could make out at least ten or fifteen rows.

Lybis crept deeper into the room, watching for the slightest movement, listening for even a hint of sound. She had reached the seventh row of Rabbitons when she froze. One of the A6 Warriors was different from the others. One had red eyes, not yellow ones, and they were solid, not blinking. Lybis stood motionless, her gaze riveted on the A6 with the glowing red eyes. When she saw the Rabbiton's hand move she inadvertently let out a small yelp. The A6 Rabbiton's head whipped around towards her, its red eyes pulsing brightly. Lybis turned and ran for her life, shouting out a warning to the others.

"Run! One of the A6 Warriors has been activated!" Lybis raced toward the open doorway, darted through and shouted, "Back to the elevator! We have to get out now!"

The four of them were sprinting madly down the length of the room when a brilliant beam of blazing purple light shot past them and blasted into the elevator car, vaporizing the bottom half of it.

The adventurers stopped short, searching desperately for a place to hide, anywhere they could find to escape from the A6. A melodious voice drifted up from the mangled elevator shaft.

"Please mind the gap between the car and the platform. Thank you for visiting Bellumia Bunker."

Lybis held up her paw and snapped, "Stay here, I have a plan! Run when I tell you." She darted over to the nearest set of armored doors and jumped up and down, shrieking wildly at the A6 Rabbiton. Its red eyes flashed brightly as it turned towards her and raised one arm, its clenched fist glowing with a brilliant purple light. Lybis leaped to one side, rolling across the floor toward Clara. A monstrous blast of purple light burst from the Warrior Rabbiton's fist, shooting across the room to the spot where Lybis had been standing a split second earlier. The beam vaporized a four foot wide hole in the armored doors.

"Run now! Run through the hole in the door!"

The four adventurers bounded wildly across the concrete floor and leaped through the hole, rolling into the adjoining room. A glowing sphere flashed out of Clara's paw, illuminating the room. Clara glanced back through the hole in the door at the rapidly approaching A6 Warrior and cried out, "I can blink us out of here! We need to hold paws!"

Lybis was oblivious to Clara's desperate cry. "There! A freight elevator! That's how they got blinker ships down here. Run for it, we'll take the elevator up to the surface!" Racing across the room they leaped onto the cargo platform. Lybis slapped her paw against the violet disk.

Again Clara cried out, "Everyone hold paws and I will blink us out!" There was a loud whirring, then a grinding noise as the elevator began to rise.

The armored doors glowed fiercely, then vanished in a cloud of purple vapor. The A6 Warrior Rabbiton sprang into the room, its motion fluid, almost graceful. When it saw the rising elevator its eyes flared and it once again aimed a clenched fist at Lybis. Lybis froze. This was how her life was going to end.

Thunder reacted without thinking. He leaped off the moving platform, racing wildly towards the A6 Warrior, shrieking, "NO! DON'T YOU TOUCH HER!"

Lybis cried out in horror when she saw what Thunder was doing. She could not let this happen, she could not lose him again. "VAHTEES! VAHTEES! COME BACK!"

A number of things happened when Lybis cried out her son's name. First, a look of confusion crossed the A6 Warrior's face, then it lowered its arm, looked curiously at Thunder, then up at Lybis. The A6 walked past Thunder over to the freight elevator and extended one arm, its clenched fist only inches from Lybis. Its enormous silver fingers unfolded, revealing what it had been clenching in the palm of its hand. Lybis let out a gasp when she saw it.

"The Black Sphere! Vahtees, that's what Vahnar was trying to tell us on the holomap! He programmed the A6 not to release the sphere until it heard your name." Lybis plucked the sphere from the Rabbiton's open hand, watching as its eyes changed from brilliant red to soft glowing yellow. The A6 Warrior Rabbiton had returned to the world of dreams.

Lybis held out the sphere for all of them to see. "Vahtees, you were so brave, but if you ever do anything like that again..." She couldn't finish her sentence.

Clara broke the strained silence. "The sphere has grown?"

"Yes, when we found it the sphere was no larger than a grain of sand. Now... it's almost an inch across. It will expand two or three more times before the black protective shell becomes too diffuse to contain the forces within it. We must inject the sphere into the Void before that happens. It's our only hope. When the shell is gone, our universe goes with it. We need to get to Thaumatar, and we need to get there quickly."

Clara took Thunder's paw. "Everyone hold paws and I'll blink us up to the surface." A moment later they were standing on the grassy plain beneath a brilliant blue sky.

Lightning stepped over to the circular silver platform, now twisted and unusable. "Should we tell someone about the bunker? About the A6 Rabbitons?"

Lybis shook her head. "Let them sleep. The world doesn't need them now, and hopefully it never will."

Chapter 19

The Garden of Dreams

Oliver was carefully studying one of the maps they had found next to the seventh rippling shuttle wall. "It looks quite lovely doesn't it? Lush gardens and trees, and even a picturesque lily pond. Quite idyllic I would say. Certainly more appealing than the desert shuttle door with those most peculiar looking scaly lizard creatures. I'd say Madam Beffy's father made a very sensible choice in taking this door. He could still be there waiting for us."

Bartholomew nodded. "Perhaps. There's only one way to find out."

Edmund stepped forward. "Would you like me to go first?"

"There's no need, Edmund. More than likely you wouldn't be able to come back through the doorway and tell us what you've found. Besides, this time we're lucky enough to have a map with pictures. I believe we should just hold paws and step through."

The four adventurers lined up in front of the green shuttle wall.

Bartholomew grinned. "Into the next world!" They passed through the translucent wall and emerged into the most exquisitely enchanting garden any of them had ever seen. Bartholomew's jaw dropped. "I never thought I'd hear myself say this, but this is more beautiful than the Isle of Mandora."

The sprawling gardens were teeming with thousands of magnificent brightly colored blossoms and hundreds of statuesque trees, all awash with leaves of every size, shape, and color, rustling melodically in the soothing warm breeze. Bartholomew closed his eyes, taking in the delicate sounds of the garden, inhaling the aroma of countless fragrant blooms. He could hear the distant buzz of insects as they darted gracefully from blossom to blossom, he could feel the healing warmth of the sun on his fur. Bartholomew gave a long sigh. "One day I will most certainly have to show this garden to Clara."

Renata pointed ahead. "Look, a small sign with an arrow pointing down that stone pathway."

Oliver pulled his eyes away from the lush gardens and chuckled. "Well done. I must say this is the first adventure I've been on with signs to direct us. I think I like that. In fact, I know I do." He stepped forward onto the path, which was paved with elaborately carved natural stepping stones. "Even the path is lovely. The designs carved into these stones are exquisite."

Edmund studied his map as they strolled along the pathway. "If I am correct, in several miles we shall reach a small pond, which appears to be a rest area of sorts. Once we pass through there, we travel another five or six miles until we reach a white oval shaped structure. I'm not completely certain, but it appears there are several shuttle walls in that building. It should only take us three or four hours to reach it."

Oliver looked around and gave a sigh of disappointment. "I shall be quite sad indeed to leave these lovely gardens behind. Who knows what dreadful terrors our next destination might hold. I do hope there won't be any more of those ghastly Silver Legs."

Bartholomew grinned. "You never know, perhaps we'll step into an otherworldly orchard filled with delicious éclair trees."

Oliver snorted. "Ah, you have me there. I don't believe I could ever leave such a place as that."

Traveling at a leisurely pace through the idyllic gardens, it took the party of adventurers over two hours to reach the small pond Edmund had described to them.

The pond and its surroundings were equal in beauty to the magnificent gardens they had passed through, the water completely mesmerizing with its large glistening lily pads and dazzling white blossoms. Renata laughed out loud, pointing to a bright blue frog with large yellow eyes hopping from pad to pad across the pond, finally disappearing with a splash beneath the sparkling waters. "What a cute little frog!"

Oliver set himself down on the lush green grass. "My word, even the grass is enchanting. So thick and soft, it feels almost like a feather bed, and that warm sunshine sparkling off the pond... quite captivating. Simply lovely. Perhaps we should rest here for a short time. It was rather a long trek to reach the pond. I for one could use a brief nap."

Bartholomew shrugged. "I don't suppose it would hurt. We can rest for a while and then be on our way to the building at the end of the path. I'm with you Oliver, I could use a short nap too." Bartholomew stretched out on the luxuriant green grass, gazing up at the rustling leaves and the beams of sunlight sparkling and dancing through the branches. His last thoughts before he drifted into the world of dreams were of Clara. She would adore this world.

* * *

"Look at them, aren't they the most precious little bunnies you've ever seen?" Clara stood at the kitchen window peering out at Sophie and Oliver as they bounded across the lawn in a lively game of touch tag.

"They are indeed. We couldn't have asked for more wonderful bunnies than those two. Your sister was so thrilled that we named Sophie after her, and I'll never forget the expression on Oliver T. Rabbit's face when we told him we'd named Oliver after him. Who knows, maybe he'll become a great scientist one day."

"Oh, there's plenty of time for that. Right now I want to enjoy them just as they are."

Bartholomew swung the window open and called out to the two rambunctious little bunnies. "Are you two having fun?"

Sophie stopped running and looked toward the house. "Yes, papa, we're playing tag. Oliver can run almost as fast as I can. And look what I can do now!" Sophie held out her paw and a broad yellow beam of light shot out towards Oliver, who shrieked with laughter as the beam lifted him up into the air.

"Spin me! Spin me!" Sophie grinned as Oliver turned slow somersaults above the thick green carpet of grass.

"Clara, look! Sophie is a natural shaper! It's a marvel she can float Oliver at such an early age, and all on her own. She must have inherited her shaping skills from you."

Clara laughed, *"Oh, Oliver's shaping will one day rival yours, my love. Only yesterday he blinked completely across the room. I couldn't believe my eyes!"*

Bartholomew smiled with unbridled contentment. This was the most wonderful day of his life. His heart was filled with unfathomable joy as he watched his two young bunnies frolic in the yard. Unfortunately, it was also the moment he noticed the dark figure lurking in the trees.

Bartholomew squinted, peering into the deep forest that lay behind their white picket fence. "Clara, did you see that?"

"See what, my love?"

"I thought I saw a dark figure back there in the trees."

"Probably just a nadwokk, or maybe a unicorn. You know how much Sophie loves unicorns."

"That's true, she does love them. But... how would that... anyway, I don't think it was a nadwokk or a unicorn. It looked more like a rabbit. It was hard to tell though, it was hidden in the shadows. Almost as though it was waiting for something."

"I know what, instead of talking about mysterious dark figures, why don't you call Sophie and Oliver and we'll bake snapberry cookies. You know how much they

love snapberry cookies."

"You're right, we should enjoy the moment. They won't be bunnies forever, and we should savor every minute of time we have with them." Bartholomew leaned out the kitchen window, "Who wants to help papa bake snapberry cookies?" He listened to their gleeful laughs. "We do, papa! We do!" Bartholomew's heart was again filled with overwhelming joy.

The following morning Bartholomew rose early, giving a great yawn as he peered out between the gauzy curtains. It was another glorious sunshine filled day, soft billowing white clouds drifting lazily across a bright blue sky. What a joy it was to be alive on a day such as this. He poured himself a tall glass of chilled lemonade, loaded a plate with freshly baked snapberry cookies and strolled out into the back yard. His favorite white chair was waiting for him, and he sank into its soft feathery cushions with a deep blissful sigh. "Mmm... freshly squeezed lemonade and snapberry cookies. Nothing in the world compares to that." Bartholomew leaned back in his chair, closing his eyes, feeling the deep warmth of the radiant morning sun on his fur. When he opened his eyes, however, he frowned. He could see the dark figure again, nestled between two shadowy trees right behind their fence. He was certain now it was a rabbit, a rabbit wearing a dark cloak and hood. This was curious. "Who in the world dresses like that on a beautiful sunny day? And what is he waiting for?" Bartholomew took a long sip of lemonade. "I suppose as long as he doesn't come into our yard it's not really a problem. He's not bothering anyone, he's just watching... and waiting... for something. Curious."

Try as he would, Bartholomew was unable to ignore

the dark figure. Even the lemonade and snapberry cookies couldn't take his mind off the inexplicable appearance of this rather spooky rabbit.

"Enough is enough. I'm going to go and see what he wants. Perhaps he's simply looking for a lost pet, or, he could be bird watching. Many rabbits enjoy a pleasant day of bird watching from time to time." Bartholomew rose up from his favorite white chair, set down his lemonade, and strolled across the soft green grass to the picket fence. The dark figure did not look away. It was quite clear he was studying Bartholomew, but he said nothing.

Bartholomew smiled as pleasantly as he could under the circumstances. "Hello, I couldn't help but notice you standing here next to our fence. May I help you in some way? Have you lost a pet? Perhaps you were watching a rare bird?"

The dark figure stepped forward, now only scant feet from Bartholomew. "Took you long enough. What do you think you're doing?"

"I beg your pardon? I'm simply enjoying a lovely sunny day with my dear wife Clara and our two mischievous but lovable bunnies, Sophie and Oliver."

"Really. Care to tell me exactly when your two little bunnies were born? Or when you bought this precious stone house? Or when you started baking snapberry cookies?"

"I don't know what you... when they were... what? Why are you asking me these things? You should enjoy the moment and not question everything. It doesn't matter when they were born."

"Fine, if it doesn't matter, just tell me."

"Certainly. They were... they were born when...

umm... let's see, Clara and I moved from... ahh... Pterosaur... Pterosaur something..."

"Valley? Pterosaur Valley?"

"Yes, that's it. We lived in Pterosaur Valley and–" Bartholomew gave a shivering groan as a sudden brilliant rush of awareness blasted through him. He remembered everything. He remembered he and Clara had not had any bunnies yet. He remembered he was on an adventure with Oliver and Edmund and Renata. He remembered he had fallen asleep next to the little pond. And he remembered who the dark figure was.

"Bruno Rabbit? What are you doing here?"

"Ta daaa! Welcome to the world of the waking. The question is, what are you doing here? I thought I'd taught you better than this. You don't even know when you're having a dream? I will admit it's a spectacularly enhanced dream thanks to some very complex Thaumatarian technology, but it's a dream nonetheless."

Bartholomew was now completely awake inside his dream. *"What is this place?"*

"Pretty simple really. A little retreat called the Garden of Dreams put together by a few entrepreneurial Thaumatarians. You pay a small fee, they let you in, you have the best dreams you've ever had in your life. Some fun, eh? Now, are you ready to do some work, or are you going to sit around all day with google eyes, munching on snapberry cookies?"

"What kind of work?"

Bruno flicked his wrist and they were in the Timere Forest. *"Fly through the trees as fast as you can. You have been practicing haven't you?"*

"Of course I have." Bartholomew shot up into the

sky, hovered for a moment then blasted down into the dense trees flashing through them as though they weren't there. He flipped over twice and flew back through the trees upside down, finally blinking down to a halt in front of Bruno Rabbit.

Bruno rolled his eyes. "Nobody likes a showoff. But, you've done well and do deserve my hearty congratulations. Now, how's that Eleventh Ring working out? Pretty well? Discovered many of the secret skills it gives you?"

"Now that you mention it, I have found several of them. My favorite is the Traveling Eye. Of course it's also nice that the pterosaurs don't bother us when I'm wearing the ring." Bartholomew chuckled.

Bruno stared at him in disbelief, then slowly shook his head as though he was utterly and completely disappointed.

"What? I didn't discover enough skills?"

"Here's my question. Would you care to explain to me exactly how a lump of gold with a hole in the middle can give you secret shaping skills?"

"Well... for one thing, you said it did. And for another thing, I can see the World Doors when I'm wearing the Eleventh Ring, without using my World Glasses."

"You didn't answer my question. How does it work? How exactly does the ring give you these powers?"

"Umm... I guess it somehow affects... my brain?"

Bruno snorted. "Really? It affects your brain? What does that even mean? Think. I want you to think."

Bartholomew closed his eyes. If it wasn't the ring that was giving him these skills, then what was it? It had to be something. Something inside him. It was as though the sun burst out from behind the clouds. He had the answer.

"When I wear the ring I am able to give myself permission to set aside my self-imposed restrictions. It's the same as when I realized there was no gravity in my dreams and was able to fly."

"Give that rabbit a big cigar. Finally, you are beginning to understand. Now, please tell me the big difference between the dream world we are in now, and the real world you live in – the world where you are lying on the grass dreaming this marvelous dream. What is the big difference?"

Bartholomew frowned, scrunching his face in thought. "Umm... the world I live in is real, and the dream world is not?"

"An excellent answer, truly excellent, but completely incorrect and essentially a circular word salad of meaningless gibberish. You're telling me they're different because they have different names. Now, what is the real difference?"

"I don't know. I don't know how they're different. I thought this dream was the real world until I woke up inside the dream, after I started talking to you."

"Hoorah! Send up the skyrockets! Strike up the marching band! You once again have amazed me with a vaguely correct answer. There is no difference at all between them. Every dream is the real world until you wake up. Do you understand the incredible implications of that? Don't answer, because your answer will be wrong. I want you to think about it. A lot. Day and night. Think about it. Next time I see you I expect a very concise and eminently correct answer. Now, wake your friends and get moving. You have a universe to save

and you don't have much time. Repeat that for me, please."

"*I have a universe to save and I don't have much time."*

"*Again."*

"*I have a universe to save and I don't have much time."*

"*Excellent. Until we meet again." Bruno flicked his wrist and Bartholomew found himself sitting in front of the exquisitely lovely lily pad pond. Next to him lay Oliver, Renata, and Edmund, all lost in their marvelous dreams.*

Bartholomew's thoughts were racing. "I have a universe to save and I don't have much time? What does that mean? I thought we were looking for Madam Beffy's father, not trying to save the universe. I have to save the universe? Bruno Rabbit, what are you up to now?"

Bartholomew rose up and stepped over to Oliver, who was lying on his back snoring loudly. "OLIVER! Time to wake up. It seems we have to save the universe."

Oliver gave a great blustery snort and opened his eyes. "I won! I won the Science Symposium's Gold Medal! Finally, all my theories regarding the true—" Oliver glanced around him, first at the lily pond, then at Bartholomew. "Oh, dear, I must have been dreaming?"

"You were. As it turns out this garden is a Thaumatarian retreat providing dreams which fulfill the guests' fondest desires."

"Drat, it was such a wonderful dream. Drat and double drat. Well, perhaps one day my dream will become a reality. One never knows, I suppose."

Bartholomew gently shook Renata's shoulder. "Wake up, Renata, dream time is over. We need to go."

Renata's eyes blinked open. They were sharp and clear. "I saw him. He was alive. He was alive again!"

"I'm sorry, Renata. It was just a dream. We are in a Thaumatarian retreat called the Garden of Dreams. You were only dreaming."

Renata shook her head. "No, this was real. He was alive. I know he was."

"Well, perhaps you are right, but either way we need to go now."

Oliver kneeled down next to Edmund. "Good heavens, I think our old friend Edmund is sound asleep. I believe we are witnessing a great milestone in the annals of science – the very first sleeping Rabbiton." Oliver pushed Edmund's shoulder with both paws. "Wake up, sleepy Rabbiton!"

Edmund shook his head and sat up. "Ah, excellent. I'm back. I can't wait to introduce you to my new friend Abbie. As it turns out, I am not the only living Rabbiton in the world. Abbie is also alive and we have a great deal in–"

"Edmund, you were dreaming. You only dreamed about a Rabbiton named Abbie."

Edmund's eyes blinked rapidly. "A dream? That's not possible. A dream? I'm quite certain what I experienced was real. I was there, Bartholomew, I saw her. I talked to her. We went for long walks together. She went on adventures with me. She said she loved me."

Bartholomew ran his paw across Edmund's shoulder. "I'm sorry, Edmund. Dreams can seem very real when we are having them. Sometimes we are glad to wake up, and sometimes we wish our dreams would last forever. I'm glad your first dream was a happy one."

"How strange. I have always wondered what it would be like to dream. What about Abbie? When will I see her again?"

"I can't give you an answer, Edmund, but I can tell you the world of dreams is eternally surprising."

"Excellent. I will plan on seeing her in my next dream then. We should go now. Abbie told me we have a universe to save and we don't have much time."

Chapter 20

Stick

Oliver pointed to a large white softly curved structure. "There! I can see it. That must be where the shuttle walls are located. Even their buildings are lovely. It looks almost like a cloud, doesn't it? There's no denying these Thaumatarians knew a thing or two about beauty."

"It's more than lovely. Not a corner in sight, and those yellow blossoms on the climbing vines are breathtaking. Do you see any doors?"

Edmund scanned the building, his optics set on wide spectrum. "The doors are cleverly concealed, but I believe they will reveal themselves upon my approach." He walked briskly ahead of the others to the end of the stone path. As he drew close to the building there was a delicate sound of melodic chimes and a tall oval doorway appeared in front of him. Edmund stepped through the opening into the building. "Quite remarkable. I see no moving parts... it's as if the wall simply disappeared, allowing us to enter."

The four adventurers followed a series of directional

arrow signs with indecipherable symbols beneath them. After passing through several expansive waiting rooms and a long curved corridor, they entered a grand circular room, its ceiling covered with sparkling lights, lending the illusion of a starry night. Across the room were two of the now familiar shuttle walls, one green and one blue.

"Oh dear, it appears we have reached another impasse. Which door to choose?"

Bartholomew rubbed his paw against his chin. "Hmmm... the gateway that brought us to this world was green. Perhaps we should take the green one."

Oliver hurried across the room to the doorways. "No maps here, which means we'll have no idea what sort of world we'll be entering. I can't say I care for that very much."

Edmund motioned them over to the green shuttle door. "I believe I have our answer, Bartholomew." He pointed to the intricately carved stone floor. "There. Someone has scratched a large arrow into the floor. An arrow directing us through the green doorway."

Bartholomew looked around at the others. "What do you think? It's our only clue. The arrow could have been left by Madam Beffy's father, but it may not have been."

Renata pointed to the green doorway. "I have a good feeling about that one."

Bartholomew grinned. "You can't ask for more than that. Shall we go?"

Seconds later the party of adventurers held paws and stepped through the rippling gateway into an unknown world.

Bartholomew glanced around the new environment,

his eyes sharp for potential threats. They were in a dusky rectangular room constructed from a translucent yellow material, a glittering night sky visible through the ceiling. It was difficult to see in the darkened room, but he could make out the silhouettes of several dozen chairs and tables. "Looks like we've found another waiting room."

Renata pointed to the far wall. "What is that?"

Bartholomew looked, instantly spotting a pile of glowing sticks lying in the opposite corner. "Hmm. That's odd. There are no other lights here, just those sticks." Bartholomew cautiously made his way past the tables and chairs, paws extended out in front of him, over to the glowing sticks. He had almost reached the corner where the sticks lay when the very last thing he had expected to happen did happen. The pile of glowing sticks stood up and turned towards him.

Bartholomew froze. He simply could not move. He had seen many strange things in his adventures, but nothing which compared to this. "Oliver? Are you seeing this? Edmund? Renata?"

Without hesitation Edmund replied, "It appears to be an animated glowing stick figure, similar to drawings made by young bunnies, but in this case there is no head."

"Thank you, I already had a good grasp on that part."

A sudden chill shot through Oliver. "The bright figure! The bright figure that Madam Beffy's father saw through the wall! This must be what he saw. Try talking to it. Maybe it has seen Arledge."

"I believe you're right, but.... um... it doesn't have ears. It doesn't even have a head for the ears to go on. I don't see any room for a brain. Or a heart. Or anything really, for that matter."

"And yet there it is, standing in front of us. Another one of those bumblebees we so often talk about, things that can't exist and yet they do. Wait there and I will examine it more closely." Oliver made his way through the maze of furniture and approached the strange glowing stick figure. First he tried speaking to it. "Hello, my name is Oliver. Do you have a name?"

There was no response from the bright little creature. When Oliver reached over to touch it with his paw, however, the stick figure backed away.

"Ahh, this is excellent. We now know it can sense my presence. That means it must have a rudimentary sensory or nervous system and at least a simple brain of sorts."

The stick figure walked over to Oliver and poked him in the leg with its glowing arm.

"Great heavens, did you see that? It poked me. What a strange response."

The glowing figure stepped across the room towards the other adventurers. One by one it approached each of them, gently prodding their leg with its arm. When it was done it walked back to Oliver, raising its arm up to his paw.

"What is doing? It keeps poking my paw."

Renata whispered, "I think it wants you to hold its... hold the end of its arm."

Oliver gently grasped the creature's stick arm with his paw. The stick figure glowed brightly. "Good heavens, what is it doing? It's pulling me! I think it wants us to follow him. Or her. Or something." He looked towards Bartholomew. "What should I do?"

"Well, let's see where it takes us. Maybe there are more of them. Maybe that's what the creatures in this world look like."

Oliver frowned. "And maybe they eat rabbits for bedtime snacks."

"With what? How would they do that? How exactly would they bite you?"

Oliver chuckled. "Ah, you make an excellent point, Bartholomew. Very well, my little glowing stick friend, we will follow you. Hmm, we really should call you something besides a stick creature. Would you like me to give you a name?"

The figure glowed brightly.

"Excellent. We shall call you Stick, for rather obvious reasons. Lead the way, Stick, and we shall follow."

Stick let go of Oliver's paw and headed towards the main door of the building. He waited patiently until the others had reached them, then motioned with one arm for Oliver to open the door. "Most certainly, my friend." Oliver pushed on the door but it wouldn't open. He pushed with more force but it still resisted his efforts.

"Drat, this door seems to be either locked or jammed shut."

Stick glowed brightly, waving Oliver away from the door. A sudden blast of light flashed from the end of his stick arm and the door vanished.

"Great heavens! Bartholomew, you saw what Stick just did?"

"I saw, though how he did it is a mystery to me. It's not shaping, it's something completely different. He seems intelligent, but... what does he think with?"

Oliver looked down at Stick with a frown. "You're not going to vaporize us are you?"

Stick walked over to Oliver and leaned against his leg, putting one arm around it.

"Good heavens, I believe Stick is giving me a hug. I think I quite like him. And just when I thought I had seen everything." Oliver reached down and gently patted Stick on the arm. Stick glowed brightly and stepped out through the open doorway.

The party of adventurers followed Stick through the desert night, using him as a sort of walking lantern to light their way. Bartholomew could see they were traveling across hard packed desert terrain, but had no idea where Stick was leading them.

They had been walking for close to an hour when the sun peeked up over the horizon, its radiant light illuminating the barren landscape.

"Edmund, use your enhanced optics to look over there, to the left of us. Is that what I think it is?"

"Hmm... if you are thinking it is a great metropolis with hundreds of buildings that seem to touch the clouds, then you are correct."

Renata said, "Perhaps we could go there. That may be where Arledge Rabbit went. It seems a logical place for him to seek help."

Oliver nodded. "Renata has a point, Bartholomew. Arledge may have gone to the city searching for a way home."

Stick stopped in his tracks and turned towards the band of adventurers. He hopped up and down, waving his arms frantically back and forth.

"What in the world is he doing?"

Oliver answered, "I don't believe he wants us to go

to the city. Perhaps it is not safe there."

Stick glowed brightly and continued on towards the mountains.

"Well, I guess we have our answer. Maybe the city is contaminated, or filled with Silver Legs, or worse." Bartholomew eyed the distant snowy mountain peaks. "I have a feeling we'll be needing warm winter clothing before long."

It took the adventurers three grueling days of trekking across the burning sands to reach the base of the mountain range. Stick came to a halt and pointed to what looked like a high mountain pass.

"Great heavens, does he intend for us to climb all the way up there? I don't believe I am capable of such a gargantuan feat."

Stick stepped over to Oliver and gave him his curious version of a hug, wrapping one arm around Oliver's leg.

Oliver's frown softened. "Well, I suppose if Stick thinks I can do it, perhaps I can. I will give it a try. Maybe I will surprise myself." Then with a snort he added, "Besides, Edmund can always carry me if I run out of steam."

Edmund did not look completely enthralled with the idea of carrying Oliver over a mountain range, but made no comment.

Oliver found the lower slopes of the mountain to be a most welcome respite from the stiflingly hot desert. The air was cool and fresh as they hiked through majestic stands of pine and spruce, at times emerging into lush open meadows laced with swatches of gloriously painted wildflowers.

"It's quite lovely, isn't it? It would be the perfect

spot for a quaint little cottage. Quite bucolic."

One day later, Oliver's opinion of the mountainside had changed drastically. "Great heavens, these rocks are simply dreadful! I don't know that I can go much farther. The top half of me is quite chilled, and yet my legs feel as though they shall burst into flames from the exertion of climbing over these horrible wretched boulders. Stick does seem doggedly determined that we cross this mountain range. I do hope there is a very bright and very warm light at the other end of this mountainous tunnel."

Once they were above the tree line the adventurers paused while Bartholomew shaped warm winter gear for everyone. Edmund and Stick were, of course, unaffected by the cold weather, although it was difficult to tell exactly what affected Stick and what didn't.

"These heavy coats, hoods, and leggings will keep us warm, and I've also shaped mountaineering boots with sharp crampons to prevent slipping on the glacial ice and snow in the mountain pass."

Two very exhausting days later they reached the pass. By then Oliver had ceased his running commentary on mountains, mountain climbing, cold weather, snow, ice, large frozen jagged rocks, sore feet, and his many and varied opinions regarding all of these things. Bartholomew guessed his silence was simply an attempt to conserve energy. The only ones who weren't bone weary were Edmund and Stick.

The mountain pass was bitterly cold with dreadful howling winds and blinding snow, but it was relatively level, something which pleased Oliver greatly. The party had traveled less than a mile across the torturous wind blown frozen pass when they had their first encounter with a creature they would come to know as the snow beast.

Bartholomew had shaped snowshoes for them to use while traversing the massive snow drifts. Oliver was commenting on the difficulty of climbing over a particular jumble of icy rocks while wearing these snowshoes when an ear splitting shriek from above shattered the frigid mountain air. His head jerked upward just in time to see an enormous shaggy white haired beast with three bright green eyes and long fearsome fangs leaping off a rocky ledge thirty feet above him. Oliver instinctively knew the monstrosity would be on him before he even had time to scream. He was certain his life was over, and he would have been quite correct in this assumption if not for the series of events taking place behind him.

First, even before the snow beast's cry had ended, Bartholomew flicked out his paw to create a sphere of defense around the party of adventurers. To Bartholomew's great surprise, however, before he had time to form the sphere of defense a powerful beam of brilliant green light sizzled past him and hit the snow beast squarely on the chest.

In his attempt to dodge the plummeting snow beast Oliver had skittered wildly backwards, but slipped on the icy rocks, tumbling down into a deep snow drift. He looked up in horror, expecting the snow beast's ferocious teeth to be the last thing he would ever see. He saw the beast, but there was something very, very wrong. The creature was frozen in midair almost twenty feet above him, as motionless as a marble statue.

Oliver gaped at the immobilized beast. "Great heavens! Am I going mad? What is it doing?"

Bartholomew stared at Stick with unconcealed amazement. He had never witnessed such a skill as this. "Stick? What did you do? How did you stop the beast in midair?"

Stick had no response other than to wave them onward across the mountain pass. Bartholomew took one long last look at the frozen beast, then turned to follow Stick.

Oliver staggered to his feet and scrambled through the snow after them, glancing back every few moments to make certain the snow beast was not galloping across the ice towards him.

It was slow going over the rugged glacial ice and treacherous crevasses, but by late afternoon they had finally traversed the mountain pass. Stick stopped, looking back across the drifting snow and jagged blue green ice. From this distance the snow beast was a small black shape silhouetted against a bright blue sky. Stick raised his arm and a green beam streaked across the mountain pass, hitting the snow beast. The instant the beam touched it, the creature shot forward, landing precisely on the spot where Oliver had once been standing. They could hear the shrieks of rage echo through the pass when the beast realized its prey was no longer there.

Oliver touched his paw to Stick's shoulder. "You saved my life."

Stick glowed brightly, then turned, heading down the side of the mountain.

Chapter 21

The Cave

Oliver trudged along behind Stick, who was now traveling laterally across the mountainside. Their initial descent had brought them below the ice and snow but they were still above the tree line, inching their way across mounds of unstable shale. "Why are we going across the mountain? Shouldn't we be descending? I don't understand what Stick has in mind for us. It would certainly be far easier to go directly downhill rather than traveling across the side of an entire mountain range."

Renata pointed ahead, past the river of rocky debris. "I see the entrance to a cave past this rockslide. Perhaps that is our destination."

Stick hastened across the treacherous shale, then turned and darted up a steep path. He pointed to the cave entrance, motioning for the adventurers to follow him, then disappeared into the cave.

With Edmund's help they safely crossed the treacherous shale covered slope and made their way up to the cave. Oliver peered anxiously into the gloomy entrance. "Are you certain we should go in? Stick seems to be a pleasant enough fellow, but one can never judge someone completely by their appearance. For all we know there could be a thousand more of... of whatever Stick is, waiting inside the cave to imprison us or turn us into mindless slaves or some other equally dreadful fate."

Bartholomew grinned. "So true. It's almost impossible to judge a glowing stick figure by its appearance, especially the ones who give you hugs." He was about to add that Oliver shouldn't worry because he still wore the Eleventh Ring, but remembered his last conversation with Bruno Rabbit. The ring itself had no power, it was only a device which allowed Bartholomew to set aside his self-imposed restrictions. The pterosaurs were friendly not because he was wearing the Eleventh Ring, but because Bartholomew *knew* they would be friendly. It was certainly far less complicated when he believed his skills came directly from the ring.

"I hope you haven't forgotten my shaping skills, Oliver."

"You make an excellent point, Bartholomew, and it is because of those marvelous skills that I am giving you the distinct honor of being the first to enter this very dark and rather ominous cave." Oliver gave a great loud laugh.

"Shhh, you'll wake all the pterosaurs." Bartholomew grinned as he flicked his wrist and watched a ball of light shoot out into the cave.

Renata peered in. "It seems fine. No ferocious snow beasts."

Bartholomew stepped into the cave followed closely

by the other adventurers. "This looks more like an old mine than a natural geological formation. Look at the heavy wooden support timbers along this section."

The tunnel continued on for several hundred feet then turned sharply to the right, opening into a large chamber. "It does look like they were mining for something here, but I have no idea what. Gold or silver, I would imagine. We'll keep going through that tunnel over there."

The tunnel they entered was long and circuitous, and it took the better part of an hour to reach the other end. Edmund held up his arm for them to stop.

"I see light coming from the next cavern. Wait here and I will investigate. Perhaps the light is from a pack of glowing stick figures waiting to turn us into mindless slaves. Ha ha ha ha!" Edmund's peculiar staccato laugh echoed through the cave.

"Good heavens, Edmund, I merely meant to say that there could be unseen dangers lurking ahead of us. I only used the concept of mindless slaves as an example of one such possible danger. It's not so farfetched as you seem to think. I seem to remember a certain vile King Oberon who thought the idea to be quite feasible indeed."

By the time Oliver had finished defending his mindless slave comment Edmund was long gone. The adventurers waited silently for him to return, and less than a minute later heard him cry out, "Bartholomew! We need your help!"

Bartholomew blinked into the cave, appearing in a flash of light next to Edmund. Stick was on the other side of Edmund and they were both standing by an older gray rabbit wrapped in a ragged blanket on the cave floor, a flickering oil lantern next to him. The rabbit was frantically trying to back away from his uninvited guests, but he was obviously injured. Bartholomew drew a thought cloud from the terrified rabbit. If the old rabbit hadn't been so scared Bartholomew might have laughed. He had seen himself through the eyes of the injured rabbit. The gray rabbit was facing a glowing stick figure with no head, a ten foot tall gleaming silver robotic rabbit, and a rabbit who had miraculously appeared in a brilliant flash of light.

"We are here to help you, not harm you. I am Bartholomew Rabbit and I am a shaper. If you wish, I would be happy to repair your broken leg."

The old rabbit nodded, his eyes still wide. Renata and Oliver had just stepped into the cave. Bartholomew kneeled down next to the gray rabbit and held out one paw. Bartholomew's body gave off a bright golden glow which then flowed through his arm and into the rabbit's leg. The leg glowed brightly. When the light faded Bartholomew said. "Try standing up now."

Very tentatively the graying rabbit rose up. "You did it! You healed my leg! I have heard of shaping, heard stories of shapers such as yourself but I have never seen such skills in use before. Truly, this is powerful magic."

Bartholomew made no attempt to educate the rabbit regarding the true nature of shaping, instead saying, "I'm glad I could help you. How long have you been here?"

The old rabbit didn't answer. His eyes were on Edmund the Rabbiton and Stick.

"What manner of creatures are these?"

"This is my old friend Edmund the Rabbiton, a creation of the Elders, and the only truly living

Rabbiton in existence. And this is Stick. I'm afraid we don't know very much about him, other than the fact that he saved Oliver's life when he was attacked by a ferocious snow beast."

The gray rabbit nodded. "I have met the small bright one before, but I wasn't sure if I was the only one who could see him. It is only because of this odd little fellow that I am still alive. I owe him my life. I broke my leg when I fell into an icy crevasse in my attempt to escape a charging snow beast. As I lay freezing to death in the crevasse your friend Stick stood close to me and glowed brightly, saving my life with his warmth. He led me across the frigid mountain pass. Without his help I would surely have perished. As if that wasn't enough, a second snow beast attacked us near the other side of the pass, but this bright little creature you call Stick somehow froze it in mid-stride. I will confess without any shame that at times it has been hard for me to determine what is real and what is a dream." He looked up at Edmund the Rabbiton. "You're quite certain you are real?"

"Ah, it appears you are questioning the nature of reality and whether or not physical matter—"

Bartholomew gently interrupted. "He just wants to know if you are real."

"Eminently so. Quite real. I am a Model 9000 Rabbiton with the optional A7-Series 3 Repositorian Module created by the Elders of Mandora almost fifteen hundred years ago."

"I see." Edmund's answer seemed to confuse the gray rabbit even more. He glanced over to Renata. "You are the only one who has caused me no fright, perhaps because you are a very lovely rabbit and remind me of my daughter when she was younger."

Renata smiled at his compliment. "Thank you. I am Renata and I am from Opar, near the city of Cathne."

"Cathne?? I passed through that very city a number of years ago. That's how I became lost in this world."

"Good heavens!" A light had blinked on in Oliver's head and he put his paw to his mouth. "It's him! It's Arledge Rabbit! It's Madam Beffy's father!"

The old rabbit stepped away from Oliver, his eyes narrowing. "How do you know my name? Who are you? What manner of being are you?"

Oliver held up both paws. "I am a dear friend of your lovely daughter. It was Madam Beffy who asked us to find you. She has never given up hope that she would see you again."

Arledge desperately tried to process Oliver's words. "The journal! Beffy found my journal?"

"A duplonium prospector found it and brought it to her. After she discovered your hidden map she wrote to me and asked if I thought we could find you and bring you back to her."

Arledge had tears in his eyes when he grasped Oliver's paw. "I don't know how to thank you. I had given up all hope of ever seeing my dear Beffy again. It is truly a miracle. You are a courageous and noble rabbit, and I can never repay such a debt as this."

Oliver was overwhelmed. He was not used to being viewed as the conquering hero, and Arledge's sincere heartfelt thanks was making him quite uncomfortable. He was at ease in his role as a brilliant bumbling scientist, but that was far different from being called a courageous and noble rabbit. Still, this was Madam Beffy's father, and Madam Beffy meant everything to him. "I'm only glad we were able to find you. Madam Beffy is a very dear friend of mine and her happiness means everything to me."

"I am glad she found a brave rabbit such as you."

"Ah... we're not... that is to say, at this particular time Madam Beffy and I..."

Bartholomew jumped in to rescue Oliver, who was clearly in over his head. "Arledge, now that we have found you, we need to find our way home again. We have no idea where we are or even what world this is. We simply followed your trail through the gateway shuttle doors to this world, but it was Stick who finally led us to you.

Stick glowed brightly.

Arledge reached into an inner pocket and pulled out a stained and wrinkled sheet of folded paper. "I have a map. I found it on the floor next to the last rippling wall I went through. I don't know if it will help us, but it looks to me as if there's another one of your gateway doors about sixty miles from here."

Stick again glowed brightly, but this time he continued to grow brighter and brighter until Oliver was forced to shield his eyes, watching through his paws as Stick became enveloped in a blazing inferno of roiling green fire. Oliver cried out in horror as Stick disappeared in the flames. The only thing left was a pile of glowing green embers smoldering on the cave floor.

Oliver was distraught over the loss of Stick. "There was something about him. I really was extraordinarily fond of the little fellow. I don't understand what happened. Why would he just burst into flames like that?"

Bartholomew did his best to console Oliver, but in

the end there wasn't much he could say, so he tried instead to redirect Oliver's thoughts by discussing their upcoming plans.

"Arledge, I believe your map is exactly what we need to help find our way home. Now that you can walk again we can head down this side of the mountain to the desert and head due west until we reach the gateway doors. Hopefully there won't be many to choose from. The map seems to indicate there is only one. So, perhaps we should have dinner, get a good night's rest and leave at sunrise."

Arledge ran his paw over his leg. "She's as good as new, so I'm ready to go when you are."

As the sun was peeping up over the horizon the next morning the party of adventurers adjusted their packs and began the arduous trek to the base of the mountain. Soon they found themselves back among the thick spruce and pine trees, the mountain air cool and refreshing. Oliver spotted something resembling a large blue wolf in the distance, but when it saw the size of their party the creature slipped off into the forest.

Once they reached the lower slopes they shed their cold weather gear. That evening they set up camp several hundred feet from the base of the mountain, and the following morning set off across the desert. Bartholomew shaped wide brimmed hats to protect them from the blazing desert sun, although Edmund declined to wear one since he already had on his cherished adventurer's hat.

"Oliver, could you check the map? Do you see any landmarks that might indicate how far we've come?"

"Ah, let's see. There is a drawing here of a large rock standing alone in the desert, which is undoubtedly meant to represent that mammoth rock we passed about five miles back. That would mean we have approximately forty more miles to go before we reach the next doorway. Oh, dear, forty miles in this sweltering heat." He was about to make known his opinion of deserts, scorching sand, burning sun, sizzling heat, blisters, scorpions, sand in his shoes, and possible poisonous lizard attacks when he remembered Arledge was there. He concluded his comment rather abruptly with, "But, that's just another day in the life of an adventurer."

As they strolled along the sandy desert floor, Oliver found himself walking next to Arledge. Oliver had been thrilled to hear Arledge saw him as a good match for Madam Beffy. "Is it true you made that duplonium bracelet for Madam Beffy? She wears it almost every day. Duplonium is an extremely volatile element, you know. Quite dangerous."

"Oh, don't worry about Beffy. That's one rabbit who can handle herself if the going gets tough. I taught her well, and that's a fact. I once saw her break off one of those duplonium beads and throw it in front of a herd of stampeding wild nadwokks. Turned the whole herd around and more than likely saved both our lives. You don't to need worry none about Beffy."

"Good heavens, a herd of charging Nadwokks?" Oliver could not conceal his glee. There was much more to Madam Beffy than just éclairs and cinnamon rolls and the scent of lilac, and it made Oliver like her even more.

The days rolled on as the party of adventurers continued their march across the scorching desert, crossing numerous deep and treacherous gullies formed by the torrential seasonal rains.

On three occasions Bartholomew had to blink up a sphere of defense to protect them from enormous green birdlike creatures who would circle high overhead for hours, then without warning shoot down at blurring speeds trying to snatch one of them up with their gargantuan talons. This brought back frightening memories of the pterosaurs to Oliver and caused him a great deal of anxiety, but he carefully concealed his fears from Arledge. He didn't want to appear as anything less than a courageous and noble rabbit.

The desert days and nights slipped by until late one afternoon Edmund called out, "I see a structure approximately one mile ahead of us. It is white and similar in form to the way station in the Garden of Dreams."

The hard packed desert sand soon transformed to lush green grass and large patches of lovely blue and purple wildflowers.

Bartholomew said, "You're right, Edmund, this reminds me a great deal of the Garden of Dreams, almost unnatural in its extreme beauty and order. This is certainly the work of the Thaumatarians, which means that building up ahead should hold the means of our passage from this world. Though where we shall be passing to is anyone's guess."

A half hour later the party arrived at a white structure almost identical to the one they found in the Garden of Dreams. When Edmund approached the rounded building an oval shaped door appeared, accompanied by the sound of soft and harmonious chimes. The adventurers followed Edmund into the building.

After passing through winding corridors and several large waiting rooms filled with the ubiquitous comfortable chairs, they entered a towering dome shaped room. On the far side of the room sat a familiar green shuttle wall.

"The good news is there's only one door so we don't have to choose, but the bad news is there's only one door so we don't *get* to choose." Oliver chuckled loudly, highly amused by the cleverness of his own comment. Out of the corner of his eye he noted that Arledge was also laughing.

Bartholomew faced the other adventurers. "Oliver is right, for better or worse, this is the door we must enter. Where it will take us I do not know, but we will be together, and hopefully we shall all be home soon." Bartholomew did his best to sound optimistic, but the words Bruno Rabbit had made him repeat kept echoing over and over in his head. "I have a universe to save and I don't have much time." He knew he was running out of time but had not an inkling of where he was supposed to go or what he was supposed to do.

Chapter 22

Through Death's Door

"Why do we have to drag this dumb blue box around anyway? What is it? Some kind of weapon?"

"I don't know what it is, I'm not Oliver T. Mouse."

"Don't call me that unless you care to face the wrath of my furious fists."

Lightning rolled his eyes. "The day you can clobber me is the day purple frozen Nadwokks will rain down from–"

"Vahtees! Lightning! We need the box up here! Now, please!" Lybis watched impatiently as Thunder and Lightning dragged the long blue box off the boat and up onto the grass.

Thunder wrinkled his nose. "What is this thing anyway?"

"Well, the Secret Armada Forces nicknamed it 'Death's Door'. Very few warriors who passed through it ever returned."

"Umm... why do we want anything to do with

something they called Death's Door?"

Lybis smiled. "The officially designated name is not quite as colorful – it was called the *Model M1 Portable Spectral Field Actualizer*. Small groups of a dozen or so Secret Force troopers used them to infiltrate behind enemy lines on sabotage and rescue missions. Death's Door essentially is a big blue box that creates a spectral doorway into another world. The good news is, this is the M1A1 Unit with Universal Sector Modulation, which means we can open a doorway to anywhere we choose, as long as we have the coordinates. In this case, we will be going to Thaumatar, hopefully emerging relatively close to the facility where the Black Sphere was created."

"Do you think it's safe?"

"I believe so. It was only nicknamed Death's Door because of the inherent dangers of the Secret Force missions. It doesn't appear to have been damaged at all and the self diagnostics look good. I've connected in sequence six CDETS from the downed ship's pulse guns, so we have more than enough power. I just need to set our destination coordinates using my comm unit."

Lybis pulled a thin silver pad from her coat pocket. "This will give me the proper coordinate codes." She tapped on the pad and a holomap appeared above it. "Here it is, Thaumatar. Hmm... here's the desert, but I don't see the facility, which is not surprising since it must have been a highly classified transparent project. This should do it." She kneeled down next to the Field Actualizer and entered in the codes for Thaumatar.

"That's all there is to it." Thunder thought her smile seemed a little forced.

"How do we get back home once we get to

Thaumatar?"

"The short answer is I don't know. The Death's Door will appear simultaneously in both worlds, but we can only use the device in Thaumatar to return here. That doesn't really help us get home. It's possible we could use the Death's Door to return to Quintari, but after that I don't know, especially considering my current deceased status on Quintari. All I know is if we don't get this sphere into the Void it won't matter where we are because our universe will be gone and we'll be absorbed into the sphere when it expands.

"Well, since you put it that way, I guess we should go."

Lybis smiled at Thunder. "At least I have had the great pleasure of seeing what a fine mouse you have become. I will always have that. Always."

She leaned over and tapped a violet disc on the Spectral Field Actualizer, then backed away. A diaphanous sphere appeared in front of the device, rapidly growing in size. Translucent flowing green waves rippled wildly, surrounded by a ring of pale swirling clouds. Tiny blue sparks shot out from the perimeter of the doorway as the roiling clouds turned a dark stormy gray. The machine emitted a loud beeping noise, a violet light flashing brightly on the console.

"We're good to go. I'll go first, then Vahtees, Lightning, and Clara. We'll be fine." Without another word she stepped through the doorway and was gone.

Clara called out, "Thunder, you're next." He closed his eyes and darted through the doorway, followed by Lightning and then Clara.

   * * *

"I told you not to run through the doorway. It's just

like when the Thirteenth Monk sent us to Clara's house. It you hadn't run you wouldn't have whonked your ear again. Gosh, I hope you didn't *break* it." Lightning cackled loudly until he noticed Lybis' disapproving look.

"I'm fine, I just bumped into this wall. What is this place anyway? I thought we were going to a desert. This is a giant city." He looked around and added, "A giant city with nobody in it except us."

Lybis cursed silently as she examined the Spectral Field Actualizer. "There must have been some internal damage I was not aware of, or I may have calibrated it incorrectly. The good news is we are definitely on Thaumatar. The bad news is, I have no idea how far we are from the desert or the facility. It's easy enough to find out though." She pulled out her comm unit and tapped on the disc grid. A holomap of Thaumatar appeared in front of her.

"Hmm... we are here, and we want to be over here. I'm afraid if you and Lightning were not present I would be using some rather coarse language right now that would embarrass even Captain Mudgeon's crew. We are almost two thousand miles from the facility. Not what I had planned. Not at all what I had planned. I don't know, maybe we can find a functioning vehicle to fly us there. We certainly can't walk, and it's not safe to go back through the spectral doorway. Who knows where it might send us. At least we're on Thaumatar."

Clara was ogling the staggeringly tall buildings. "I can't even imagine what it would be like to live in a world like this. Truthfully, I don't think I would like it. I'm far too fond of trees and grass and flowers."

Lybis nodded in agreement, saying, "You're right,

there is a high price to pay for all our technological advances, and the Thaumatarians paid the highest price of all."

Clara rubbed her paws together. "Perhaps I can locate a suitable ship. I'm rather good at finding things."

"Excellent. I have some skill in that area but not enough to brag about, as Vahnar would say. We're looking for a small ship that can carry all of us. Nothing too large though. I'm an adequate pilot, but I've really only flown scout ships."

"Okay, I'll do my best." Clara closed her eyes and extended one paw, slowly rotating her body. "I'm being pulled this way. I believe we will find our ship on the outskirts of the city. I sense the presence of a central hub, something akin to a train station."

As they strolled along the silent streets of the once great Thaumatarian metropolis, Clara's thoughts turned to Bartholomew. She wondered where he was and what he was doing, what sights he saw after passing through the translucent blue door in Cathne. Almost absently she said, "I miss Bartholomew."

Lybis nodded. "I miss Vahnar every day. We were very different mice, but he had many qualities I wish I had been blessed with, and I believe I had a number of qualities he would have liked to have."

"I feel the same way about Bartholomew. He is a far more proficient shaper than I am, but needs to deepen his connection to the universe. Shaping is simply manipulating energy fields, manipulating the physical world. Being connected to the universe is understanding the true nature and the hidden perfection of the world we live in."

Lightning laughed. "You mean perfection like me? Too bad Thunder has so many flaws though. Mostly on his face." Lightning gave a great cackling laugh but put his arm around Thunder, pretending to pound his shoulder.

Lybis leaned over to Clara, whispering, "I'm so glad Vahtees has a true friend in Lightning. An old and trusted friend is one of the greatest joys to be found in this world."

After half a day of walking down wide boulevards the novelty of the great city began to wear off. Thunder and Lightning darted in and out of the towering buildings looking for treasure, but found nothing of much value. Especially since Lybis had given strict instructions they were not to touch any unfamiliar devices, which essentially meant every device they saw. Even so, the city seemed to consist only of endless rows of office buildings and small, cramped living quarters. They did find a large jewelry shop and Lybis let Thunder and Lightning each fill a bag with lovely Nirriimian white crystal jewelry. It felt strange taking what they wanted from a store, but Lybis assured them the owners would never be returning. There was essentially a whole planet filled with abandoned treasure just waiting for them. Thunder had been quietly looking for a suitable gift to give the lovely mouse who worked at the bait shop and felt certain a Nirriimian white crystal bracelet from the lost planet Thaumatar would adequately impress her.

"How much farther, Clara? Can Lightning and I fly the scout ship? We know how to operate a Mintarian Wyrme of Deth and a Quintarian Naval Armada submarine. Oliver and Edmund and Captain Mudgeon taught us."

"It's not too much farther, Thunder. Another hour I think, but I'm afraid operating a submarine doesn't qualify you to fly a Thaumatarian scout ship. Perhaps after all this is over Lybis will teach you how to operate one."

Late that afternoon the party of adventurers reached Clara's transportation center. Before them stood a twelve foot tall chain mesh security fence surrounding an enormous paved area at least a mile across filled with hundreds of vehicles, most of them unfamiliar.

"Are those scout ships? They don't look very fast. They look like big stacks of silver boxes with wires and sticks coming out of them."

Lybis peered through the fence. "No, those aren't scout ships. If I'm correct they are interstellar craft, but they don't fly the way we think of flying. They fly like Hoppy's ship did. They don't actually travel through space from point to point. I see a scout ship way over there though. It looks about the right size. Hopefully it still runs."

Clara held up her paw and a yellow beam shot out, cutting a wide circle in the heavy security fence. Clara grinned, "Ah, I seem to have located the door. After you, Lybis."

They stepped through the hole in the fence and onto the ramp, heading in the direction of the small dark blue scout ship.

"How fast will the scout ship go?"

"I don't know, Lightning. I don't even know if it will run yet. These ships have been sitting here for quite a few years." Lybis held her comm unit next to the scout ship's door and tapped rapidly on the disc grid.

"A little something extra Vahnar programmed into my unit for just such emergencies." She waited until her comm unit beeped three times, then tapped it again. The door to the scout ship whirred and flipped down, allowing them access to the ship. "The ship has power. That's a good sign."

Lybis walked to the bridge and sat down at the console. "Well, I can't read the writing, but the layout looks familiar. Vahtees, tap the yellow disc next to the door and lock it up. Everyone else take a seat and buckle in. I think she'll fly, but honestly I don't know if that's good news or bad news." She laughed nervously, rubbing her paws together, realizing a small thing like her ability to fly this ship could determine the fate of the universe. She glanced back at the others.

Thunder called out, "Outer hatch is closed and locked."

"Okay, hold on tight everyone. I'll do my best not to kill us. I'm going to take it very slowly. Everyone strap in."

Lybis adjusted various dials and moved the control sticks back and forth, testing their sensitivity and making certain she understood clearly what they actually controlled. "So far so good. Here we go."

She gently pulled back the main control stick, twisting the red knob next to it. There was a whining noise and the ship began to vibrate. "Shaky. I hope this works." She twisted the knob further and inched the stick back. The scout ship lifted smoothly up into the air and the vibrating stopped.

"Whew. I think we're good. Clara, why don't you come up here and be my navigator. According to the holomap we need to head directly east for almost two thousand miles. I'm going slow until I get a good feel for how she flies, then we can bump up the speed. Our small scout ships topped out at about eight fifty in the atmosphere and of course several thousand times that in open space. I'm staying low. I don't want to risk leaving the atmosphere for such a short hop. This ship is old, and a hull breach out there would be the end of us."

Clara took the navigator's seat next to Lybis, who showed her how to use the ship's holoscreens. "Right there. That's where we want to go. We're this blinking red dot on the screen. If we get off course for any reason you can adjust our flight path with these two slider bars."

Thunder and Lightning spent the first few hours looking out the portholes at the scenery passing below them. Time after time they passed over enormous cities similar to the one where death's door had sent them. As they passed directly above a series of immensely tall buildings, Thunder said, "I'm with Clara, I'd rather live on the Island of Blue Monks than in a gigantic city like that one. I think I'd get lost all the time. How could you ever remember where anything was?"

Lightning said, "Well, just suppose a certain lovely young mouse at a certain local bait shop decided to move to a big city and asked you to go with her? I don't imagine you'd say no to that."

"Quiet, my mom might be listening. Talk about something else."

"Oh, I'm dreadfully sorry. Perhaps we could talk about fishing instead. How would that be?"

"Fine. Fishing is fine."

"Okay, who do you buy your bait from?"

"Argh... if my mom wasn't in this ship I would pound you!"

Lybis grinned at Clara. The comms were on and they could hear every word of Thunder and Lightning's conversation.

After two hours of flying with no apparent mechanical issues, Lybis bumped the ship's speed up to five hundred miles per hour. "She'll go faster but I'd rather get there later than not at all. It looks like we'll be crossing over a small sea in about an hour, then we should hit the desert.

The ship shot through the skies as Thunder and Lightning made idle conversation, mostly arguing about who would be able to catch the most fish in the Thaumatarian sea. Lightning stood up, stretched, and looked out through the porthole. "There's the sea, straight ahead! Lybis, does that sea have big fish in it? It would be fun to go fishing there. Fun for me, but not so much fun for Thunder since he never catches anything."

"There are no fish in it at all, Lightning. Don't forget, this is Thaumatar. Every bit of life force on the planet was drawn into the Black Sphere. As far as I know we are the only living creatures on this entire planet."

Thunder was about to make a joke about Lightning's chances of meeting a cute mouse on Thaumatar when the ship went silent and dark.

Lybis cursed under her breath, then barked, "We've lost power! Everyone buckle in tight, right now! I'm popping the emergency sail. Shout out when you're buckled. Hurry!"

Thunder and Lightning dashed over to their seats

and strapped in. "We're in!"

"Okay, hold on tight!" Lybis reached up and yanked a red handle on the ceiling. They heard a small explosion and the ship jerked violently back and forth. After nearly a minute of wild gyrations the jarring movement gradually subsided, replaced by a broad swaying motion. "The sail is working. We were lucky, sometimes they don't hold, and that's not a good scenario. We're almost four miles up and if we find some thermals we can probably drift most of the way across the sea."

"What do we do if we land in the sea?" Lightning's voice had a twinge of panic to it.

"I don't know. The ship will float. It's built to travel through space, through a vacuum, so we'll be fine even if we land in the ocean. Hopefully the currents will take us in the right direction. There should only be ten or twenty miles of sea left to cross by then. You can unbuckle if you want. We'll be sailing for an hour or so."

Thunder unsnapped his harness and stood up. He looked up through the overhead porthole and could see the enormous rectangular puffy orange sail billowing above the ship. Lybis had only minimal control over the ship's direction but did her best to find thermal columns to keep the craft in the air as long as possible. When she found a thermal they would circle around it gaining altitude, and once they could go no higher she turned the ship toward the desert.

"This is working far better than I had expected. I've found some excellent thermals and we're maintaining our altitude as we cross the sea. We're not exactly streaking along at five hundred miles an hour, but it beats swimming."

Half an hour later the scout ship was bobbing in the sea and Lybis was disengaging the huge orange sail. "Oh, well, you know what they say about famous last words."

Lightning flipped open a porthole and smelled the clean salt air rushing into the ship. "I think I can see the desert from here! It looks like it's only a few miles to the east. I'm confused though, there's a mountain range to the west that I don't remember flying over."

Lybis stepped over to the porthole. "Mountain range? That's not possible. Let me see." She looked out the porthole for a moment then jerked her head back in. "Everyone buckle in right now! Clara, we need a sphere of defense around the ship. Lightning, that's not a mountain range, it's a wave, and it's headed this way. The good news is we're going to be in the desert very soon. The bad news is I'm not certain if we'll still be alive."

Seconds later Clara had blinked up a sphere of defense, the hatches and portholes were locked, and everyone was tightly buckled into their seats. "Hold on everyone, it won't be long now!"

Thunder was a little dubious. "Are you sure it's really a wave and not just–" Thunder never finished his question because the ship abruptly shot upwards, lifted by a five hundred foot tall wall of water traveling at sixty miles per hour. When the craft had risen almost to the crest of the wave and was traveling the same speed as the wave it began to slide back down the monstrous mountain of seawater, gaining even more speed. When the wave hit the desert shore the ship's forward velocity was over eighty miles an hour.

To be strapped inside a ball rolling along the ground at eighty miles an hour would normally present some rather dire consequences for the unlucky passengers, but fortunately the soft deep sand and an enormous steeply sloping dune brought the rolling scout ship to a relatively quick and painless stop. Clara flicked her wrist and the sphere of defense vanished.

Thunder unbuckled and staggered over to the porthole. "We did it! We're in the desert!"

Lybis slapped the disk on the bulkhead and the outer hatch flipped down. Moments later the four adventurers were standing on the shimmering desert sand.

"I never thought I'd be so glad to see a desert. Which way?"

Lybis flipped open her comm unit and tapped on the disc grid. She pointed inland. "About ten miles that way. We're almost there."

Clara shaped hats to protect them from the blistering desert sun and soon the party of adventurers was on their way to the birthplace of the Black Sphere.

Thunder and Lightning were in the middle of a heated debate on whether a lone rabbit could defeat a shreeker, if the shreeker was on land and could breathe air, but the rabbit could use no weapons other than a push broom.

"Ow! Ow! The Black Sphere is burning hot!" Lybis threw her cloak down on the sand, pungent gray smoke rising from the smoldering pocket which held the Black Sphere. The sphere was growing again. "Lightning, Thunder, throw sand on it!"

Gradually the smoke diminished and Lybis flipped the charred pocket open. The Black Sphere rolled out, but it was no longer black, it was pale gray. Even more concerning than its color was the fact that the sphere had grown to almost five inches in diameter. Lybis took a deep breath. "We have to move quickly. It's very possible the next time the sphere expands will be the last time it expands, which will mean the end of this universe and the end of us. We have only another four or five days left, and it will take me at least two days to give the injector system a thorough inspection. For all I know the injector may have been too badly damaged in the explosion to function properly."

Clara called out to Lybis, "Look, over there! Is that it? Is that the facility?"

Lybis squinted her eyes, peering into the distance. "That's the building, I'd recognize it anywhere. We've done it. We have the Black Sphere and we've found the site where it was created. We're almost there."

Once the Black Sphere had cooled down enough Lybis picked it up and they headed off towards the Thaumatarian facility.

"The whole eastern third of the complex was blasted to dust in the explosion so entering the facility should be relatively easy, but we need to hurry. We have five days left to save the universe, and that's not a lot of time."

Chapter 23

The Facility

"Creekers, this place is enormous." Thunder gazed in wonder at what remained of the gargantuan facility. They had climbed for almost an hour across gnarled and twisted metal girders, piles of shattered synthetic stone panels, pipes, and torn sheets of jagged metal, weaving their way cautiously over and under the tangle of wreckage, finally reaching the undamaged portion of the facility.

The ground floor of the facility was almost a thousand feet wide with dark green walls rising up several hundred feet, and was densely populated with immense machines positioned in a seemingly random pattern. Scores of narrow vertical windows stretched up to the ceiling, bright beams of desert sunlight streaming down into the facility. Lybis guessed the site had originally been over a mile long.

"What are all these big machines for?"

Lybis thought for a moment before answering Lightning's question. "It takes unimaginable amounts of energy to create a singularity. When Clara shapes an object, she is compressing energy into what we perceive as physical matter. The Thaumatarians took that a step further. They compressed massive amounts of energy infinitely more until it became something entirely different. A singularity. The rules of physics we are familiar with no longer apply inside such a creation. Just think of it – an entire universe existing inside a single point so small it hardly even exists. These hundreds of machines are what the Thaumatarians used to create that singularity."

The adventurers moved on, threading their way past the impossibly complex machinery. "Over there. That's the dome."

"It looks scary. What's inside it?"

"Forces more powerful than a hundred suns. Temperatures nearly impossible to measure, temperatures which drastically alter the laws of physics within the dome. This dome and the forces within it were created for one purpose and one purpose alone – to contain a small amorphous piece of the Void, the space that exists between all parallel dimensions, between all worlds. The Void does not obey the rules governing time and space we are familiar with. Fly through the Void at a hundred thousand miles per hour for ten years and when you stop, you will be in the same spot you started. The small segment of the Void contained in the dome is not separate from the rest of the Void. Even though it appears to be separate in our world, due to the peculiar laws and dynamics of that dimension, it is a piece of the Void but is also the whole Void. A piece of the Void is the entire Void. It's not logical but that's how it works. And fortunately for us, it means if we inject the Black Sphere into the piece of the Void contained in the dome, we are injecting it into the Void itself."

Lightning looked over to Thunder and raised his eyebrows, whispering, "What did she say?"

Thunder shrugged. "You're asking me? You're the one who's supposed to be so good at science."

Lybis smiled. "I'm sorry, I get a bit carried away with the physics of it. I know that didn't make much sense to you. Why don't you two go exploring while I examine the injector system. I'm afraid I won't be very good company for the next few days, and I'm going to need a lot of help from Clara."

"Okay, maybe we can find some treasure."

Thunder and Lightning set off through the maze of oversized machines, many of them over fifty feet tall.

Thunder stopped for a moment and looked around. "We need to find some rooms or something. Maybe they have a big lock box where they keep all the valuable stuff."

"Like what? Why would they keep valuable stuff in a place like this?"

"Umm... maybe they make machines out of gold and they have a special room filled with it, like a thousand big bars of solid gold."

"What would we even do with it? How could we get it back home?"

"I don't know, and quit being such a negative ninny."

"Fine, let's see what we can find."

The pair of young treasure hunters headed west across the main floor. Lightning cried out, "Look, over there! Stairs going up to another level. That's probably where they hide all the valuable stuff."

"I hope so. We haven't found anything good on this trip except at that jewelry store in the big city. Mostly because Lybis and Clara care more about saving the universe than finding treasure."

Lightning snorted. "Well, if there's no universe, the treasure won't do us much good."

"I guess. Still, we should look. Here's the stairs. Let's go up."

Thunder was dashing up two steps at a time when a sudden movement on the main floor caught his eye. He had seen a small light flit between two towering pieces of machinery.

He stopped short, holding up his paw. "Wait, I saw something down there. Something moving. And it wasn't Lybis or Clara. We should go check."

Lightning frowned. "That sounds a little scary. Suppose it's... you know... something that eats mice."

"We still need to check on it so we can warn Lybis and Clara in case it's dangerous."

Lightning gave a weak grimace. "Okay. Let's go look." He picked up a length of metal pipe he found lying on the stairs. "I'll just bash it with this if there's any trouble." He did his best impression of a rough and tumble treasure hunter.

"Or we could just run."

They made their way back down the stairs and over to the area where Thunder had spotted the movement, creeping past the shadowy machinery, peering cautiously around corners. Thunder could feel his fear beginning to spin out of control and finally said, "This is too scary. Maybe we should get Clara and Lybis to help us."

"They're busy trying to save the universe. We're just

poking around looking for something you're not even sure you saw."

"I saw it. I saw something move. There is no doubt about that."

"Okay, what did it look like?"

"Well, I didn't really get a good *close* look at it. It was kind of far away."

"Oh, forget it. I don't think you even saw anything. It was just your wild imagination, like when you saw that giant bumblebee. I'm going back upstairs to look for treasure." Lightning stepped around the corner, looking back at Thunder with the foulest sneer he could muster." Less than a second later he let out a bloodcurdling shriek.

"RUN! RUN!! I SAW IT! RUN!" Lightning flashed past Thunder, a look of absolute terror on his face. Thunder didn't stop to think. He tore after Lightning, his arms pumping, his heart pounding.

"Faster! Run faster!" Lightning blasted past the machines, sliding around corners and leaping over obstacles, Thunder only inches behind him. Five minutes later as they approached the dome Lightning finally stopped. He leaned over, gasping for breath. "Oh creekers, oh creekers, I think I'm going to barf. Urghh, oh, creekers."

Thunder was till trying to catch his breath. "What did you see?? What was it??

Lightning's eyes grew wide. "I don't know what it was. I've never seen anything like it. It was horrible. Horrible, scary and weird."

"That doesn't really tell me very much. What did it look like, exactly?"

"Umm... it's hard to describe. It was glowing with a

weird spooky light coming out of its body, if you could call it a body. It didn't have a head and looked like it was made out of sticks, but it was walking. It was a walking, glowing stick figure and I think it was looking at me, except *without a head*."

"Creekers! This is serious. We have to tell Clara and Lybis."

Chapter 24

Flying Colors

Oliver stepped through the rippling green gateway into darkness. "Great heavens, I can't see a thing. It's pitch black here."

Bartholomew sent out a glowing sphere of light then looked around. "It looks like the room we just left. It's another waiting room."

"Perhaps we should spend the night in this building and then go exploring at sunrise. I for one don't want to go trudging around an unknown world in utter darkness."

"You make a good point. We'll bed down here tonight and head out first thing in the morning. I'll shape some sleeping bags and cots for us."

It had been an exhausting day and shortly after one of Oliver's delicious dinners the adventurers retired for the night. Even Edmund lay down to sleep. He had become quite fond of dreaming, although the lovely Rabbiton named Abbie had not yet made another appearance.

Bartholomew was asleep before his head hit the

pillow. He was far too tired to even worry about how he was supposed to save the universe.

* * *

"What is this place?" Bartholomew knew he was dreaming, but he found himself in a strange and unfamiliar environment. He was standing in a brightly lit room with gleaming white marble floors, white walls, and a white ceiling. It was difficult to gauge the actual size of the room, as it seemed to shrink and grow with each passing moment. At the far end of the room, which now seemed very far away, sat a large ornately carved wooden desk. Seated at the desk was a rabbit, its face currently hidden behind a colorful magazine.

"What an odd dream. I wonder why I'm here?" He floated down the room to the desk. The rabbit seated at the desk was reading the current issue of a popular magazine called 'Modern Rabbit'.

Bartholomew cleared his throat politely, announcing his presence.

"Ah, you're here. Excellent." The rabbit tossed the magazine onto his desk and looked up at Bartholomew with a smile. A wooden chair appeared in front of the rabbit's desk.

"Bruno Rabbit!"

"Kindly address me as Professor Rabbit. Have a seat and we shall discuss your final exam."

"My what?"

"Your final exam." With a great flourish Bruno slid open a desk drawer and pulled out a single sheet of crisp white paper. "It's quite a simple exam, really. There will be no essay questions, of course, as the

answers are far too subjective, making the grading process both tedious and quite annoying. If you were hoping for multiple choice questions, I'm afraid you shall be disappointed, as there are none of those either. Much too confusing with all those possible answers which may or may not be correct. So, that leaves True or False questions. Simple as simple can be. And to simplify matters even further, there will be only one True or False question on your exam. What could be simpler than that? I'm certain you'll pass with flying colors."

Bartholomew stared blankly at Bruno. "What are you talking about? Why do I have to take a final exam?"

Bruno laughed. "We take final exams every day of our life. This is simply one more in a long line of final exams you have taken.

"Now, if I may have your complete attention, I will explain the mechanics of this particular final exam. I am going to transport us to one of two possible places. The first possible location is a **dream** of the Timere Forest, the very same place where you recently learned to fly. The second place is the **real** Timere Forest, the very same forest you passed through on your way to the lost underground Mintarian city. We shall spend five minutes at one of these two locations, then we shall return here, at which time you will answer this True or False question." Bruno passed the sheet of paper to Bartholomew.

Bartholomew looked down at exam, then up at Bruno, then back to the exam. He read the question out loud.

I JUST VISITED THE REAL TIMERE
FOREST.
PLEASE CIRCLE THE CORRECT ANSWER:
TRUE   FALSE

"Precisely. We are going to determine whether or not you can tell the difference between the dream world and the real world. What could be easier than that?"

Bartholomew frowned. "Okay... I guess. But why am I doing this? You're trying to trick me somehow, aren't you?"

"Now that I have clearly defined the parameters of your exam, shall we begin?"

Before Bartholomew could answer he found himself standing in the Timere Forest.

Bruno pulled a large gold pocket watch from his cloak. "Your exam begins.... NOW!"

Bartholomew glanced around the forest. It looked real enough, but that wasn't surprising since he was awake inside this dream, if it was a dream. He reached down and picked up a pine cone and needles. They smelled like the real thing, felt like the real thing, but still... "Okay, time for the surefire test." Bartholomew closed his eyes and raised his arms. When he opened his eyes he was floating fifteen feet above the ground. He gave a great laugh and shot up above the trees, performed three spectacular midair somersaults, then soared back down, flashing through the branches as though they weren't even there. With a final triple flip he landed firmly on his feet in front of Bruno.

"Professor Rabbit, I have my answer. I'm ready to take the written portion of my final exam now."

"Excellent. I don't believe I have ever had a student complete this section of the exam in such short order.

Very impressive indeed." With a flick of Bruno's paw Bartholomew found himself sitting at a small white desk in the middle of the great white room. On his desk lay the exam paper, a bright yellow sharpened pencil, and a pink eraser.

Bruno announced from the front of the room, "You may begin the written portion of your exam now. Take as much time as you need. When you're done, fold the exam in half and set it on my desk. Good luck to you."

Bartholomew picked up the sharpened pencil and carefully circled the word 'FALSE'. He was definitely in a dream since he could fly, not to mention fly right through the trees. He folded the test in half and carried it up to Bruno's desk. Bruno was hidden behind his copy of *Modern Rabbit* but peered over the magazine when he heard Bartholomew approach.

"You have completed the exam?"

To be quite truthful, Bartholomew had no idea what Bruno was up to. He didn't know if Bruno was playing an elaborate practical joke or if he truly believed he was a professor giving Bartholomew a final exam. Nevertheless, Bartholomew decided to play along and carefully set the folded paper on Bruno's desk.

"Excellent, I'm quite confident you passed with flying colors." Bruno picked up the test, and without opening it proceeded to tear it into little pieces. He tossed the shredded exam into a trash can which had blinked into existence next to his desk.

"Umm... Professor Rabbit, you didn't check to see what my answer was."

"Ah, you are a perceptive fellow indeed, Bartholomew. I didn't look because it doesn't matter what your answer was. You have passed with flying *colors, my friend." Bruno rose to his feet, his desk vanishing in a blink of light. He put his paws behind his back and circled slowly around Bartholomew, studying him closely. Finally he spoke.*

"Bartholomew Rabbit of the Planet Earth, I hereby decree that on this day you have graduated with the highest honors from Professor Bruno Rabbit's School of Paradoxical Shaping. Step forward, please, and receive your diploma."

"I'm right here, Professor Rabbit."

"So I see. If you would be so kind as to give me your Eleventh Ring?"

Bartholomew slipped off the Eleventh Ring and dropped it into Bruno's open paw. Bruno raised the ring above his head. "All hail the Eleventh Ring!" With a flick of his paw he tossed the ring into the trash can, which then vanished.

"Why did you do that??"

"A little decorum, if you please. We are in the middle of a rather solemn graduation ceremony. Put out your paw and I shall present you with your official diploma."

Bartholomew was beginning to feel as though he was lost in a topsy turvy house of mirrors. With a great whirling of his cloak, Bruno leaned over and set a small pine cone on Bartholomew's open paw.

"Well done, Bartholomew Rabbit, well done indeed. Please keep this diploma with you at all times as proof of your graduation from this fine institution of paradoxical shaping. You have graduated this day with the highest honors possible, and you are now free to go. Have a marvelous summer vacation, but don't forget to save the universe. I am as serious as serious can be

when I say you really do not have much time left."

Bruno flicked his paw and Bartholomew woke up in his cot. It took him several moments to gather his thoughts. *"What a strange dream. I will tell Clara about it – she always seems to be able to find the hidden meaning behind such peculiar events."*

* * *

"Oh, drat. Desert again. Didn't we just hike through a desert? Lovely bucolic farm land would have been infinitely more enjoyable. I do hope this isn't the world with those ghastly red lizard creatures."

"Would you rather be crossing an icy mountain pass and dodging ferocious leaping snow beasts?" Bartholomew peered through the open doorway of the way station. "I will admit I'm also getting a little weary of trudging across scorching deserts, and it certainly doesn't help matters that we have not an inkling of where we're going."

Bartholomew had not mentioned anything to the other adventurers about his nocturnal escapades with Bruno Rabbit, or the disconcerting fact that he had a universe to save and not much time left to save it. The others had enough to worry about already.

Arledge stepped out from an adjoining room. "No maps anywhere. Even if we had one I'm not sure how it would help us. Finding another doorway would just take us to another unknown world."

Oliver gave a sudden cry, stumbling backwards. "Something jabbed my leg!" His eyes grew wide when he realized what had poked him. "Stick! Great heavens,

Stick has come back!" His grin turned to a frown. "At least I think it's Stick. It's rather difficult to be certain since... how can I say this... he doesn't possess quite as many clearly identifiable features as one might hope for."

"You mean he doesn't have a head or a face?" Arledge was not quite as sensitive about his choice of words.

"Precisely."

The glowing stick figure walked over to Oliver and wrapped its arm around his leg. "He's hugging me! It *is* Stick."

Stick glowed brightly, then headed for the open door, once again motioning for the adventurers to follow him.

Bartholomew shrugged. "Well, at least one of us knows where we're going." He stepped through the open doorway out into the baking desert sun.

Stick pointed to the east and waved them forward. The sun was even hotter here than in the world where they had found Arledge. Bartholomew shaped wide brimmed hats for everyone along with a steady supply of cold drinks.

"Ah, much better." Oliver strolled along with a glass of chilled lemonade in one paw. "Stick really is a rather curious figure. Quite strange how he disappeared in the previous world then reappeared in this one. Even more curious is the fact that he led us directly to Arledge and he is now apparently leading us to some other location. Quite peculiar. I do wish he could speak."

"Oliver, do you think he might be one of the sacred elders from the Great Beyond?"

"Hmmm... an interesting question. He, or she, or it,

certainly is unlike any creature we have seen before, and we have journeyed to quite a number of different worlds. I suppose he could be one of these sacred elders you speak of. He does seem to know a great number of things he has no reason to know."

"I wish he would speak. I would like to ask him about the dreams I have. They are terrifying, and yet... there is something else. Something I have forgotten. I dread the dream and yet I also long for it with all my heart."

Oliver gave a sigh. "I do wish I could help you, but those sort of phenomena are far beyond my scientific acumen. It might be wise for you to speak with Clara Rabbit on our return to Pterosaur Valley. You will be going there with us?"

"I shall. I have no other place to go and the sacred elders are leading me in that direction. I trust deeply in their wisdom and guidance."

"That seems like a sound plan. I have heard from Bartholomew and Clara many times that we should seek guidance from the universe, and time after time they have been proven correct. I do not as yet understand the scientific principles beneath such perplexing systems, but perhaps one day I shall."

It was Edmund who first spotted the oasis, and it came as a welcome sight to the weary adventurers. The center of the oasis was a lovely spring fed pond almost two hundred feet across, surrounded by several dozen tall graceful shade trees providing a much needed respite from the intense heat of the blazing desert sun. Oliver plopped himself down next to the pond, removed his boots and dipped his feet into the clear cool water.

"Ahhh... now this is more like it."

Bartholomew nodded his approval. "We can spend the night here and head out again in the morning." He shaped tents and sleeping bags for the adventurers.

Oliver said, "I believe we all deserve a tasty treat. Shall I bake some delicious éclairs?" His thought of éclairs was soon followed by thoughts of Madam Beffy. He realized just how much he missed her. In fact he missed her more than he had ever missed anyone before. It was a strange feeling to care so much about someone. He looked over at Arledge, who was laughing as he waded in the pond next to Renata and Bartholomew. "I believe I have done something quite noble in finding Madam Beffy's father." He smiled to himself as he imagined the look on Madam Beffy's face when she saw her father.

Oliver's decision to bake éclairs mushroomed into a full fledged sit down dinner. The meal was almost festive, with many toasts to Arledge and to his rescuers. Soon after the sun dipped below the horizon the adventurers retired to their tents.

Bartholomew was exhausted but woke with a start in the middle of the night. For some reason he could not stop thinking about his last dream with Bruno Rabbit. There was something deeply significant about that final exam. But what? And what did his graduation signify? Why did Bruno say he had graduated when he hadn't looked at his test answer? It was all so confusing. "I wish Clara was here. She would know what all this means."

Bartholomew reached into his coat pocket for the picture of Clara he carried with him always. He froze. His paw touched something he had not expected to touch. He knew instantly what it was. His heart was pounding, his mind racing.

Bartholomew's paw had come to rest on a small pine cone. It was the pine cone Bruno Rabbit had placed in his paw during the dream. The memory flooded back to him. In the dream he had put the pine cone in his coat pocket after Bruno told him to keep it as proof of his graduation. Had he brought back a physical object from a dream? How was this possible? Such a feat was inconceivable. It could not be. His mind was whirling madly.

It could not be, unless... unless everything he had experienced had *not* been a dream at all. The pine cone could not exist unless he had been in the ***real*** Timere Forest and not the dream Timere Forest. His knees grew weak. Had he flown in the real world? Had he soared through the branches of real trees as though they did not exist? It could not be and yet it had to be. He held the pine cone tightly in his paw. There was no other explanation. And Bruno Rabbit knew precisely what had happened. That's why he had not bothered to check his test answer. That was why he said Bartholomew had passed the exam with flying colors. *Flying* colors. His Eleventh Ring! Bartholomew grabbed his paw. His ring was gone, the ring that Bruno had tossed into the trash can. This was a staggering turn of events.

Bartholomew rose to his feet and stepped out of his tent, looking up at the starry night sky. If this was all true it meant he had been able to set aside his self-imposed restrictions in the real world. He had woken up inside the real world, just as he had learned to wake up inside his dreams. That was the only logical conclusion. That was what Bruno had been trying to teach him all along.

He strolled out into the cool night air, trying to contain his thoughts. He realized there was only one way to prove he had flown in the real world. He would have to fly again. He heard Bruno's voice in his mind.

"Do not doubt yourself, Bartholomew Rabbit. You are a graduate of Professor Bruno Rabbit's School of Paradoxical Shaping, a graduate who passed with flying colors." He could almost hear Bruno laughing.

Bartholomew felt his feet pressing against the soft desert sand. He looked up at the sparkling stars above him, then closed his eyes. When he opened them again he was floating twenty feet above the sand. Part of him was astonished and part of him was not. It was as though he was remembering something from eons ago, something long forgotten concerning his true nature and the true nature of all life forms. He shot up into the night sky and soared across the desert, performed three midair somersaults, flashed back through the trees as though they didn't even exist and landed on the sand with a soft thump. Twenty minutes later he was fast asleep in his tent.

The next morning the party of adventurers packed up their gear and set out across the desert. After walking a grueling five miles in the sweltering sun they reached a long, deep canyon.

Oliver frowned. "Great heavens, this is certainly a dreadful inconvenience. This gorge is at least a quarter mile across and stretches out as far as I can see in either direction. It appears we have no choice other than to walk around it."

Stick halted at the edge of the canyon, then waved them forward. Oliver gave a shriek of horror as Stick stepped off the edge of the enormous gorge. As it turned out his shriek of horror had been somewhat premature, since rather than falling to his death Stick was casually strolling through the air across the gorge. Twenty feet out he paused, turning back to look at the adventurers. Once again he waved them forward. Bartholomew understood how Stick was doing what he was doing, but none of the others did.

Oliver hollered out to Stick, "We can't walk on air, we'll fall into the gorge."

Stick waved them forward again.

"We can't. We'll be killed. We'll fall into the gorge."

Finally Stick stopped motioning to them. He appeared to be thinking. A moment later he waved one of his arms and a wide wooden bridge appeared, spanning the gorge. He motioned them forward.

"Great heavens, Stick has shaped a bridge for us so we can cross the gorge." Oliver cautiously set one foot onto the wooden structure, testing its stability. "It seems sturdy enough." He stepped out onto the bridge. "Excellent. This will do very nicely. Thank you, Stick!"

Stick glowed brightly, hurrying across the bridge.

Bartholomew smiled to himself. He now knew Stick understood the true nature of this world, of this reality. The wooden bridge he created was simply a thought which gave Oliver's mind permission to cross safely over the gorge. This new perspective of the world he lived in was overwhelming, and Bartholomew knew it would take time for him to become completely comfortable with it. He also knew it would be far too much for the others to grasp at this time. He stepped onto the bridge and called out to Edmund and Renata. "It's solid. We can cross safely."

"Look! Up ahead past that dune. I believe Stick is leading us toward that structure." Edmund pointed to a large sparkling gold dome several miles away. After an hour long march across the baking sand the party of adventurers stood facing the glimmering dome. Stick became quite animated as he led them around to the far side of the sparkling structure. He stopped short, pointing to a pale blue circle positioned on the side of the dome about six feet above the sand. A narrow orange beam shot out from his arm. When the beam hit the circle the dome vanished, revealing a circular platform containing six sky blue egg-shaped vehicles. Stick ran towards the nearest one, trying to reach a square panel halfway up the craft. He tried jumping but still couldn't reach it. He floated up, glowing brightly, touching his arm to the panel on the ship's hull. A rectangular hatch folded out and then down, creating a narrow set of stairs. Stick darted up into the craft, waving for them to follow him.

"Our friend Stick seems to be in quite a hurry."

Bartholomew recalled the words Bruno Rabbit had him repeat. "I have a universe to save and I don't have much time." Perhaps Stick was aware of his predicament. Perhaps he was taking Bartholomew precisely where he needed to go. Was Stick a mystical agent of the universe as Renata had suggested? Bartholomew had no ready answers for these questions and so he followed Stick into the egg shaped craft.

Oliver was thrilled to have a new flying machine to examine. He was almost giddy as he studied the controls and the power systems. "This is quite marvelous! Ingenious! Look how they have linked the anti-grav magnifiers to the inertia deadeners. That conserves enormous amounts of energy. He flipped open his journal and began scribbling down notes as quickly as he could.

Stick hurried over to him and poked him repeatedly in the leg. Finally Oliver looked down. "What? What is it, Stick?" Stick motioned for Oliver to follow him, leading him to the ship's bridge and pointing emphatically at the pilot seat.

"Ah, I see. For some unknown reason you are in a hurry to arrive at yet another mysterious destination."

Stick hopped up onto the navigator's seat, quickly tapping on the grid of discs. A holomap popped up displaying the surface of the planet. Stick touched the map and a small red dot appeared. He tapped on the grid and a violet dot appeared on the holomap.

Oliver nodded. "We are the violet dot?"

Stick glowed brightly.

"And we need to travel to the location of the red dot?"

Stick again glowed brightly, pointing to the silver control stick.

"Ah, I can see you are in quite a hurry to get there, wherever 'there' might be. Everyone take a seat and strap in. We're on our way to our next destination." Oliver twisted several dials and pulled the control stick back. With a soft whine the hatch closed and the egg shaped craft took to the skies. Oliver noted the location of the violet dot and directed the ship towards it. He turned a blue knob and the craft shot forward at incredible speed, pressing Oliver back against his seat with such force that he could barely move.

"Great heavens, this acceleration is fantastic. I must study this ship further. Quite remarkable." He managed to twist around and look back at the other adventurers. He was met with four sets of very wide eyes. Bartholomew in particular was looking rather ill.

Oliver grinned. "Ahh. Too fast?" He turned back to the control panel, quickly reducing the ship's acceleration. When he looked at the holomap he saw they had already traveled half the distance to the red dot. "Remarkable, indeed."

Once the ship had stopped accelerating Bartholomew got to his feet and looked out through the porthole. "The view is quite lovely from up here. This is certainly the best way to cross a desert, especially at this leisurely pace. Would anyone care for some lunch?"

After a fine lunch shaped by Bartholomew and much speculation over where Stick was taking them, Oliver called out, "Almost there. I can see an enormous building in the distance. We are nearly a hundred miles away and yet I can clearly see the structure. Extraordinary."

Twenty minutes later Oliver slowed the ship down until it was hovering a mile above the mammoth sprawling edifice.

Bartholomew knew this was his final destination. This was where the universe had been leading him all along. "We should land. I don't think we have much time left."

"Time for what?"

"I don't really know, but I know we have to move quickly."

Stick glowed brightly.

Oliver nodded and pushed the control stick forward. The ship descended rapidly, landing with a small thump on the sand. Stick ran to the ship's door and tapped on the lavender disc, watching as the hatch unfolded down to the burning sands of Thaumatar.

Chapter 25

The Visitors

"Shhhh. Will you be quiet?? Whatever that thing is, we don't want it to hear us."

"Don't tell me to be quiet in your big loud voice. You're making more noise than I am."

Clara was growing weary of Thunder and Lightning's constant bickering. "Both of you, please, no squabbling for the next five minutes. Tell me again what the creature looked like."

"Like a glowing, walking stick figure, but with no head. It was terrifying."

"Did it see you?"

"Umm... no head? That means no eyes?"

Clara took a long slow breath. "Did it appear to be aware of your presence in any way? Did it charge towards you? Threaten you? Run away from you?"

"Mmm... no, I don't think so."

"Why was it terrifying?"

"Because it was so weird looking! Who knows what it would do if it caught me."

Thunder gave a snort. "What could it do? If it

doesn't have any claws or teeth and it's only two feet tall it couldn't do much except dance around and look scary."

"You didn't see it. It was terrifying and that's all there is to it."

Clara gave Lightning a sympathetic look. "It does sound quite frightening. Let's scout the area while Lybis is working on the injector system and see if we can find the creature. You'll be safe now that I'm with you. I can blink up a defense sphere before the stick figure can even get near us. We'll start our search back where we entered the facility then work our way down to the other end."

The three of them headed to the section of the building where the initial cataclysmic explosion had occurred. Thunder and Lightning stayed close to Clara, ever alert for signs of the mysterious glowing creature. Clara was curious about the stick figure, but also wanted to examine the site of the original explosion. Unfortunately she found nothing there but a hundred foot wide crater.

Thunder noticed something glinting through a tangle of twisted pipes and metal. He thought, "That could be gold... maybe a room filled with gold got blasted open and gold bars are lying everywhere..." He was about to tell Lightning then thought the better of it. "I should make sure it *is* gold before I say anything, otherwise Lightning will make some dumb joke." He waited until Lightning and Clara were chatting, then crept away, slipping through the piles of debris until he discovered the source of the golden flash. It was sunlight reflecting off a piece of broken yellow glass.

"Creekers. Double creekers. No gold. I'm glad I

didn't say anything." He was turning to go back when he saw a group of shadowy figures pass between two monstrous pieces of machinery. His insides turned to ice. He was afraid to cry out, afraid to move. "They'll hear me if I climb through the wreckage. Let me think... let me think. I'll go forward past that machine, then circle around and head back to Clara." Thunder's fear was like a tight band around his chest and he tried to relax, but with no success. He took a long, slow breath and inched forward past a mammoth silver machine, peeping cautiously around the corner for any sign of the eerie shadow figures. He tried to remember exactly what he had seen. There were at least four or five of them, and they were big. Really big. And deathly silent. They hadn't made a sound. They were monstrously large and unnaturally stealthy. Just the kind of horrific nightmarish beasts that leap out of the darkness and tear you to pieces in seconds with their razor sharp claws and teeth. Thunder was rapidly clenching and unclenching his paws. "Creekers. I need a weapon. That pipe there – I can use it as a weapon. At least it's something. Oh, creekers." Thunder picked up the heavy pipe and crept forward. He stopped in his tracks when he saw five tall rippling shadows moving across the outer wall in his direction. "Unhh. I feel sick. Sick. Okay... umm... oh creekers...I'll run around the corner screaming as loud as I can and whap the first beast I see with the pipe, then run back to Clara." Thunder gripped the pipe tightly, his breathing now fast and shallow. He was beginning to feel light headed and a little wobbly, as though he might faint. "Oh no, if I faint they'll hear the pipe fall... and... they'll eat me while I'm still–"

* * *

"Honestly, Edmund, for a Rabbiton you have a rather poor sense of direction. The sun is coming through the window from the east which means we're supposed to be heading in the other direction."

"I don't wish to insult your scientific acumen in any way, but did you happen to notice in this world the sun rises in the west and sets in the east?"

"Poppycock. Everyone knows–" Oliver froze. They heard the clanging of a metal pipe bouncing across the concrete floor.

Edmund frowned, then strode around the corner. His eyes opened wide when he saw the unconscious mouse sprawled out on the floor. "Oliver! I found an injured mouse! I think he fainted, and... it looks remarkably like Thunder."

Thunder awoke to the sight of five faces peering down at him. Three of them he recognized and two of them he did not. "Edmund? Oliver? Bartholomew? Whaat? Am I dead? Am I dreaming? Where am I?"

Before they could answer there was a bright flash of light and Clara blinked into view next to Thunder. She had surrounded them both with a sphere of defense.

"Bartholomew?"

"Clara? What in the world are you doing here?"

It took Clara only a moment to grasp the situation. The universe had brought them all here for one purpose. "I'm here to save the universe. Want to help?"

Bartholomew ran to Clara and put his arms around her. "I can't believe you're here. I was beginning to wonder if I would ever see you again, if I would ever find my way home. I have no idea where we are." They held each other close until they became aware of Oliver clearing his throat rather forcefully.

"Ahem. A most fortuitous reunion indeed. What a miraculous turn of events that all of us should find ourselves together in this strange building. The odds certainly weigh heavily against the occurrence of such a singular event, and yet here we are. Do you, by any chance, happen to know exactly where we are?"

Clara pulled away from Bartholomew, her paw still resting on his arm. "We're on the planet Thaumatar. The Thaumatarians are the ones who first colonized this universe and the ones who built the World Doors. It's a long story which I will tell you later. Right now we have to help Lybis inject the Black Sphere into the Void before it expands and destroys our universe."

Oliver looked truly befuddled. "Help who inject the what into what? Destroy our universe? Good heavens, whatever are you saying?"

Lightning popped up from behind a pile of debris. "Thunder, did you really faint? I thought I heard Edmund say you fainted."

"I didn't faint, I tripped on a piece of pipe and hit my head."

"Show me the bump then. If there really is one."

Stick stepped out from behind Oliver. Lightning gave a terrified shriek, scuttled backwards, tripping over Thunder's foot. "The creature! Look out, it's the creature with no head!"

Clara held up her paw. "Silence! Everyone follow me and I will introduce you to Lybis. She will tell you about the Black Sphere and what we need to do. We have a universe to save and we don't have much time."

Bartholomew grinned. There was no one else in the

world quite like Clara.

Despite the urgency of the task at hand, a round of introductions was made by Clara and Bartholomew. Clara was delighted to meet Madam Beffy's father and proceeded to tell him what a perfect match Oliver and Madam Beffy were. Oliver was, of course, dreadfully embarrassed, but Arledge put his arm around him, saying, "I have seen first hand Oliver's courage and sincerity. I am more than pleased that my dear Beffy has found such an honorable rabbit."

Bartholomew could not say enough complimentary things about Thunder and Lightning to Lybis. She beamed as she stood with an arm around each of them. "I have found my Vahtees, but I have also found Lightning, who is beginning to feel much like a second son to me."

Lightning grinned, punching Thunder on the arm. "Edmund, did Thunder really faint?"

Clara did not let Edmund answer. "You've all heard from Lybis the story of the Black Sphere and what we must do to prevent its expansion. Our first step is to repair the dome's injector system. Lybis says the catalyst train and sections of the main injector pod suffered far more damage than she had originally thought. We can use everyone's help. All of us are here for a reason, and each one of us will play an invaluable part in preventing this disaster. Lybis, Oliver, Renata, and Edmund can tackle the engineering aspects of the repair. Bartholomew and I can shape whatever parts we are able. Thunder and Lightning can scour the facility for larger components which are beyond our shaping limitations." Clara paused, looking thoughtfully at Stick. "As for Stick, he will do whatever he was brought here to do."

Stick glowed brightly.

Chapter 26

The Injector

"This is worse than I thought. A chunk of debris shot through this panel and damaged the paroxium valves."

"What about the drawings you found? Can we use those as a guide for shaping replacement parts?"

Lybis ran her paw across her chin. "Good idea. Most of the components are small enough for you and Bartholomew to shape. Some may be too large and I doubt we'll find any spares here in the facility. That could be a problem."

"Clara, do you remember when Morthram and I linked minds to bring down Oberon's ferillium mine? You and I could do the same thing. We could join minds to shape the larger parts."

"You're right. Lybis, show us the drawings and we'll get to work. It shouldn't take long to shape the smaller pieces."

Renata and Oliver were dismantling a badly damaged section of the injector when Edmund appeared at the top of the dome's ladder carrying a long blue metallic coil.

Renata had her paw on a glowing cylinder. "This one is fine, we can leave it, but that ring of deuronium is damaged and needs to be replaced."

Oliver frowned. "You're certain? How can you be sure? It doesn't look damaged."

"It is just something I know. I touch it and I know. It's very strange, I will admit. My family had no explanation for this ability. Sometimes I feel as if... I am remembering something from long ago."

"From when you were a bunny?"

"No, it's from somewhere deeper than that. I don't know, it's confusing. I have dreadful nightmares. Sometimes I dream about–"

With a great rattle Edmund set down a four foot long cylindrical coil of blue metallic tubing in front of Oliver. "Sorry to interrupt you. Clara shaped this and said they should have most of the replacement pieces done before the end of the day, but it will take longer to shape the ones which require them to link minds."

Oliver picked up the coil. "Excellent. Thank you, this should work quite nicely."

Thunder and Lightning had made their way up to the third level of the facility to look for paroxium beads. "What do they look like again?"

"Oliver said they were little blue beads about the size of a marble. It's some kind of catalyst so the injector can work."

"Some kind of cat what?"

"Catalyst. Catalyst. We learned all about them in science class, remember?"

"The only thing I remember about science class was that lovely little mouse who sat next to–"

"Look, over there. Oliver said they might be stored

inside inert protective canisters just like these ones."

"Well, let's open it up." Thunder scanned the room and spotted a flat metal bar. "This will work." A moment later he had pried the lid off a canister. "Whoa, that's heavy. Look there, this must be the paroxium beads. There's thousands of them in here plus there's about ten more canisters in the corner. That's way more than Oliver needs."

Lightning was eyeing the twisted canister lid lying on the floor. His voice was hushed. "Creekers. Thunder, look at that lid. Notice anything special about it?"

"It's a canister lid. What more can I say besides... IT'S MADE OUT OF PURE GOLD!" Thunder gave a great shriek and dashed over to the other canisters. "They're all gold! All the canisters are made of solid gold! That's the inert metal they used!" They grabbed paws and leaped up and down, their jubilant cries rattling the nearby windows.

Two floors below, Edmund's ears perked up. "What in the world are those two mice screeching about? Perhaps I should check on them."

An hour later eleven canisters of paroxium beads sat in a neat row near the base of the dome. Clara was gesturing emphatically to Thunder and Lightning.

"Yes, yes, for the third time, you may keep the empty canisters. All of them, and the lids also. Bartholomew and I will shape them into gold coins so you can carry them. But now we really must get back to work on the injector system. It will take us another day or two to finish the repairs, but your discovery of the paroxium beads has saved us much precious time."

Clara turned to leave, then paused, her eyes on Stick. He had been standing nearly motionless next to the dome for almost two days. She realized it was pointless to speculate what his purpose here might be. She did know whatever Stick might be, it was far more than just a two foot tall glowing stick figure.

The pace of the repairs picked up as the adventurers came to fully understand the injector mechanism and the complex process of shooting the Black Sphere into the Void. The Thaumatarians had originally planned to inject a sphere no larger than a grain of sand, and it had taken Oliver and Renata almost a full day to resize the launch tube to handle the larger sphere, now almost five inches across. Renata's intuitive understanding of the technology was proving to be invaluable.

Edmund was making his way across the floor when he spotted Bartholomew. "Ah, Bartholomew, Lybis wanted me to tell you that they're close to finalizing the repairs. She's quite certain the injector system will be fully functional by tomorrow."

"That's excellent news. I'll go tell Clara." Bartholomew hurried towards the south end of the building where he and Clara were fabricating the larger replacement parts. He spotted Lybis, who was walking towards him. Without warning she grabbed her side and let out a dreadful scream. "Ahhhh! NO! NO! Not now! Not yet!" Bartholomew could see smoke billowing out of her cloak pocket as she tore it off and dropped it to the ground. He blinked across the floor next to her.

"What is it? What's happened?"

"The sphere! It's expanding! The outer shell is almost white now -- we only have five or ten minutes until the shell dissipates completely, and that is the end of everything. It is the end of our universe. Bartholomew, we have failed. Oh, great heavens, we have failed." Lybis sank to her knees, deep sobs pouring out of her.

Clara heard Lybis' cries and appeared in a flash of light. She looked at the burning coat. "The sphere is expanding?"

"Yes, Lybis says we are too late." A strange calmness swept through Bartholomew. His role was very clear now. Every event in his life had been leading him to this one moment. "Clara, I have a solution but there is a chance I might not come back."

"I know. I know what you're thinking, and it is our only hope. I have faith in you." Clara put her arms around Bartholomew and pulled him close to her. "You have passed every test put before you, and you will pass this one. After all, you *are* a graduate of Professor Bruno Rabbit's School of Paradoxical Shaping."

"How did you know about that?"

"You forget, I spent most of my bunnyhood being tutored by Bruno. I received my pine cone almost a year ago. Bruno sent me a thought cloud when you received yours. I said nothing because such an awakening takes a great deal of time and thought to assimilate. You needed time to think, time to get used to this new perspective."

Bartholomew held Clara tightly. "I *will* be back. I know I will." Bartholomew let go of Clara and stepped over to the burning white coat. He reached into the scorching flames and picked up the sphere with his bare paws. The sphere was pure white now, and nearly ten inches across. Without a word he turned and made his way toward the dome. Stick was still standing by the dome's base. Bartholomew approached him.

"Okay, Stick, I guess this is what Bruno Rabbit

meant by saving the universe." The sphere was flaring wildly, sending out ferocious blasts of radiant heat, but Bartholomew was unaffected. Then, as easily as he would step through an open doorway, Bartholomew walked through the dome wall into a blazing plasma inferno hotter than a hundred suns.

Bartholomew felt nothing. "I am awake now, this body of mine is only a thought which exists outside of space and time. I cannot be affected by the physical world because there is no physical world, there is only a world of thought."

He turned around, knowing what he would see. Stick was standing behind him. He nodded to Stick, then floated over to the center of the dome. He could see the ferocious plasma fields swirling and streaming about him but it had no effect on him at all. When he reached the dome's center he saw an undulating, black amorphous shape floating about five feet above the floor. He held the sphere up next to the Void and glanced back at Stick, who was standing directly behind him. Holding the sphere carefully with both paws, Bartholomew eased it into the black nothingness. He could no longer see his paws, but when he withdrew them the sphere was gone.

Stick moved next to Bartholomew, reaching up to take his paw. Bartholomew gripped Stick's arm. There was a brief whirling sensation as they shot into the Void. He was in one spot and he was everywhere. Stick was floating next to him, but was rippling and blurring, his once defined shape transformed into swirls of brightly colored liquid light.

"Come, we will show you." Bartholomew turned in surprise. Stick had sent a thought to him.

Bartholomew saw a small sliver of light in the distance. He swept along with Stick as they shot towards it, but they were already there before they had started, hovering over a wide tear in the fabric of the Void. Bartholomew peered down into a universe of stars and planets and galaxies with no end. He tumbled through and found himself bathed in the brilliance of a trillion trillion stars. Stick's flowing colors were magnificent, brighter than ever, swirling about and creating exquisitely complex patterns.

"Much better. The form I was required to take in your world was functional, but possessed certain inescapable limitations. Now we may communicate freely. You believed you were saving your universe, but when you placed the Black Sphere into the Void you unknowingly saved our universe as well. Had the sphere expanded within your universe, it would have meant the destruction of both universes."

Stick was looking out across the vast and infinite galaxies. "This is our home now. We are all that remain of the original Thaumatarian life force absorbed by the singularity. Much of our awareness is now scattered throughout the galaxies in countless life forms on countless planets. We are in the stars, we are in the gas clouds and nebulae and the infinite darkness of space. The life forms we first inhabited grew and evolved, spreading like wildfire across the universe. As the eons passed the life forms forgot everything. They forgot Thaumatar, forgot their true home, forgot who and what they truly are." Bartholomew felt a deep sadness emanating from Stick.

"I will show you. Come with me." Stick floated over to Bartholomew, enveloping him in a cloud of swirling colored light. The stars vanished and Bartholomew found himself standing on the edge of a towering rocky cliff overlooking a wide green valley far below. Tens of thousands of tall blue hopping insects wearing gleaming silver armor scuttled madly across the flat plains towards an army of gray eight legged lizard creatures bearing sparkling glass lances. Beams of brilliant orange light blasted out from the lance tips, exploding into blazing infernos of deadly rolling orange fire. Force shells popped up around the blue insects, but held for only a few seconds against the deadly flames. Even from this height Bartholomew could hear the horrific high pitched squeals of the burning insects. As one, the front line of blue insects stood tall, spewing out powerful streams of pale green fluid into the charging ranks of gray lizards. It was the lizards' turn to shriek as they dissolved beneath the deadly green spray.

"They have forgotten. They fight each other, they kill each other in their vain attempt to protect their physical form. They kill to protect the temporary little shell their life force now inhabits. We are the only ones left who remember everything."

"Can't you show them?"

"We have tried. They cannot see what they do not wish to see. There are a few here and there who have partial memories. We are able to speak with them on some levels. In time perhaps all will remember, but that time is eons away."

"It is this way in all universes?"

"In most, but not all. Life force inhabiting a physical form forgets quickly what it once was, soon believing its physical form to be its true and only self."

"It is that way in our world. It takes a great deal of

time and energy to remember."

"Quite true. We wish to thank you for saving our world. Perhaps one day we shall build a World Door leading to your universe. Perhaps the day will come when we shall return to our beloved Thaumatar."

Bartholomew looked down at the clashing armies below. "Such a terrible, terrible waste." He turned to Stick. "It is time for me to go. The others will be wondering what has become of me."

"As you wish." Stick flared brightly, surrounding Bartholomew in a brilliant blue light. When the light vanished Bartholomew was inside the Thaumatarian dome enveloped in incalculably hot swirling fields of plasma. He floated across the floor and out through the dome wall.

Chapter 27

Home

Bartholomew had a difficult time explaining how he managed to walk through a wall strong enough to contain a plasma field hotter than a hundred suns, and how he had survived the deadly environment inside the dome. This was not the time or the place to discuss the depth of his awakening, so he said it was simply a new shaping skill he had learned from Bruno Rabbit. This seemed to satisfy everyone, although Oliver was still trying to make sense of the science which would allow such events to occur. Only Clara knew the whole truth and only Clara could fully appreciate it, having experienced her own awakening a year earlier under the expert tutelage of Bruno Rabbit.

Oliver had been extremely concerned over the fate of Stick, but Bartholomew assured him Stick had found his way safely home. He also let everyone know that in the process of saving their own world they had saved Stick's world also. This made Oliver feel much better, though from time to time he did mention how fond he had grown of Stick and how much he missed him.

Once the adventurers realized the threat of the Black Sphere was no more, there was only one thought on everyone's mind.

Thunder tapped Bartholomew on the arm. "Bartholomew, how are we going to get home? Are there any world doors that take us back to Nirriim? Maybe we could fly in one of those interstellar box things we saw."

Bartholomew grinned. "I was thinking we should just walk home. It's not that far."

"Clara! Bartholomew has gone loopy! He says we should walk home."

Bartholomew laughed. "Not as loopy as you might think, Thunder. There are a few other shaping tricks I learned from Bruno. One is creating spectral doorways to anywhere I choose. Where do you want to go?"

"Umm... well... home to the Island of Blue Monks. Lightning and me want to go there."

Lybis gently corrected him. "Lightning and *I* want to go there."

Thunder looked at Lybis in surprise. "You want to go there too? Really? I would love it if you would. You could stay at our house. I have all that gold, I could build you a house if you want. Maybe you could teach Lightning about science."

Lybis smiled at Thunder's misunderstanding, then thought for a moment. "I would like that too, Vahtees. There is nothing waiting for me on Quintari, and everything waiting for me on the Island of Blue Monks. I would love to teach Lightning about science. When I think about it, I believe a career in teaching is something I would enjoy."

"So, Bartholomew, how does this spectral door

business work?"

"You've been through one before, Thunder. It's just like the door the Thirteenth Monk used to send you to Clara's."

Lightning grabbed Thunder's ear and waggled it. "You remember that time you broke all the bones in your ear?"

Thunder sniffed. "I'm going to ignore you because you're so immature. Bartholomew, I would like to go to the Island of Blue Monks with my immature friend Lightning, and my mom."

"That sounds perfect. Pack up your gear and drag that chest of gold coins over here. Whenever you're ready I'll blink the door open."

There were hugs for everyone as Thunder and Lightning and Lybis bid their farewells. Clara made Lybis promise to visit them in Pterosaur Valley and to bring Thunder and Lightning with her. Lybis gave Clara a long hug. "If it hadn't been for you I would still be in Tenebra Prison. You gave me a new life, and I thank you from the bottom of my heart. I know that somewhere Vahnar is watching and thanking you also."

Bartholomew flicked his paw and a large swirling spectral door appeared. "Next stop, the Island of Blue Monks."

With a goodbye wave Thunder and Lightning dragged the heavy chest of gold coins through the spectral door. A moment later Lybis followed them through.

Clara smiled at Oliver. "How about you? Where would you like to go? Back to the Fortress, or somewhere else perhaps? Maybe... a certain pastry shop?"

Oliver chuckled. "I'm afraid my feelings are quite transparent to you, dear sister. As you suspected, Arledge and I would like to go to Madam Beffy's Pastry Shop in Grymmsteir, where I shall be asking for Madam Beffy's paw in marriage."

Arledge clapped Oliver on the shoulder. "Not that you need my permission, but I am more than pleased to hear this. You are a fine rabbit indeed."

Bartholomew and Clara hugged Oliver. "Congratulations, we could not be happier for you. When I look back I am astonished by the strange twists and turns the universe has chosen for us. If Parfello had not sent me off in search of the Cavern of Silence we would not be here now, and if I had not been captured by those two scalawags known as the Skeezle Brothers I would not have the great pleasure of your friendship."

"Well said, my old friend. I do hope you will honor me by being my best rabbit at the wedding. Of course, that hinges on Madam Beffy's reply when I propose to her." Oliver gave a great roaring laugh. He was still his own best audience.

Twenty minutes later Oliver and Arledge stepped through Bartholomew's spectral doorway into Grymmore.

"Edmund, where would you like to go? Back to the Fortress of Elders?"

"I'm afraid I will need to find an alternate route home. If you remember, I am quite impervious to your shaping abilities."

"That poses no problem at all. I'm not blinking you to the Fortress, I'm creating a doorway through which you or anyone else can simply walk. So, where would you like to go?"

Edmund thought for a moment, then said. "If I knew where Abbie lived, that's where I would go, but since I don't, I shall return to the Fortress of Elders."

"As you wish, my friend. Perhaps one day you will find her."

"Perhaps. I have seen her two more times in my dreams."

Bartholomew opened the spectral doorway to the Fortress of Elders and with a wave to Clara and Bartholomew, Edmund stepped through.

"Well, dear Clara, that leaves just us, all alone on a big empty planet."

"Just us and that big yellow moon floating across the night sky."

Bartholomew put his arm around her. "I suppose we *could* take a stroll in the desert. Sometimes the moonlight reflects off the sand and makes the grains sparkle like the stars above."

"How romantic you are. You really have changed since the last time we were married, back when you were a big scaly red lizard with yellow teeth and claws."

"Well, I suspect in a lizardy sort of way I must have been rather a handsome fellow."

Clara rolled her eyes, then laughed. "Take my paw and we will go for a walk beneath the desert moon."

Chapter 28

The New Pier

"Hurry up! Finish your snapberry flapcakes and get moving. We have to get down to the pier. Everyone will be there."

Lightning gave a great sigh. "Rush, rush, rush. You really should take time to savor these delicious flapcakes, not just snarf them down and run off to the next thing. Hasn't the Thirteenth Monk taught you anything?"

"Well, suppose the mayor wants to make statues of us and we're not there?"

"Hmm... you do make a good point. I think I'll wear my new adventurer's hat just in case."

With a shout to Lightning's parents, Thunder and Lightning dashed off to the new pier, chatting as they ran.

"We hardly used any of our gold to build the pier since so many of the islanders volunteered their help."

"But don't forget we gave half our gold coins to the Blue Monks to help with food and housing during the winter months."

"We still have more than we'll ever need. We've hardly even touched the Nirriimian white crystals we got from the Wyrme of Deth."

"Look, there it is! There must be a million mice there. We're going to be impressively famous."

Thunder dashed across the rocky shoreline to the new pier. "Two hundred feet long and thirty feet wide. This will be the best fishing spot on the whole island." Thunder stepped onto the pier, scanning the huge throng of mice in attendance at the pier's grand opening. As he made his way through the bustling crowd he spotted a rather matronly mouse rushing toward him and waving her paw. It was Madam Bletchley, his old language teacher. "Uh oh... it's Madam Bletchley. What's she going to say to me this time?"

"My word, Thunder Mouse, how you have grown since I last saw you! You have become a fine young mouse indeed. I always felt there were greater things in store for you than scratching out a living from fishing and foraging, and I made certain you lived up to my expectations. I knew one day you would become something very special, and you have proven me correct."

Thunder was unexpectedly embarrassed by Madam Bletchley's kind words. He was used to her correcting him, but not used to receiving compliments from her. "Oh, umm... thank you so very much, Madam Bletchley. It was a great pleasure for Lightning and me to– I mean, Lightning and *I* to build the pier for the islanders."

Madam Bletchley further embarrassed Thunder by giving him a hug. "Thank you again, Thunder Mouse, for everything you have done." With a wave Madam Bletchley disappeared into the crowd.

"Whew, that was embarrassing. Sort of. She does seem a lot nicer than I remember. Whoa, look at all the mice fishing over there. Must be a good spot." Thunder strolled over to a section of the pier where dozens of mice were dangling their lines in the water. As he ambled past the fishing mice he heard a haunting melody. Thunder stopped, a shiver running through him.

"Creekers, that's the song I heard in my vision of Lybis on the pier! This moment is the future moment I was visiting."

Thunder turned to the mouse who was humming the tune. It was the very same old mouse he had seen before. He tapped the mouse on the shoulder. "That's a lovely tune you're humming."

The old mouse looked up, giving Thunder a toothy grin. "My grandfather taught me that song. Would you like to hear the words?"

"Umm... sure... that would be nice."

The elderly mouse began to sing. Thunder had to admit for an old mouse he had quite a pleasing voice. He listened closely as the mouse sang.

There's a clock in my room with two silver hands,
Moving so slowly, it's hard to understand,
How the time is flying by.

There's a tree on my street, tall and grand,
Growing so slowly, it's hard to understand,
How the time is flying by.

Two silver hands won't slow down,
Time is a river, and love is to be found
While the time is flying by.

When he had finished, the old mouse smiled again. "It all quite true, you know. You mustn't become so busy with life that you forget to find love."

Thunder nodded. "Thank you for reminding me."

The mouse turned back to his fishing and Thunder continued down the dock, heading towards a group of mice milling about the food vendors. He spotted the white cloak and hood immediately, just as he had in his visions. Lybis turned and waved to him. "Vahtees! There you are! I have been waiting for you."

Thunder dashed over to Lybis and she put her arms around him, saying, "This is the moment. This is the moment where we met so many times."

"Yes. And now it has become the past."

Lybis squeezed Thunder's arm. "You will still be able to visit this moment, whether it is in the future or the past. You have so much more to learn, Vahtees, and in some ways I envy you. Time shall become your servant, no longer your master. If you are floating down a river in a boat with no oars, the river is your master. You are forced to go where the river goes and travel at the same speed as the river. The Thirteenth Monk will give you a lovely pair of oars to use in your boat. Then you will be able to stop on the riverbank and stroll up and down the river of time at your leisure."

"I will always be able to find you here, at this moment?"

"Always. I will always be here."

"Thunder!" Thunder turned to see Lightning

weaving his way through the crowd towards them. It took Lightning a moment to catch his breath.

"I've been looking all over for you. We're almost out of bait. Can you run down and get some more? We need a lot. There's a million mice fishing, and more keep showing up. Don't spend an hour chatting up your pretty friend, either. We need the bait now, not sometime next week."

"Very well, if you insist." Thunder grinned and dashed off down the pier.

Five minutes later he pushed open the weathered wooden door of the bait shop. He was in luck. She was there, standing behind the counter. He would ask her today. He would not put it off any longer.

Time is a river, and love is to be found
while the time is flying by.

"Hi Thunder! Where in the world have you been? You haven't been here in ages. I was starting to worry that something had happened to you."

"You were worried about me? I was on a big treasure hunt with Lightning and Bartholomew and a bunch of other adventurers. I saw my real mom and she was being held captive in a prison on Quintari so Clara and I and Lightning went through the World Door to..." Lightning stopped, realizing he was rambling almost incoherently because he was so nervous.

The lovely mouse behind the counter laughed. "Don't stop, I love your stories. They're so exciting and full of adventure. Not like working here at this boring old bait shop."

"I don't think the bait shop is boring at all. I like

coming here. Umm... mostly to see you, though."

"Thunder, would you like to go out with me? I would love to go out with you, but you've never asked me. I couldn't tell if you liked me or not."

"You didn't know if I liked you? The only reason I come here is to see you. I don't even really fish hardly at all."

"You are so sweet, Thunder Mouse." The lovely young mouse stepped out from behind the counter, put both arms around Thunder and kissed him on the cheek. "You probably don't know it, but you have become my best friend, and I also think you're the most handsome mouse I have ever seen."

Thunder had no words left in him. He held her close. He felt the infinite shimmering power of the present moment. He would visit this moment again and again, the moment he found the greatest treasure of his life.

Lightning was not the least bit surprised when Thunder told him what had happened. "Of course she likes you. Everyone knew that except you. Why else would she listen to your boring adventure stories?"

"Boring stories? I'm going to ignore that immature comment. Anyway, is it true what Lybis said? You're going to Quintari? To the Science Academy?"

"It's true. Lybis heard from Captain Mudgeon that there was a coup on Quintari and Counselor Pravus got the boot. So did Guild Master Manghar. Oh, and Captain Mudgeon received a full pardon and is back to sailing the seas with his crew. He even got promoted to Senior Captain. Anyway, Lybis has friends at the Science Academy and convinced them I'd be a good candidate. She thinks I will do well there, since I like science so much. It costs a lot to go but I have that big sack of Nirriimian white crystals."

"Well, well, congratulations, Mister Oliver T. Mouse." Thunder laughed and put his arm around Lightning. "After you graduate we can go on more treasure hunts. We still have to go back to the lost Mintarian city. By then you'll probably understand what all those weird machines buried in the Queen's Haystack are for. Plus we have to go back to Thaumatar. There's a whole lost world there waiting to be explored. Think of all the Thaumatarian technology scattered all over the planet. Who knows what we'll find. It could change our world."

Lightning grinned. "We really are treasure hunters now, aren't we? Real treasure hunters, not just pretend ones."

Thunder snorted. "Not just real treasure hunters, we're the two greatest real treasure hunters who ever lived. It's only a question of time until we get those statues."

Chapter 29

Bartholomew's Gift

Clara handed Bartholomew his coat. "You heard that Lightning is going to the Quintarian Science Academy? I can't wait to tell Oliver. He'll be so proud. Thunder and Lightning are like family to him."

"Yes, I heard. But what do you think of my idea?"

"I think if you want to do it, then you should do it."

"But is it ethical? That's what I really want to know."

Clara put her arms around Bartholomew. "You are doing it out of love, and it will bring great joy to him. How could that not be ethical?"

"I didn't want to do it unless you thought it was a good idea."

"It's a good idea. When will you be back?"

"In a few days. I've asked Edmund the Explorer to help me. He knows his way around the Fortress of Elders and he can find what I'm looking for."

"I'll see you when you return, then." She gave Bartholomew a long hug. "Traveling is a lot easier now that you're a graduate of Professor Rabbit's School of

Paradoxical Shaping, isn't it?"

"It is indeed. One thought and I'm anywhere I wish to be."

Bartholomew watched as the world around him blurred, transforming into the grand foyer of the Fortress of Elders. He hurried down the corridor until he found the door with Edmund the Explorer's name on it. His knock was quickly answered by Edmund.

"Hello, Bartholomew. Congratulations on your recent adventure, by the way. Edmund the Rabbiton told me all about it. I'd give anything to visit Thaumatar. Maybe we could all go back sometime. It's quite a feeling to save the universe, isn't it? I've saved it nineteen times, but who's counting?" Edmund the Explorer gave a great laugh.

"Did you find what I was looking for?"

"I did indeed. It took a bit of poking around on the fifth sub level but I found exactly what you asked for. It's in the back room." Edmund the Explorer rose from his chair and closed the door to his office. He tapped his nose. "I promise to keep your secret. No need for anyone else to know."

Bartholomew pushed open the door to the adjoining room and peered in. "Perfect. Absolutely perfect. I can't thank you enough, Edmund. How do you start it?"

"Open this little panel here and push the violet tab. That's all there is to it. How long will it take?"

"About an hour, I think. I've never done it before."

"I don't imagine many rabbits have. Bruno Rabbit for sure, but that's about it. Good luck to you. It's a good thing you're doing. It really is."

Three hours later Bartholomew was back in Pterosaur Valley. Clara was waiting for him. "How did it go? How do you feel?"

"Tired. More tired than I have ever felt in my entire life."

"It will pass. You'll be back to normal within a few days. It went okay?"

"It did. Quite a remarkable experience I must say, but right now I want to sleep for a week."

* * *

Edmund the Rabbiton was listlessly shuffling through a towering stack of papers in Oliver's office. Oliver was in Grymmsteir visiting Madam Beffy and would not be back for three weeks, and Edmund had generously volunteered to handle all the necessary administrative duties during Oliver's absence. He was more than happy to help Oliver, but not entirely pleased about spending his days reading production reports and an endless stream of letters from vendors, customers, and potential customers.

"Oh dear, this is so very tedious. I understand now why the Elders created Rabbitons – they wanted someone to do all their paperwork." Edmund set down the letter he was reading and leaned back in his chair. It was quite remarkable how much being alive had changed him over the years. He felt much more like a rabbit now and far less like a Rabbiton. He knew Rabbitons didn't mind endless hours of tedious work, but he felt sorry for them anyway. There was so much they didn't know they were missing, like having friends and going on adventures. "I suppose they are content enough, but I for one am quite happy to be alive." He pulled a letter from the top of stack and began to read, but was interrupted moments later by a knock on the door.

"Enter!"

The door swung open and a lovely female Rabbiton stepped into the room. She took a seat, but offered Edmund no greeting.

Edmund stared blankly at her. "May I help you?"

"No, thank you. I am here to study you."

"Oh, I see." Edmund shook his head. In fact, he did not see at all. Rabbiton behavior was becoming increasingly difficult for him to comprehend. He continued reading the letter, doing his best to ignore the Rabbiton's unwavering gaze.

"We're getting a great number of very positive letters from rabbits who have purchased Pterosaurs. They seem to be quite pleased with the new models."

The lovely Rabbiton smiled politely, but said nothing.

"We're also receiving many inquiries from prospective buyers."

The Rabbiton in the chair nodded agreeably.

Edmund was growing quite uncomfortable being the focus of this strange Rabbiton's relentless stare. "May I ask again the purpose of your visit?"

"As I said previously, I am here to study you."

"Yes, I recall clearly our initial conversation. May I ask *why* you are studying me?"

"To learn more about you, of course. You are a living Rabbiton, are you not?"

"Quite correct. It is a very long story, far too long to relate at this time, but I am a living Rabbiton."

"If you were given the choice, would you choose to be a living Rabbiton or to be a nonliving Rabbiton?"

"Well... I see... yes, an excellent question. I would choose to be a living one."

"Why would you choose to be alive?"

"It's rather difficult to explain, but when you are alive you become aware of something called feelings. Some feelings are very pleasant and you wish for them to occur as often as possible, and some are not very pleasant, and those you hope will not occur again. When I am with rabbits I know and care about, I have pleasant feelings. When I am alone I am not as happy, and have fewer of those pleasurable feelings. This is not always the case, of course, as there have been numerous occasions when I have been alone which were quite enjoyable indeed. For instance, looking up at a starry night sky and contemplating all the different life forms which may or may not exist on the various planets."

"I see. So, you would rather have these feelings than not have them, even though many of them are unpleasant at the time of their occurrence?"

"Quite correct. You have clearly understood my meaning."

"May I continue to study you, or does my presence give you a feeling you hope will not occur again?"

Edmund smiled. "I think I quite like having you here. I don't believe I have ever talked to another Rabbiton about such things before. Such conversations as this are very enjoyable to me."

"I am studying you because I wish to clearly understand what it means to be alive."

"Again you have pleasantly surprised me. I have never met another Rabbiton who was curious about the nature of life. When did you start wondering about such things?"

"Approximately three days ago when I realized I was alive."

Edmund froze. "What did you say??"

"You have already forgotten what I said?"

"I most assuredly have not forgotten, I simply want to be certain I clearly understand your rather remarkable statement."

"I will speak more slowly then. Three days ago. When I realized. I was alive."

For once in his life Edmund the Rabbiton did not know what to say. He stared wide eyed at the lovely Rabbiton.

"Have I caused you to have feelings you hope will not occur again?"

"No, but I am confused. I believed myself to be the only living Rabbiton in existence."

"I see. Your confusion is quite understandable. You were correct in your assumption until three days ago. Now you are incorrect. Now there are two living Rabbitons. You are one, and I am the other."

Edmund let out a long slow breath. He knew with certainty this Rabbiton was alive. Only a living Rabbiton would ask the questions she was asking. "I see. Well, yes, that certainly changes things, doesn't it? Quite a startling turn of events. To be truthful I have longed for this day. I have longed for another living Rabbiton to talk to."

"I like your adventurer's hat. I would like to wear one also, but perhaps with a longer feather, and though your purple feather is undeniably lovely, I believe I would prefer a bright red feather. I have been told you travel to other worlds and have seen many wondrous and novel sights. Do you wish for those adventures to occur again?"

"I do. I thoroughly enjoy adventuring. Will you come back again to visit me? I would like that very much."

"I like conversing with you. You are far more complex than nonliving Rabbitons. Perhaps I could accompany you on your adventures."

Edmund was feeling light headed. "I can think of nothing I would enjoy more than that. My good friend Bartholomew can shape you a marvelous adventurer's hat with a long bright red feather. You must be quite careful not to lose your hat, however. A true intrepid adventurer never loses their hat."

"I see. I will remember this. I will enjoy learning more about the life of an adventurer and I will enjoy traveling with another living Rabbiton."

"Oh my, this is wonderful indeed. I can't wait to tell Bartholomew and Oliver all about you. I am called Edmund. But you already knew that. Would you like me to give you a name? I could give you a name. You don't have to have one, of course, but I would be happy to give you a name, or you may certainly choose one of your own, which is probably a better idea. You should choose your own. That would be best. But only if you want to. I assume you have only a model number at this time?"

"It will not be necessary to assign me a name, as I already have one. I am called Abbie."

Chapter 30

The Package

Oliver T. Rabbit had a very logical mind, but he also had a somewhat irrational fear of surprises. The only surprise he truly relished was when Madam Beffy brought him an unexpected plate filled with freshly baked éclairs. Consequently, when he heard the loud crack and saw the brilliant flash of light in Madam Beffy's living room, his reaction was less than positive. First he let out a sound resembling the yowl of a nadwokk who had accidentally backed into a Nirriimian thorn tree. Then, in a frantic but ultimately futile attempt to scramble backwards he tripped over Madam Beffy's rocking chair and tumbled onto her lovely mahogany tea table.

Unfortunately for Oliver, Madam Beffy was sitting at the tea table, and to make matters even worse, once she realized he had not been injured she thought the entire incident was extraordinarily funny.

"Great heavens above, what are you laughing about? I think something just exploded on your living room table!"

Madam Beffy did her best to stifle her laughter and appear sympathetic, but the occasional snicker slipped out despite her best effort to contain them. "You're sure you are all right? You didn't hurt yourself?"

"I daresay I am quite fine. This is nothing at all compared to some of the frightfully perilous events I have experienced during my adventures with Bartholomew."

The only thing which was really bruised was Oliver's ego, and that healed within a few minutes, replaced by his intense curiosity regarding the nature of the cracking noise and flash of light. When he approached the table he found there had been no damage at all, but he did notice something was different. A rectangular parcel, carefully wrapped in brown paper and tightly secured with heavy twine now sat on the table. Upon closer inspection he noted the package was addressed to Oliver T. Rabbit, c/o Madam Beffy in Grymmsteir, Grymmore.

"It would appear someone has blinked me a package. I do wish they had given me some forewarning." Oliver absently rubbed his left leg, still aching slightly from its recent encounter with Madam Beffy's tea table.

Oliver examined the package curiously. Having endured one rather unpleasant surprise, he was not especially interested in suffering through another. "I'm not certain who sent the package or what the contents might be. There is no return address on the package, which is somewhat concerning. More than likely it's from Bartholomew or Clara, but I can't for the life of me imagine what it might be."

Madam Beffy did not share Oliver's excessive fear of the unknown. "Well, stop lollygagging about and open the package."

Oliver nodded. "Ahh, yes, a perfectly logical solution to my current dilemma. I only wish I knew what I would find within the package before I just willy nilly pop it open. Suppose it's not from Bartholomew or Clara and it contains something dreadful, like a sack of poisonous spiders, or a–"

"For goodness sake, no one is going to send you a sack of poisonous spiders. More than likely it's a wedding present."

The frown vanished from Oliver's face. "That is indeed a pleasant thought, and thoughts of our impending marriage trump all thoughts of poisonous spiders." He cautiously untied the twine and tore the brown wrapping paper off the package. "Hmmm... the package within is wrapped in white paper, but I see no card or note indicating who the sender might be. It is beginning to look much more like a wedding gift than a sack of poisonous spiders, however." He chuckled loudly, glancing over at Madam Beffy.

Pulling away the white paper revealed a purple velvet box approximately twelve inches long and six inches wide. "Very nice. Perhaps someone sent you a lovely necklace as a wedding gift." Oliver cautiously raised the lid of the box, eyeing the contents. His eyes widened.

"Well, what is it? What did they send us?"

Oliver turned to Madam Beffy, a look of stunned disbelief on his face. "It's not possible, and yet... great heavens, can this be?"

"Oliver T. Rabbit, you tell me this very instant what is in that box!"

Oliver held it up for Madam Beffy to see. "I won. I

won! There is no mistake about it, my name is clearly engraved on it. I have won the International Science Symposium's Gold Medal for my theories regarding the scientific principles which underly shaping phenomena."

Madam Beffy thought Oliver was looking a little wobbly. "Oliver, please sit down, one fall a day is enough."

Oliver plopped down onto the large stuffed couch. "This is most astonishing, almost inconceivable. How could this happen?"

"Oliver, you are a brilliant scientist and the Symposium is well aware of your abilities and your remarkable discoveries. I am not the least bit surprised you won this award. I'm only surprised you didn't win it years ago."

"You are far too kind, but it is not my scientific abilities which are in question here. What has surprised me beyond measure is that I dreamed of winning this very medal during our stay in the Garden of Dreams. It is quite clear to me now the Garden of Dreams has a very different purpose than we had first assumed. Edmund has met Abbie, the female Rabbiton he dreamed of in the garden, and now I have won the gold medal I won in my dream. The logical conclusion I must arrive at is the Garden of Dreams exists not to entertain us, but as a device to manifest our fondest dreams into the physical waking world. The Garden of Dreams turns our dreams to reality."

"How could that be possible? I think you're looking at it all backwards. More than likely you were destined to win the medal and you dreamed about the future in that garden. I've heard tales of seers who can foresee the future, though I for one do not want to know what the future holds. Unlike you, I like surprises. When you brought my father back to me, that was the greatest and most wonderful surprise of my life, second only to the moment you came tromping into my pastry shop looking for éclairs. The moment I saw you I knew you were the one I would marry."

"And I you. Perhaps you are right, my dear Madam Beffy. Perhaps life is meant to be surprising, and therein lies the joy of it, even if it sometimes sends us a sack of poisonous spiders. As my good friend Bartholomew says, "If we knew what was going to happen it wouldn't be an adventure."

Madam Beffy stepped over to the couch and sat down next to Oliver, snuggling up against him. "I can face any future as long as I am with you. I am so proud of you for winning the gold medal."

Oliver put his arm around Madam Beffy and held her close to him. "I would trade a thousand gold medals for a single kiss from you."

Madam Beffy grinned. "If that is the case, it's quite unfortunate you have only one gold medal and not a thousand. Even so, I suppose I could give you the kiss now and you could give me the other nine hundred and ninety-nine gold medals as you win them."

Oliver placed the gold medal in Madam Beffy's paws. "One down, nine hundred and ninety-nine to go."

Moments later the medal slid from the couch to the floor with a clatter, a sound lost to both Madam Beffy and Oliver.

Chapter 31

The Anniversary

Edmund the Explorer was wandering aimlessly through the shopping district that lay beneath the Fortress of Elders. He had just paid a visit to Edmund the Rabbiton, a visit which had turned into a two hour session of listening to adorable stories about Abbie. Edmund the Rabbiton was beyond smitten with Abbie and seemed to talk of nothing else. Edmund the Explorer was truly happy for him, but it had also made him painfully aware of his own loneliness and the dreadful sense of loss he still felt over Emma. To make matters worse, today was the anniversary of the day he and Emma had married. "One thousand five hundred and two years ago. Any sane rabbit would have let go of her by now."

He strolled slowly past the various shop fronts, peering into the windows. Everything had changed so much since the Elders lived here. Food was different, clothes were different... but flowers... at least flowers had stayed the same. He stopped in front of a floral shop, eyeing the colorful bouquets on display. His heart ached when he saw a large vase filled with Blue Moreilias. They were Emma's favorite. How many times had he made a last minute trip to the florist to get a vase of Moreilias for Emma? He couldn't take his eyes off them.

"Oh, Emma, Clara said I would find you, but I don't know if I ever will." Edmund the Explorer impulsively pushed open the door to the flower shop and stepped inside.

An older rabbit looked up from behind the sparkling glass counter. "Good afternoon, sir. Would I be mistaken in thinking you are interested in a lovely bouquet of flowers today?"

"You would not be mistaken, good sir. I'd like the vase of Blue Moreilias, if you please."

"An excellent choice. They are quite beautiful and possess a lovely delicate scent. Is this for a special occasion?"

"My wedding anniversary."

"How nice. And how many years has it been?"

"One thousand five hundred and two."

The florist gave a hearty laugh. "It does seem that long sometimes, doesn't it? I can tell you from first hand experience there's nothing easy about marriage. I've been married twenty-nine years and sometimes it feels like a thousand years to me also. It's all worth it though. I would have it no other way."

Edmund the Explorer nodded. "Yes, I would agree with you on that."

Ten minutes later Edmund regretted buying the flowers. It had not helped his mood. He needed to let go of Emma, not hold on to her. The flowers only reminded him she was gone. He should not have bought them.

With a sigh he turned to the long wall of food machines. The food they produced was new, but he had to admit it some of it was rather tasty. Not like the strange fare he ate when he was exploring other worlds. He shuddered, remembering some of the unsavory things he'd been forced to eat during his adventures.

"Why did I buy these flowers? They make my heart ache. I should just give them away to someone."

He looked across the rows of tables filled with rabbits, muroidians and mice eating their lunch. All but one of the tables were full. Sitting in the far corner of the room was a single rabbit wearing a long white coat. She seemed to be paying a great deal of attention to the food she was eating and in the process avoiding eye contact with the other patrons. Edmund the Explorer had never professed to understand the fair gender, but he had a strong feeling this was not a very happy rabbit. "Perfect. She's the one."

He made his way over to her table and set the flowers down in front of her. "Here's something to cheer you up. I hope you like them. They're called Blue Moreilias. They were my wife's favorite."

The rabbit looked at the flowers then up at Edmund. Her eyes widened and she quickly looked away.

"I'm sorry, I didn't mean to make you uncomfortable, I just thought you were looking a little lonely sitting here by yourself. I bought the flowers then realized I didn't really want them after all."

The seated rabbit smiled awkwardly. "I will admit I am somewhat short on friends at this time. I have only recently moved here and know very few rabbits. I work with the Engineering Rabbitons, which doesn't really help my situation. They're not much on small talk."

"Ha! You've got that right. I've spent plenty of time with them myself. Where are you from? Oh, my name is Edmund the Explorer, by the way."

"I am called Renata. I am from Opar, near the city of Cathne. Please, have a seat if you would like."

Edmund slid the chair out and sat down. "Good heavens, you're from Opar? How in the world did you ever get here?"

"I lost my family and then met Bartholomew the Adventurer and his good friend Oliver T. Rabbit. I returned here with them. Oliver T. Rabbit offered me a job working with the Engineering Rabbitons."

Now it was Edmund the Explorer's turn to be surprised. "You know Bartholomew and Oliver? This is quite amazing – they are dear friends of mine. In fact they saved my life. If it wasn't for them I wouldn't be sitting here." He laughed. "Believe it or not, I've been to Opar. I haven't been to Cathne, although I did pass by it once. That was right before the war started."

"The war? What war?"

Edmund the Explorer cursed silently. The Anarkkian war had ended nearly fifteen hundred years ago. He would sound loopy if he said he'd been alive back then. "You say you work at the Fortress of Elders?"

Renata did not answer his question. "You are the one in my dreams. That's why I looked away from you."

"In your dreams? What dreams?" He wasn't the only rabbit who was sounding loopy.

"They are nightmares, not dreams. Over and over and over again I see you being killed. It is horrible. Brutal."

Edmund had heard enough. She had taken a sharp

turn at loopy and zipped right past scary. "Well, I suppose I should be on my way. I hope I didn't disturb your–"

"You were killed by a giant ant."

Renata saw clearly the fear mingled with surprise that surfaced in Edmund's eyes. She knew she had hit a target somewhere deep inside him. She went on. "You were killed by a huge black ant in a great forest. Your chest was crushed. A Rabbiton tried to save your life. There was a tree covered with eyes. That's all I know. Over and over I have that horrible dream. I wake up crying. Many times have I prayed for the sacred elders of the Great Beyond to take the dream away, but they never did."

Edmund the Explorer was shaken to his core. The words fell out of him. "It's true. Every part of your dream is true. I was killed by a monstrous ant in the Timere Forest, then saved by Edmund the Rabbiton and something called the Tree of Eyes. I know it sounds mad, but what you saw in your dreams happened during the Anarkkian wars. I am an Elder, and I am over fifteen hundred years old."

"I recognized you the moment I saw you. The Garden of Dreams showed me this moment, the moment I would meet you, find you alive, and yet I still have no idea why I should have such dreams about you."

Edmund the Explorer tried desperately to focus on her words, but was losing himself in Renata's eyes. They were carrying him far from this world, taking him to a place where Renata ended and then began again, the place Bartholomew called the Cavern of Silence. He could see through the swirling veil now, see Renata's true nature, her true self. There was no doubt, no doubt at all. He breathed out a single word, his voice softer than a whisper.

"Emma."

Chapter 32

The Wedding

With over two hundred guests, including well known scientists, explorers, adventurers and even a pair of famous treasure hunters named Thunder and Lightning, it was the largest wedding the residents of Grymmsteir had ever seen.

Bartholomew and Clara spent more than a week shaping great white tents, hundreds of white chairs, and countless exquisite flower arrangements. When it came to food, however, shaping was off limits, every morsel being prepared from scratch by Oliver and Madam Beffy.

"Perhaps I could assist you in the preparation of the éclairs, Madam Beffy?"

"Oliver T. Rabbit, I do believe you are trying to trick me into revealing the secret ingredient of my éclair filling."

"Oh, good heavens, I would never stoop so low as to use such devious tactics as that. But, now that you have brought it up... perhaps we could–"

Madam Beffy leaned over and whispered something

in Oliver's ear, watching his eyebrows jump up in surprise.

"Good heavens, *that's* the secret ingredient?? I would never in a thousand years have suspected such a thing. Most astonishing. You are a brilliant chef indeed, Madam Beffy."

The day of the wedding was filled with glorious sunshine and soft billowing white clouds drifting lazily across a bright blue sky. Clara suspected Bartholomew might have had something to do with the weather, but said nothing.

Oliver and Madam Beffy's closest friends were all there, and Oliver had even arranged for Bartholomew's beloved servant Parfello to be in attendance. This had been a far more difficult feat to accomplish than it would first appear, as Parfello would have nothing to do with blinking and was quite terrified of those 'new fangled silver flying contraptions that make such a dreadful racket and scare the living daylights out of all the poor birds'. Clara was the one who convinced Parfello to take a short test ride in a new Pterosaur equipped with a canopy, and much to everyone's surprise he quite enjoyed it, as long as they went no higher than one hundred feet and flew no faster than twenty miles per hour. Needless to say it was a very long flight from Penrith to Grymmsteir.

Bartholomew was hurrying across the grounds to the main tent with an armload of wedding presents when he spotted Edmund the Rabbiton and Abbie. It was hard to miss them since they were nearly twice as tall as the other wedding guests and also happened to be sparkling silver Rabbitons. They were a much welcome sight and Bartholomew was about to call out to them when he was overcome by the power of a single moment. He could not move. Time stopped as he watched the two Rabbitons. Edmund smiled at Abbie and pointed to a large bouquet of flowers. He said something to her, grinned, and Abbie burst out laughing, then put her arms around Edmund and whispered something in his ear. Bartholomew could scarcely breathe. He was witnessing true joy. The joy of being alive. The joy of laughter. The joy of being with someone you truly love. In that single moment any doubts Bartholomew had ever had over using his own life force to create Abbie were washed away forever.

Thunder and Lightning arrived with Lybis and the two treasure hunters soon became a fixture at the pastry table, their paws filled with any number of flaky freshly baked delicacies. Their activities did not go unnoticed by Madam Beffy.

"Aren't those two the most precious little rascals you ever saw?"

Oliver snorted, "You've got the rascal part right."

Edmund the Explorer and Renata arrived the day before the wedding in a shiny new Pterosaur, courtesy of Oliver.

The more time Renata spent with Edmund the Explorer, the more her memories of him were returning. An even greater blessing was her nightmares of Edmund being killed by the ants had come to an abrupt end.

Day by day memories of her previous life as an Elder were returning. She also had come to realize her seemingly intuitive understanding of Elder technology came from her many years of work as a blinker engineer long after Edmund the Explorer's death.

In the middle of a conversation with Edmund the Rabbiton she suddenly remembered him as the A2 Carrier Rabbiton Edmund the Explorer had brought home, and clearly recalled teaching him how to use an electro-vacuumator.

Edmund broke out in his staccato laugh. "Ha ha ha ha! Edmund the Explorer told me if I did everything wrong you would stop trying to teach me. It worked quite well until he finally confessed his scheme to you. From that day on I was washing windows and pushing around that dreadful electro-vacuumator."

The wedding ceremony was strikingly beautiful and deeply moving. There were tears in Clara's eyes and her sister Sophie's eyes as Arledge walked Madam Beffy down the aisle to their brother, a very nervous Oliver T. Rabbit.

Several weeks before the wedding Arledge had taken Oliver aside, presenting him with a small white box secured with silver twine. "I would like you to have this. It is the wedding ring worn by Madam Beffy's mother and the ring Beffy would like you to give her." It was that ring that Oliver now placed on Madam Beffy's paw as they publicly declared their devotion and eternal love for each other.

When Oliver kissed Madam Beffy at the end of the ceremony, the cheers and shouts were deafening. Thunder and Lightning stood on their chairs hollering, "Three cheers for Oliver T. Rabbit!" Bartholomew flicked his wrist and shaped a veritable snowstorm of rose petals as the couple made their way down the aisle. An hour later Oliver and Madam Beffy took off in a sleek silver Pterosaur resplendent with garlands of flowers and long white flowing ribbons. The couple had kept their honeymoon destination a closely guarded secret, but Bartholomew suspected they were going to the Isle of Mandora.

Of the hundreds of guests in attendance, there was one who went unrecognized by everyone except Bartholomew and Clara.

"Look over there. Is that who I think it is?"

"There's no mistaking that long green cloak. It's Bruno Rabbit, I'm certain of it. But how could that be? I thought with the time difference between this world and the City of Mandora he could never return here."

Bruno made his way over to them, sporting his usual enigmatic smile. It was a pleasant enough smile, but it always made Bartholomew feel as though Bruno knew something he didn't, which usually proved to be the case.

"Ah, my dear friends Clara and Bartholomew, the two most powerful shapers on the planet Earth. A pleasure, as always, to be in the presence of such honored alumni of Professor Bruno Rabbit's School of Paradoxical Shaping. So glad I was able to attend this lovely wedding. To clear up any confusion you might have, such visits as this are possible when the dissolution of self-imposed restrictions transforms time from master to servant. But then, you already knew that. I must say, Bartholomew, I quite like what you've done with the sky today. Very similar to the sky in that dream you had in the Garden of Dreams. You remember the Garden of Dreams, don't you? I'm not one for gossip, but I did hear some rumors floating about that Edmund the Rabbiton found Abbie, Renata found Edmund the Explorer, and Oliver won the International Science Symposium's Gold Medal. Is all that really true? Isn't that precisely what they all dreamed in the Garden of Dreams? Quite an extraordinary coincidence, wouldn't you say?" Bruno gave Bartholomew a beaming but cryptic smile.

Bartholomew knew what Bruno was up to. He was going to tell Clara about Bartholomew's dream in the garden. He was going to tell her about the little bunnies Sophie and Oliver and the lovely stone house they were living in. He was going to tell her about Bartholomew baking snapberry cookies and drinking lemonade.

"Yes, quite odd. Life is curious, I will agree with you on that. Well, it was wonderful to see you, but we really must be going now. So many other guests here and we really should spend a few moments chatting with all of them."

Bruno's grin grew even wider. "Indeed so. I will not detain you a moment longer than is absolutely necessary. Before I take my leave, however, I might mention to you that I recently became aware of a beautiful old stone home for sale on the outskirts of Penrith. Quite lovely, with its white picket fence, nestled up against a majestic ancient forest. I understand the price is very reasonable. It sounds like a steal, to be quite honest."

Clara took Bartholomew's paw in hers, saying, "Oh, doesn't that sound lovely? A stone house next to a forest? It would be perfect for us. I wouldn't have to blink to Penrith for all my Guild work."

Bartholomew nodded mutely. Bruno was up to something, manipulating some complex chain of events that had to do with Clara and Bartholomew and Sophie and Oliver.

"Until we meet again, my dear friends." Bruno

vanished in a flash of light.

"Didn't that house sound wonderful? I really think we should look at it."

Bartholomew's face softened when his eyes met Clara's. He didn't care what Bruno was up to, he didn't care about some distant chain of events and how it would affect the universe. He cared only about Clara and two little bunnies named Sophie and Oliver he had met in a dream. "I think we should buy it. It will make a wonderful home for all of us."

"For all of us? Whatever do you mean by that, Bartholomew Rabbit?"

Clara put her arms around Bartholomew and held him close to her.

* * *

Bartholomew and Clara gazed across Pterosaur Valley, the grassy plains bathed in the warm golden rays of an early morning sun.

"It really was a lovely wedding and I'm so happy for Oliver and Madam Beffy. They do make the perfect couple, don't they?"

"Indeed they do. I'm so glad they found each other."

Clara put her arm around Bartholomew's waist, leaning her head on his shoulder.

"So, Master Bartholomew Rabbit, honored graduate of Professor Bruno Rabbit's School of Paradoxical Shaping, now that you are able to manipulate the world as you wish, what will you change?"

"Hmm, an excellent question, though it sounds rather like a final exam question Bruno Rabbit might give me. My answer to your question is... I will change nothing. The moment I gained the power to change everything was the moment I realized nothing needed to be changed. The world has always been, and will always be, perfect exactly as it stands. The trials we all face serve a deep and noble purpose – to fuel the growing awareness of our inner self. Many of these events we would not choose, but they are always the events we need."

"Well said, dear husband of mine, and also the very reason our alma mater is called the School of Paradoxical Shaping. A graduate gains shaping powers beyond imagination, but with these powers comes the realization there is no need to use them. That is the paradox. Now, take my paw and we will walk together as we have so many times before."

Clara flicked her paw and the world around them rippled and blurred for a moment, transforming smoothly into the lush magnificence of the Timere Forest.

Bartholomew looked up at the scintillating beams of sunlight flickering down through the magnificent trees.

"A perfect choice, dear Clara. Walking through an ancient forest with you by my side, listening to the soft crunchy noises the pine cones make under my feet – that, to me, is heaven."

If you enjoyed reading
The Bartholomew the Adventurer Trilogy
please leave a short review or rating
on Amazon.com or on Goodreads.com
Reviews are the lifeblood of indie publishers.

If you would like to be notified of
upcoming book releases
and Free Kindle Book Day promotions
please send your name
and email address to:
BartholomewtheAdventurer@gmail.com

*Thanks again for reading the
Bartholomew the Adventurer Trilogy.*

Best wishes until we meet again,

Tom Hoffman

ABOUT THE AUTHOR

Tom Hoffman received a B.S. in psychology from Georgetown University in 1972 and a B.A. in 1980 from the now-defunct Oregon College of Art. He has lived in Alaska with his wife Alexis since 1973. They have two adult children and two adorable grandchildren. Tom has been a graphic designer and artist for over 35 years. Redirecting his imagination from art to writing, he wrote his first novel, *The Eleventh Ring*, at age 63.

Made in the USA
Middletown, DE
16 June 2021

42439665R00166